OH NO IT ISN'T!

Bernice was doing a quick head count of her hosts, who were now sitting around their kitchen table, each at a chair with their name on the back. 'Lazy, Moody, Laddish, Gushy, Bitchy, Liberal and Cute. Seven of you, and I knew that before I was told. How is that possible?'

Wolsey shrugged a languid cat shrug. 'Perhaps they've escaped from some travelling show. I hear the King has a new plan to deal with such as the [illegible] *alled Care in the Entertainment Community.'*

'We have not escap [illegible] *aimed Moody. 'We work in ou* [illegible] *nd diamonds that we fin* [illegible]

Bernice [illegible] *et for precious stones in a s* [illegible]

The dwarv [illegible] *blankly.*

THE NEW

ADVENTURES

OH NO IT ISN'T!

Paul Cornell

First published in Great Britain in 1997 by
Virgin Publishing Ltd
332 Ladbroke Grove
London W10 5AH

Bernice Summerfield originally created by Paul Cornell

Cover illustration by Jon Sullivan

ISBN 0 426 20507 3

Typeset by Galleon Typesetting, Ipswich
Printed and bound in Great Britain by
Mackays of Chatham PLC

Thanks to Gareth Roberts and Penny List, Jackie Mulligan, Jac Rayner and Steven Moffat, without whom there would be no book and no me.

Thanks also to: Russell Davies, Jason Haigh-Ellery, Craig Hinton, Matt Jones, Rebecca Levene, Claire Longhurst, John McLaughlin, Paul Marquess, Carrie O'Grady, Kate Orman, Dave Owen, Gary Russell, Carla Tsampiras, Sam Walke, Jo Ware, Peter Ware, and Mark Wyman.

For Jac Rayner

Laughter is a celebration of our failings. That's what clowns are for. And that's what I am.

Emma Thompson

Chapter 1

Porterhatch Blues

The great red building in the shape of a barrel had grown dark in the rain, the natural tan of its bricks staining with the water. The rain had washed its steamed-up windows, fallen through its drainpipes and flowed along its gutterings all night. Now it was morning, but the sky was still full with storm clouds.

The building was made of old mud, baked hard in modern kilns, bonded brick to brick at an atomic level. Each brick had been blessed by the High Priest of Knowledge of the Tashwari Regime. Satellite feeds and aerials and data terminals had been knocked through the brick by Tashwari workers, swinging from girders around the block by their hands and tails. The bricks had been painted with a rain-tight solution. Doors and arches with electronic keys and entry systems had been driven into the barrel, a vast staircase lowered through the roof as a slab and unfurled like a card shuffle, and a big, friendly, fusion boiler tunnelled into the ground underneath.

The future Garland College Hall of Residence of St Oscar's University was completed and blessed in under ten of the days of the planet Dellah. It was not named at that point. The Sultan of the Tashwari had put on a pair of stout boots and stamped about the site, his advisers at his side, quoting from an old book he carried. He pointed at and named all the nine colleges, and the university itself, after things which would bring the children of Earth to his world. Then he closed the book, took the mud of construction in both hands, and held it to the sky in hope. Then he had tea.

The children of Earth had been a problem for the Sultan. His world sat too close to their territory. Every year, a nearby world would align itself to, or be annexed by, the Earth's 'Empire'. The Sultan knew Earth was ruled by an elected president, but he had heard the term 'Empire' used so casually by human explorers that he became wary. A people that were fundamentally at odds as to the nature of that which ruled them . . . you could not turn your side to them and reach for tea. And with the ships of the human Spacefleet came their corporations, settling on to worlds like swarms of feeding creatures, sucking away the goodness and seeing the people of those worlds as something glimpsed from a speeding sailpod.

Even if Dellah had been a united world, it could not have fought the humans off. But it was not. As well as the Tashwari Regime, there were two other large power blocs: the monarchy of Goll and the Sylan Federation. These three nations alone included seven separate intelligent species, of vastly differing biological types. There were, including all the cults and splinter groups, over five hundred officially registered religions on the planet. To unite all that would be beyond even the Sultan's charm.

So the Sultan did something very clever. He swiftly established trade links with several of the major human corporations, sending learned advisers to them – Tashwari who had spent all their time learning about the humans from their communications. These ambassadors acted as if relations with Earth were already at an advanced stage, as if genuinely mutual trade agreements and treaties were already in place. They talked about the latest share prices, and celebrities and the wonderful human game called cricket, pitches for which already dotted the meadows of the Sultan's lands.

Thanks to the chaos of the frontier, and the humans' capacity for delusion, these words soon became truths. The Earth's sphere of influence swept by Dellah, counting it as taken, civilized, urbane, even. The Galactic War, in which the humans and their allies struggled with an alien species that fundamentally disagreed with them, missed the planet completely. With the destruction of many lines of communication and the razing of many civilized worlds, Dellah's status as a place of relative safety was confirmed. There never was an invasion. The Sultan sacrificed an eye to his gods in thanks for that, in the process of a vigil in a cave deep under his palace. After he did so, numb from the shock, his other two eyes saw a vision. A vision of an establishment that would affirm and cement the peace that he had made.

A university. A place where all species, including many of the humans, would come and learn, under the palm of his hand.

A place that could never be a target.

Within days, all the major corporations were involved in sponsorship negotiations. Krytell himself, greatest of the many great entrepreneurs who had profited from the Galactic War, visited Dellah and, over tea, was persuaded of the R&D opportunities offered by a place where knowledge was free. Well, as free as the corporations wanted it to be.

The campus of nine colleges was built across a chain of hilly islands, a site agreed upon by the various countries and tribes of Dellah as being absolutely neutral, and of no possible strategic worth . . . at the moment. The others had never fully given credit to the Sultan for his saving of the planet, and were puzzled, more than anything else, by his latest vision.

St Oscar's University had its own spaceport, at the insistence of the corporations – Dellah's first, a silver needle at the northern end of the islands that reached all the way up into orbit. When the final brick was placed in the base of that construction, when the first parties of academics, and then students began to arrive . . . each time the Sultan prostrated himself before his gods, more certain that he had saved his world.

And the cost was not too high, for was the university not made in the Tashwari style, blessed and baked and red?

The gods extracted but one price: the needle of the spaceport made it rain much more often than it had.

Hence the conditions over, and the presence of, the Barrel, as the humans called it, that morning of the human year 2593.

Hence the woman who slept in one set of rooms there, dreaming of Earth, oblivious to the rain and the leaves of alien autumn that were splattering against her window.

She was finally woken only by a bad dream . . .

Professor Bernice Surprise Summerfield woke up, stretched, and groaned. The stretch had brought on the groan. That was nothing to do with the look of the day: she'd got used to the torrents of the Dellahan autumn. The groan was to do with the crunch of muscles at the back of her neck, and the weight that had been settled in the middle of her head during sleep, which had now rolled over to smack against the inside of her forehead.

Surprisingly, she hadn't been drinking last night.

With her eyes tight shut, she reached out to the cabinet beside the bed, and laid her fingers on her glasses. Sheer affectation, these, a product of the same urge that had lined every one of her rooms with books, and had made her order a dozen trad jazz discs from Earth, at the vast prices of ancient vinyl.

Bernice was trying very hard to be old.

Judging by the feeling down her spine this morning, she was succeeding.

She dropped the spectacles on to her nose, and opened her eyes. She was only in her mid-thirties, but this last few weeks she had found herself desiring to be much, much older. To have a body that was like one of the leaves that the suspensor fields were fluttering off the window, all brown and curled, and a mind that was without desire. This age thing, and the spine thing, were both products of not having a body beside her under this double duvet, after having got used to that feeling. Her husband then was her husband no longer. At least, they were no longer married. And, though she had cried and cried, and the parting had been her decision, she still regretted it every day. That was also the cause of a band of whiter flesh around her ring finger.

Breaking up, Bernice was discovering, was hard to do. Harder than getting one's tights on after swimming. Harder than table football. Harder than a lump of something that lay over your ribs in the night. Bernice was an archaeologist of some fame, the author of the bestselling coffee-table book that everybody had bought but nobody had read: *Down Among The Dead Men*. After the heartache and the separation, she'd jumped at the chance of a teaching post at St Oscar's. St Oscar's, following their policy of recruiting the most glamorous – if not necessarily the most learned – scholars, had jumped at having her. Her head of department, Dr Follett, an aged reptilian who purposely didn't regulate the cloud of chlorine that surrounded him when Bernice was in his office, hadn't been so keen. But at St Oscar's the Shilling was mightier than academic respect. Writing a similarly bestselling sequel to her book, with lots of mentions of the quality of the archaeology department at St Oscar's, had been written into Bernice's contract of employment for taking up the Edward Watkinson Chair of Archaeology. She had a title for the new work: *So Vast A*

Pile, but that was about it. Even at this early stage, the publishing arm of the university had started to write her nervous letters concerning the delivery of the manuscript, hinting that they might eventually get someone else to write it, want their investment back, or even one day maybe sue her. Oh well. She was sure that she'd get around to writing it one day. If the publishers got too concerned, she'd just tell them she'd had a system crash and lost the manuscript. Or something.

And all this was good, because it provided something to do, some security, some people to talk to. Somewhere to stop being so bloody rooted in depression and start living again. Jason had gone, and he was, in all probability, not going to come back. Unless she asked him. And she didn't even know what part of the galaxy he was in these days, so . . . no. It didn't matter that every time she thought of something they'd done together she felt bruised, that she associated whole countries, genres of music and the actual experience of watching old cinema with him and him only, and that every time one of those things crossed her mind her face clouded and her students asked her what was wrong. She'd got so used to having a little bundle of thoughts that boiled down to 'and Jason too' at the end of her musings. Such as, 'What colour should I paint my study . . . what would Jason like?' and, 'That was a good play . . . I must tell Jason about it.'

And these thoughts were with her this morning as they always were, like vultures round her bed.

There was absolutely no point in being depressed, she told herself as she hugged the pillow. Depression was counterproductive, and why should she give him that satisfaction? Not that it was anything to do with him any more; not that he'd ever know . . .

She took her first deep breath of the morning, and convinced herself that she was old and wise and felt better. 'Wolsey?' she called, clicking her tongue against the roof of her mouth. That was the name of her tabby tomcat. 'Where is he?'

'I'm afraid I don't know, Rector.' A white sphere, about the size of a billiard ball, drifted towards the bed. This was Joseph, her Porter, whose presence had started to irritate Bernice a month ago. That was on the day after she'd moved in. The whole business of being the Rector of Garland College, in charge of the moral wellbeing of a thousand young beings, was a bit of a bugger too.

Bernice threw the duvet over her head. 'Lullaby of Birdland . . .' she mumbled.

'As you wish.' The Porter floated towards an ancient vinyl record player. The arm lifted itself, and dropped on to a record that sat there. The gentle tune soothed out from the speakers, one placed on top of the wall bookshelf and one beside the collection of empty and half-empty wine bottles.

'You have a tutorial at noon, Rector,' said the Porter. 'And, of course, tomorrow is the expedition to Perfecton, for which you have not yet begun to pack.'

'Um-hm.'

'Your Head of Department also wishes to remind his staff about the later field trip, only, he emphasizes, accommodating two students, which –'

'Nobody wants to do because it's too boring. I know, Joseph. Right now, I want tea, the *Campus Bulletin* and love.'

The sphere paused. 'Please, Rector.'

'Please what?'

'Tea, the *Campus Bulletin* and love . . . please.'

Bernice peered out from her duvet cave. 'Please, Joseph. Bring me all those things.'

'Very well, Rector.' The Porter floated out through the Porterhatch at the top of the door.

Bernice pushed off the duvet and put her feet down on the carpet, searching without looking for her newly purchased carpet slippers.

If Joseph was going to bring her love, she definitely wanted to get to the bathroom before it arrived.

Part two of an everyday waking up in the Garland College Rector's Rooms: the ordeal of the bathroom mirror.

Before she was married and divorced, Bernice had mocked the fatty concerns of lesser women. She'd known then that she was gorgeous, a certainty that sprang from an internal well of gorgeousness. Hubby had dipped his ladle into that well a few too many times, and had taken some of the gorgeousness away with him. When she married Jason, Bernice had completely cast aside the thought that she might ever want to be stared at by eighteen-year-old boys. Now she was surrounded by them, her students, and, as far as she could tell, they simply were not staring.

She pulled a face, a big pout. Her short-cut dark hair was spiked up by the pillows. Her girlish complexion, until recently free of make-up, had a dusting of lines across the cheekbones. Under her eyes was darkness.

She looked like a howler monkey.

The bath was a blessed relief, as baths to Bernice always were. She'd been in the field, and up to her armpits in mud, often enough that the terms that she'd had written into her contract included provision of a vast bathroom and appropriately vast bath.

The Porter returned, after a blissful ten minutes, carrying a steaming cup and a datascreen on a silver tray. Benny caught the datascreen as Joseph dropped it into her hand, wondering as she did so if a miss would have electrocuted her, leaving the Porter with its non-existent hands clean of her murder. The headlines of the *Campus Bulletin* scrolled with her eyeline. They'd reduced the journey time to Earth to eleven months, and the celebrity burglar known as the Cat's Paw had been briefly thought to have been responsible for a burglary in Rigg College Halls, resulting in a security operation that had only succeeded in capturing one of the Dean's pet honking birds. She sighed as she inhaled the aroma of the cup of tea that levitated gently on to the bottle shelf beside the bath. 'Do you think I should be getting older, Joseph?'

'If you are not, Rector, then you are unique.'

Bernice settled back into the bath, wedging the datascreen between her toes, and sucking the surface off the tea without using her hands. 'I'm just trying to age gracefully. As a full Professor, I feel that one ought to abandon one's speeder-pod and buy a proper bicycle. Most newly separated women would, I fancy, begin a desperate scramble to regain their youth. I am different. I am thoughtful. I have decided to get old instead.'

'Very clever, Rector.'

'I wonder if I should have a breast enlargement.'

The Porter gave a little mechanical whine, its internal gears trying to formulate a response.

Bernice looked up before it could. 'Any sign of Wolsey yet?'

'No, Rector.'

'That's so strange. He's normally here for his biccies, eight on the dot. I hope he hasn't got into a fight.' Bernice sloshed a bit, picked up the tea, drank deeply of it, and managed her first smile of the day. 'Why are you still hovering there, Joseph?'

'I was waiting for a moment to interject. The remainder of your request is waiting.'

'The . . . you mean "love", don't you?' Benny slowly lowered the teacup.

'The young gentleman is in the study.'

Bernice screamed.

Ten minutes later, very fully dressed, Bernice cautiously poked her head around her study door. An incredibly well-dressed thin boy with a flop of brown hair over his eyes was standing in the corner, idly toying with the globe of Dellah that Bernice had placed atop the fridge.

It was Doran. Joseph, with its obscene sense of humour, had brought her Doran.

The boy was in her tutorial group, an absurdly waiflike teenager with a vast knowledge of theoretical archaeology and a pair of extraordinary azure eyes. Every now and then he asked Bernice questions that she couldn't answer. He'd even, according to the computer records that Bernice had hacked into by chance one day, read some of her articles.

Goodness, this was an ugly boy. Ugly ugly ugly. Get-somebody-thrown-out-of-St-Oscar's-University ugly.

Bernice forced her face into a frown, and made a humphing noise. She was pleased by the way Doran jumped. 'Yes?' she queried testily, marching into the room. 'What do you want at this time in the morning?' She plucked a book from the shelf, as if that was what she'd come in to do, and found that it was her own. Bernice studied it anyway, and then, with the precision of a pre-emptive nuclear strike, glanced up at the student over her glasses. 'Speak.'

'I . . . the Porter asked me here. It . . . I . . . I'm . . .'

'Oh!' Bernice cut in a moment into his blush. 'You're Michael Doran, aren't you?'

'Yes, Professor Summerfield.'

'Thought I recognized you. I wanted to lend you a book.'

'Couldn't you have done that at the tutorial?'

'What? Oh, no no no no no!' Bernice randomly plucked another book from the shelf, flapping her arms to try to appear even more wilfully eccentric and hide her own fluster. 'Too many books in the bag already, young man. I'd like you to study this in detail, and tell me what you think.' She pressed the book into his hand.

He looked at the title page for a moment. '*Make Dangerous Love to Me – The Erotic Poetry of Carla Tsampiras*.'

Bernice bit her bottom lip. 'There are bits about archaeology.'

'Oh.' Doran nodded and smiled innocently. 'By the way, I think I saw your cat on the way over here. He was up a tree, and –'

'Oh was he I'd better go and rescue him see you at the tutorial.' The door slammed so loudly behind her that it made Doran jump again.

Bernice whizzed down the red-brick incline that marked the edge of Goodyear College on her bicycle, following the route that Doran must have taken to get to her rooms. The search for Wolsey wasn't entirely motivated by a desire to get out of a nervy situation. Bernice and her archaeology tutorial group left on an expedition to the planet Perfecton tomorrow, and if Wolsey wasn't found by then, Bernice wondered if she could still go. The archaeological treasures of a previously unexplored world were one thing – losing one's cat was another. But that fear was, as yet, still at the back of her mind. The air tasted dark and spicy this morning, fresh with the smell of wet leaves. It was good to feel the rain.

Jason had always loved this time of year.

He probably still did.

She scattered a group of students as the bicycle careered down into a courtyard. One Ootsoi boy in a suit of red feathers dropped his books, and she stopped for a moment to help him pick them up.

The campus was certainly crowded for the start of the new academic year. Professors who'd been here longer than Bernice told her that, in the early years, there had been very few students. It had taken the financial might of the corporate sponsors to lure academics to the place, to build centres of excellence in half a dozen different disciplines. Again, that was down to the will of the Sultan to protect his planet and its culture, inoculating his world with a small sample of the outside to save it from the plague. Secure the mind, as Bernice's just-begun monograph about the history of this place put it, and the rest will follow.

Nobody had seen a cat. They probably thought she was mad for using an antique vehicle, when there were underground speed pavements, flyer pads, the carrier tunnels between the islands. But Bernice's bicycle was old and sturdy, with a basket on the front, a big brass bell, and a little gravitic motor to help with the hills. It got her out into the world, made her work her calves, made her breathe a bit harder. She went on her way again.

The bad dream last night had been unusual. It wasn't one of the regular ones about missing the last spaceship, dropping valuable vases over cliffs, not catching the elephant that had leapt from the other trapeze. It was about being on stage. An audience was watching her, bored and grumbling, as she tried to reach out to them with a dramatic piece. She knew that what she had to say was passionate and profound, but on her lips the words had become too concrete and crude. She died on stage, and started to cry, asking the watchers just what they expected of her. Asking how much longer she had to go on, how much harder she was expected to try.

Good to be awake out of that one.

Bernice saw a familiar figure ahead of her. He was marching towards the lecture theatres in his long black coat, carrying a bundle of leads and tubes over his shoulder. His walk, as always, was that of somebody who felt that he was about to be disturbed in the midst of doing something that, even if quite innocent, he felt he ought not to be doing. He had an aesthetic, high-cheekboned face, with a mop of brown hair that, because of an unfortunate double crown, could never be put into anything resembling a style. He was always freshly shaved, and always had shaving cuts. This was Menlove Stokes, Professor of

Applied Art, a fellow new arrival, and somebody whom Bernice had taken an instant liking to, because he was thoroughly harmless and, more than any other sort of person, she loved the company of the harmless. He was, like her, something of an intellectual celebrity, the host of the popular weekly art transmission *Paint Along With Menlove*.

'Morning, Menlove,' she said, slowing her bicycle to a walking pace beside him. 'Have you seen a cat this morning?'

'A cat?' Stokes looked as if he was being accused of stealing one. 'No. Why, have you lost Wolsey?'

'Yes, and it's starting to worry me.'

'How awful. I'm so terribly sorry.'

Bernice nodded at the things hanging over Stokes's shoulder. 'So what are the tubes for? Should I ask?'

'My new project.' Stokes looked to his left and right, and then whispered conspiratorially to Bernice. 'I intend to shove them up my every orifice.'

'Goodness, I don't think you should take your critics so much to heart.'

Stokes ignored the barb. 'Pictoscopic sampling is at the cutting edge of art, an aesthetic location of which I am the natural inhabitant. The liquids which I extract from the centre of my being I shall use to fashion my paintings of the surface of Perfecton. The human fluid in alien circumstances.'

'Bile in space.'

'You understand.'

Bernice agreed that she did, and bicycled on.

There were places on the campus that one couldn't go: not without a security badge and a lot of electronic checks. The Advanced Research Department was one. It had been built as an extension of Pracatan College, but had only one entrance – a forbidding pair of jet-black doors – with a security guard standing there twenty-six hours a day. Bernice stopped outside the doors and talked to the Goll on guard. She wasn't a Goll fundamentalist, obviously, or she wouldn't have been there, but the Goll physique, particularly that of the females, was valued across Dellah for mercenaries and bodyguards. Behind her, a camera watched from a security panel. Bernice knew that there would be questions asked of her in the senate for even stopping here, but the whole business of secrecy and security irritated her, particularly in a centre of learning, and she took the opportunity to tie her bootlaces and smile at the camera every time she passed.

Whatever they were working on in there, it brought finance to Dellah from off-planet. Campus legends spoke of the whole building being kept in darkness, of alien researchers who sometimes ventured out in the early hours, and of strange noises from the ventilation ducts that the building shared with the college.

Bernice had very little Goll, but managed to ascertain that the guard hadn't seen any small animals since lunch yesterday.

She cast a wary glance over her shoulder as she moved on, full of dark thoughts about what might happen to a cat that strayed into that place, and saw the Goll talking into the security panel behind her.

Hettie Bonistall and Lucinda Pargiter were St Oscar's joint occupiers of the Chair of Etiquette, the result of a bureaucratic error which nobody had had the courage to correct. Bernice found the two of them on the corner beside the Parapsychology labs. The two old ladies were always perfectly presented, in neat little dresses and shawls, their grey hair pinned up above their hawklike eyes, their mouths permanently curled downwards as they eyed each other. They were such clones of each other that their presence here together could only, Bernice thought, be the product of some greater plan for mischief in the universe. At this moment, they'd surrounded Professor Warrinder, the Head of Psi, a Pakhar male. The Pakhars were short and fluffy, with powerful hind limbs and little paws. They reminded Bernice of nothing more than giant hamsters, as she'd told Warrinder one night over a bowl of Kinsa seeds in the Collins College bar. He'd laughed at the photo of the hamster Bernice had once owned, and said that that had nothing to do with evolution, and everything to do with the wonderful sense of humour that the universe had. Which was probably what lay behind the coincidence of the dear ladies, too.

Warrinder was possibly the most powerful psychic that his race had ever produced. His talent was precognition, for which reason he was barracked by the Physics Department at every senate meeting. 'Predict this!' they'd shout at him, throwing their lunch at the Pakhar in an effort to prove that he couldn't possibly peep over the parapet of time.

But Warrinder persisted, and Bernice, who had a rather grand and poetic view of space and time, and had really loved her hamster, admired him for it. She believed in his powers completely. The first thing he'd said to her was, 'Yes, I can.' Bernice's reply had been: 'I hear you can predict the future?' The dear ladies of Etiquette doubtless had views of their own on precognition, but both loved Warrinder equally. Ferociously and competitively. The three-way conversation between them currently centred on whose onboard party Warrinder would attend on the way to Perfecton. A large number of academics had booked places on the archaeology trip to this particularly famous planet, and by the sound of the conversations Bernice had overheard on the subject, many of them had decided to make a cruise of it.

'I shall have the ship's captain at my party,' Hettie was assuring Professor Warrinder.

'That is entirely possible . . .' Lucinda agreed. 'If the captain can be in two places at once, since he has personally assured me –'

Bernice jumped off her bicycle and made an extravagant and sudden motion with her arms in front of the three of them. Any verbal attempt to butt into one of the warring academics' battles inevitably began a joint assault on the rudeness of the interloper. 'Excuse me. Has anybody seen my cat?'

Warrinder grabbed her hand in his paws, relieved at the interruption. 'Wolsey? Yes, I have seen him. In a dream last night.'

'So could you tell me where he is?'

The two old ladies glanced at the paws clasped around Bernice's hand, at each other, and then back to Bernice, glowering.

Warrinder's little eyes glittered for a moment. Then he nodded. 'He is in the cloisters of Pierce College.'

Bernice beamed, kissed Warrinder on his fluffy cheek, and hopped on her bicycle again. 'Thanks!' she called as she cycled off.

'Never shorten a thank you!' Hettie bellowed after her. 'Honestly, these younger academics. Such a bad example. Now, Professor Warrinder, as I was saying . . .'

Bernice crossed on to the smallest island of the campus via a travel tube. She parked her bicycle in the rack at the gates of Pierce College, thankful that the rain had eased slightly. Pierce was the college that housed the mature students, home of Philosophy and Literature of the Milky Way. It was in a quieter part of the islands.

Bernice wandered into the Pierce courtyard, glancing around at the elegantly bioengineered gardens, the trees dripping in the rain. She ran a hand through her hair, smoothing the water from it. Wolsey was nowhere in sight. There was only one person in the quad, standing by the fountains that surrounded a marble statue of a woman, her arms spread wide. The man was clad in a black academic gown, and he had his hands clasped behind his back.

The courtyard was full of the sound of water: the rain, the fountains, and the rush of it around the guttering of the roofs. Bernice was about to call to the man when he turned, opened his mouth in surprise, and then smiled at her. 'Ah. Professor Summerfield. I've been hoping to meet you.' He stepped towards her. His voice was rich and cultured, possibly an old Earth accent. He had a face that was lined with experience, the sort of face a vicar or an aged comedian might have. His eyes were extraordinary, and they held Bernice for a moment. They were dancing with interest, as if she was suddenly the most important thing in the world to this man.

'You have me at a disadvantage,' said Bernice, wondering if she'd met him at one of the many induction evenings and staff get-togethers.

'Professor Archduke,' he said, taking her hand with a cold smile. 'Earth Literature. I specialize in Obscure Theatrical Forms.'

'Pleased to meet you. I was just wondering –'

Another cat enquiry would have followed, but then something very strange happened.

From above the courtyard came the sound of a scream. A thin, high-pitched scream, increasing in volume above the noise of water. It was coming closer.

Bernice, who'd been in the odd bombardment in her life, was the first to look upwards.

A missile was falling straight towards them. A little, darker, dot against the storm clouds of the sky. It was getting bigger every second.

No, not a missile, she thought, as she threw herself at Professor Archduke and crushed him into the wet gravel, shielding him with her body, it was actually a –

The falling thing hit the statue and exploded.

Into flesh.

The body hit with a terrible thump, like meat thrown on to a butcher's slab.

And then there was silence.

Bernice and Archduke gathered themselves up, wiping bits of blue stuff off their clothing, and got to their feet. Splattered across the statue were the remains of an alien corpse. The body was humanoid, its uniformed midriff crumpled across the torso of the statue, its limbs everywhere, its head a mess in the bowl of the fountain, where the waters were already spraying blue. Bernice realized that, as she'd looked up, already moving, she'd seen its eyes, its face – there had been something odd about its face, as if it was covered in string – its expression of fear. She thought that perhaps the species was familiar, but there was no way to identify it from what remained.

'If that's something to do with Rag Week,' she told Archduke, 'then I'm resigning my post.'

They poked around the corpse as Porters came buzzing in, their little sirens disturbing the quiet of the quad. There seemed to be nothing in the sky above, nowhere the creature could have come from. Bernice was too shocked to feel horror or squeamishness. The strange nature of the creature's arrival had rendered it not quite real, and the conversation after its arrival, without the weight of any reasonable speculation to hold it down, couldn't help but turn to other things.

Bernice got the feeling from the corpse of a being sacrificed to comedy, its poor life nothing more than a punchline in the wrong place. Not even funny. It reminded her again of her dream, that inability to communicate an individual drama.

The Porters cleared away and cleaned up, and, in the end, Bernice and Archduke could only shrug at their questions.

Archduke watched as they left, carrying the remains of

the alien. He took a deep breath, and seemed to decide on a serious course of action. He turned back to Bernice. 'I wonder if you might do me a small service,' he began. 'In return for which, I shall take you to your cat. Follow me, if you would . . .'

He crooked a finger, and Bernice, surprised, followed him to his rooms.

Wolsey was eating from a soup bowl full of meat when Bernice found him, contentedly munching away in Archduke's hall. His fur was fluffed up and full of water, and he looked happy to have a place to shelter and eat. Bernice plucked him up, against his struggles, and glared at the tabby. 'There you are! Why are you here, and not at home for your biccies?'

'I'm afraid that I detained him with an offer of foodstuffs,' Archduke told her, hanging his cloak on a peg. 'It's not often that I get a visitor. Now, concerning that favour . . .'

'Anything,' Bernice declared, 'for finding Wolsey.'

Archduke grinned. 'I have written a book, of which I am rather proud, and since it concerns a theatrical form from your favourite era and planet, twentieth-century Earth, I was wondering –?'

Bernice's heart sank, but she managed a bright smile. 'Of course I'll read it. I'll need something to keep me occupied on the journey to Perfecton.'

'Ah yes, Perfecton; I am envious of you all. My slight sway with the Vice Chancellor was not enough to secure me a berth. I suppose that Earth Literature isn't the most obvious of studies for a journey to a dead civilization . . .'

'I don't think Etiquette is going to be a vital discipline in the exploration either, but we have no fewer than two specialists in that field coming along.'

'Hmm. Knowledge above all, as they say. To take one Etiquette specialist to Perfecton may be a misfortune, to take two . . .'

'Is sheer bloody nonsense,' Bernice finished.

'You know the quotation.' Archduke moved towards his library. 'I'll just get that data module. I'm sure it's compatible with the cruiser's computer.'

Once he'd gone, Bernice kissed Wolsey on the top of his head. 'See what you've made me do?' she whispered. 'You've made me read a textbook.'

Extract from the Diary of Bernice Summerfield:

After I dropped Wolsey off at my rooms, and gave him one of his *looks* right back at him when he realized that his biccie ration had been cut in half, I rushed to my noon tutorial. That, as always, faded into an afternoon beer session in the Garland College bar, the Witch and Whirlwind. There's nothing like good, rich ale when the shadows grow longer and the gold of autumn is on the land. It helps you to embrace time, makes you philosophical. Or just too pissed to care. Over a couple of pints of it, I became settled into my favourite bar-corner armchair, seven of the most devoted of my protégés gathered in an adoring circle about me. Doran was there, but I managed to resist the urge to ruffle his hair, pinch his fresh cheek or pat him on the head. An urge towards maturity should not immediately turn one into a fruity old lady. He'd already started to read the book I'd given him, and didn't question the lack of archaeological material so far.

My other six admirers were:

Arex, Polybus: a Lucidian with golden skin who wears a freedom ring through his nose, a Lucidian Power Y-shirt, and bristles at every mention I make of human achievement, insisting that the lost empire of Lucidia had been behind every major achievement in human history. He's actually right about that, but I wouldn't dream of telling him.

Rose, Anne-Marie: a human girl who dotes on my every

word and gesture, violently rowing with Arex whenever he disagrees with me. I think she may have a little bit of a crush on me, the poor thing. Hee hee hee hee hee.

Fuleep, Ockjin: a vastly chested Maldean sports student, who tries to translate everything into a bizarre philosophy he calls Common Sense and can't be bothered to work too hard. He fears change, I think.

Waspo, Jayne: a rich and offhand girl who spends all her time making sure that her dress doesn't get dirty. She seems to hang around me because she regards me as the closest thing the course has to a celebrity. Goddess knows what she'll be like in the field.

Pluse, Vitor: a bit of a lad. He keeps making Chelonian jokes, which, since I have some personal experience of that species, I suppose I should complain about. He's also, unfortunately, a Linnekerist. You get a lot of these cultists in twentieth-century studies, but this one's my first. That's the trouble with religious tolerance: it stops you from giving somebody a good slap.

Marjorie, Marjorie: a very caring and sharing young woman with pink hair and cheeks, who insists that we should all forget our differences and cooperate, and that everybody's point of view is equally valid. Whereas I tend towards the view that my point of view is rather more valid than anyone else's, her services at the more fractious moments of debate amongst this lot are welcome.

We were arguing – sorry, debating – the current vogue in archaeology for actually experiencing the times researched, via sophisticated computer recreations of the era concerned. Now, I think this is bollocks, basically, that history creeps into the book of archaeology and rewrites every line, to the point where any reading of the past distorts it. It's a sort of quantum-fridge-light-on-off-status-look-inside thing. But then I'm vastly experienced in practical archaeology, and my young charges are but students, not yet having got their hands dirty.

I held up a hand, and Rose hushed the others in expectation of my words of wisdom, her bright eyes positively staring at me from under her untended plop of blonde hair. 'You have not lived,' I told them, 'until you have been up to your thighs in mud, your mind completely on the job.'

'Really?' Doran had his chin rested on his hands, gazing at me with puppy eyes.

'Unfortunately,' said Waspo, flicking her raven-black bob away from her sharp features, 'it doesn't sound like the way to get rich and famous.'

'At the end of the day, all things considered, that sounds like the Last Chance Saloon for any title hopes,' agreed Pluse, grinning a grin of irregular and missing teeth before draining his pint.

'That's the only way we're going to understand Perfecton civilization,' I said. I took another sip from my beer, and watched the first rays of afternoon sunlight peeping through the clouds outside the window. The golden fittings on the bar looked particularly nice that afternoon, and I wondered what they would look like buried in sand, unearthed by alien fingers in a few centuries. I was prey that day, as I often am, as archaeologists in general often are, to mortal thoughts. Perhaps I had some inkling of what was later to befall me. Or perhaps not. 'The Perfectons, as we call them, because they never left a name for themselves, vanished five thousand years ago, before most currently civilized species – yes, including yours, Arex – had been into space. They had technology beyond our dreams, but didn't leave their homeworld. All we know of them is in the records left by other races who landed on Perfecton, and they're very incomplete. We don't know, for instance, why they died out.'

'They probably had a war, or created a virus, or summat.' Fuleep took another draught from his protein drink and yawned, his big face unfolding and then folding up again. He smacked his chops together a few times and laid his head on his hands, as if about to drop off.

I nodded brightly, trying to encourage these small seedlings of intelligence. 'That's why Earth Central declared Perfecton to be a Prohibited World when it was located. That order is lifted next week, and you're all utterly fortunate to be part of the first scientific landing party. Don't let the activities of our shipmates fool you. This journey is going to be about hard work, about archaeology. This is the real thing.' I threw back the last dregs of my pint. 'We leave tomorrow, so early to bed, and remember to pack your equipment.' With that, I stood up, sat down again, made a greater effort and then stood firmly on my feet.

My students gave me a round of applause.

I found the door quite easily, just as two men I didn't recognize were entering the bar. One was fat and solid-looking, the other was thin and sharp. They were dressed in identical dark suits and homburg hats, which, and I confess that I only realized this a couple of hours later, weren't stained by the rain at all. They were attempting to be inconspicuous by wearing shades.

Everybody in the bar looked at them.

They stopped when they saw me, as if they recognized me. The fat one took a step closer, looking very serious. 'We,' he whispered in my ear, 'are on a mission from God.'

'How nice for you,' I said, and left.

I often think that, if I paid more attention, I'd lead a much more comfortable life.

Diary Entry Ends

Chapter 2

New Adventures, New Danger

The IAC cruiser *Winton* was just visible in the twilight sky above the planet Perfecton, a small and swiftly circling star. Outside her tent on the planet's surface, Bernice put a hand to her brow and watched the ship twinkle as it passed through the smoke of the campfire. It had done that for two weeks now, completing an orbit every two hours, a little clock for this timeless old world.

The *Winton* was the most powerful craft available to St Oscar's University – an ex-military vessel capable of carrying a crew of one hundred. Much of this capacity, including the weapons bay that once held missiles, had been filled with scientific equipment and provisions for the expedition. The journey had taken a week through hyperspace. The official quarantine of the planet, enforced by a number of blockade satellites, had expired a day before the ship arrived. The satellites had exploded on the deadline as promised, leaving a trail of debris around the planet. Bits of that fell into the atmosphere at regular intervals, creating spectacular meteor showers.

As far as the ship's crew had established, there was nobody else in orbit around Perfecton. St Oscar's was the only academic body with a permit to land, as yet, but the reputation of the planet stretched across the civilized galaxy. Unlicensed explorers could be relied upon to arrive at some point.

Upon achieving orbit, one of the *Winton*'s jolly boats had immediately descended to the surface, the university's small team of security troops making the first landing to check for weapons systems, atmospheric poisons and other environmental problems, such as the viral contamination that had worried Fuleep. Their survey took a day, and during that time Bernice had found herself pacing the ship as if she was waiting for her date to show up, stopping at a window from time to time to gaze down at the silvery grey globe below. Wolsey – whom seeing as everybody else had treated this trip as a beano, she'd brought along in a basket – got a lot of petting that day. But even during the waiting, much to her guilt, Bernice had never got round to reading Professor Archduke's theatrical thesis. In a moment of mental strength, she had loaded it into the ship's central computer, for replay on her lectern. But something else had come up before she could actually read the first line.

The academics who'd wangled a trip on this historic mission included Professor Warrinder, who'd spent most of the journey out looking extremely worried. Bernice had asked him what was wrong, but he'd just waggled his paws, and replied that he was getting precognitive flashes whose contents he could not take seriously. He wouldn't elaborate further. Menlove Stokes had, thankfully, left his tubes at home, though he had in his luggage several suspicious-looking sample jars. He'd announced at one of the many shipboard parties that he was going to develop a new style of painting, one suited to the colours and textures of Perfecton's surface. Hettie and Lucinda had managed to secure the ship's captain for both their parties, but only because he'd dashed from one end of the ship to the other when Hettie was looking the other way. And Bernice had been delighted to make the acquaintance of a

Professor Arthur Candy, a chubby and jolly academic whose subject of study she hadn't managed to discover.

This group, and the fifty other academics who'd managed to blag passage on this trip, had descended in the third boat. The second boat, at Bernice's request, was reserved for herself and her tutorial group, who would, after all, be doing all the hard work in the next three weeks.

She'd stepped out on to the surface of this new, old world and lifted her foot to inspect the imprint that her boot had made in the silver dust. 'That's one small step for a single woman,' she whispered.

And, looking up into the face of a spectacular Perfecton sunset, she'd stretched to her greatest height, fallen back against the chattering gang of her students and whooped to the sky.

That had got an interesting, if rather scared, look from Doran.

The reality had been as good as the anticipation. The surface of the planet was covered in a soft, grey dust. It formed dunes that stretched to every horizon, that shifted and whispered under the gentle winds of a thoroughly breathable and, indeed, invigorating atmosphere. It was the opposite of rain and, for that reason alone, the Dellah delegation were glad to be in it. Bernice's team had established a camp in the lee of one of Perfecton's major cities, a group of seven tall lozenge-shaped buildings that, eroded as they were, still managed to tower over the sand. They were golden in colour and, silhouetted against the vast red bulk of the setting sun, they were a sight that, after two weeks, still made Bernice ache. It was an ache to stay: their mission was just to map the ground, establish parameters, take some minor samples . . . and an ache for something long lost and now returned, something that she didn't dare identify.

This was where she belonged, in the field.

Because here you could work so hard you didn't get time to think about your mistakes.

Now, Bernice stretched again, luxuriating in the alien landscape. Picking up her rucksack, she headed towards the campfire. Whereas, in the drunken rush to complete her ordinary packing, Bernice had forgotten her toothbrush, her earrings and several sets of underwear, she'd got her rucksack, as she always did, absolutely right. It contained her archaeological equipment, her data-retrieval systems, and a number of carefully selected tools and ration packs, as well as the standard bottle of fine brandy. This rucksack had saved Bernice's life many times: she could pack it blindfold, and, once, owing to a mistake involving a pair of handcuffs and an alarm clock, she had.

The golden towers to the west had, by now, been thoroughly mapped by the tutorial group, and the beacons they'd left as markers across the site could be seen all the way to the base of those monuments, winking in the declining light.

The students had returned to the camp, and had collapsed around the campfire, groaning and laughing. Those were good sounds. Bernice had spent the day recording the inscriptions on a big pair of golden doors that, presumably, led into the city that she was sure lay buried under the towers. So far, her translators could make nothing of the language.

She reached in her rucksack, and found what she was looking for: an elderly, blue-bound notebook, a little frayed at the spine, its pages filled with yellow notelets. This was the latest incarnation of Bernice's diary, and the sticky-tabbed notelets were what she used to rewrite particularly dull or angst-ridden episodes into more glittering things. She opened it and, sitting cross-legged beside her students, pushed her glasses up on her nose, and poised her pen to write. 'It's the last day of our initial mapping mission,' she told the group. 'We return to the ship at midnight, for the best night's sleep any of us have had in the last two weeks. Anybody got any observations for posterity?'

'Never worked so hard in my life,' laughed Fuleep. 'My boots are full of dust.'

'Very, very messy,' agreed Waspo, who was using a spray to try to return the shine to her flat but fashionable shoes. 'But I'm looking forward to writing it all up. There's a book in this, wouldn't you say?'

Bernice met her enquiring gaze evenly. 'I'll have to see if my publisher's interested, but I'm a bit busy at the moment.'

Waspo looked shocked. 'I didn't mean –'

Bernice waved the response aside and pointed to the girl's shoes. 'Do the undersides as well, but not the heels if you're walking over sand.'

Pluse had stood up, and was gazing at the horizon, a hand to his brow. 'At the end of the day, though,' he said, 'one has to say that the performance has been nothing short of brilliant.'

'He means, like, the sunset looks good,' noted Arex. 'It's been a good few days, you know? I've had a good time.'

'We've all had a good time,' Marjorie murmured, taking the hands of her neighbours to the left and right. 'And I feel much closer to everybody here because of this bonding experience. I think it would be nice if we could all sing something to celebrate our mutual closeness.'

'Oh, can we sing?' Rose turned eagerly to Bernice, smoothing back the colourful braids in her hair. 'Can we, Professor Summerfield?'

Doran glanced laconically up from where he was tossing sticks into the fire. 'Yes, Bernice. Know any good songs?'

'Can we call her Bernice?' Rose looked between Bernice and Doran. 'Is that allowed?'

'Virtually everything is allowed,' Bernice replied, glancing at Doran over her glasses again. 'Call me whatever you're comfortable with, as long as it's flattering.'

'Then I shall call you Benny,' Rose cut in quickly. 'And I bet you know some good songs from all that time you spent exploring space.'

'I heard she was in the military,' Arex added, with a wry glance at Benny. 'Oppressing my people and anybody else who stood in Earth's way.'

Bernice closed her eyes for a moment. This must be what being a mother was like. At least Arex was now baiting her with a touch of self-mockery. 'I was conscripted, straight out of the Academy, yes, like a lot of us were during the wars. I bailed out of a troopship on the way to a battle, joined a dig by faking my qualifications, and worked my way up to being in charge of many expeditions. I gained my doctorate on the run, through experience. Any more questions?'

'Gosh,' said Rose.

'Now, as to the matter of music . . .' Bernice took off her glasses and dropped them into her top pocket. 'I know several campfire ditties, but few as appropriate as this one. Some of the words may be strange to you. They come from old English, from an era that I specialize in.' She took a deep breath, and began to sing. 'It was on the good ship Venus . . .'

On the other side of the dunes, further from the towers of the Perfecton city, Menlove Stokes looked up from his painting, and frowned. 'Is that some sort of desert creature howling?'

'Not unless it knows some very rude words,' chuckled Professor Candy as he wandered by, clutching a glass of champagne. He stopped for a moment to take a look at Stokes's canvas, winced, and moved on.

The academic staff had set up camp a mile or so from the archaeology site, and had spent the last two weeks trying to justify their presence. Stokes had his painting, of course.

Candy had been sunbathing in a pair of outsize shorts, and Hettie and Lucinda had spent the time arguing over the best word to describe the beautiful desolation that surrounded them. They'd got to the point of agreeing that it should be a new word, a word never heard before. Hettie had settled on 'lituminous', Lucinda on 'scithering', and from that point both ladies had become entrenched in their points of view. They were now settled in sofas at opposite ends of a wilderness barbecue and wine tasting, a crowd of other academics milling around them.

Professor Epstein, who was a specialist in Chelonian Literature, with a neat little beard and a pair of tape-repaired glasses permanently attached to his nose, was waving a vegetarian sausage meaningfully, and explaining the nature of his work to Professor Owl, an elderly, rather buxom cosmologist, who used a monocle and was never without her grey cardigan. 'They don't have a word for comedy. That's the whole schtick with these martial races, they have to take themselves so seriously, because, if they don't, their society collapses. They're almost an adolescent race, and you know adolescents –'

'Once.'

'They think that the only art form that's valid is melodrama, a bunch of serious individuals yelling at each other about serious subjects. And those subjects invariably require those characters to use and carry weapons. The mark of a sane society, Professor, of any sane person, is comedy. The ability to laugh at oneself. You introduce a hint of comedy into a culture like the Chelonian, and –' he made a vast deflating gesture '– the whole thing falls apart.'

Candy had been listening, nodding. 'Ooh, that's exactly what my academic speciality is about,' he began, and started enthusing to them.

Professor Warrinder was scampering from one end of the party to the other, trying to please both Hettie and

Lucinda with his choice of wines.

He arrived at a hop to fill Stokes's outstretched glass, and gazed at the artist's canvas in wonder. 'Why, it's lovely,' he chittered.

Stokes stopped painting and blinked at him, astonished. This wasn't the normal reaction to his work. 'Do you really think so?'

'Yes, it reminds me of a dream I once had. A surreal thing, full of fear and vertigo.'

'It's a self-portrait,' said Stokes.

'I'm sure it could be that, too.'

'Are you still getting those headaches?' Stokes asked, a little too sharply.

'Indeed.' The Pakhar settled for a moment, and tapped his skull with his paw. 'My precognitive abilities keep on telling me that something strange and wonderful is about to happen, but when I try to ascertain just what that is . . . the images I get are . . . bizarre.'

Stokes shrugged. He wasn't really used to the company of academics, not having been one for very long. It was difficult to tell the reality from the pose sometimes. More than anything else, Stokes detested pretentious people. 'Perhaps you're just visualizing my next work. It's going to be a painting that will encompass the entire visual experience of this planet. I'm going to paint it tonight, on a precipice I've found that lies above a magnificent valley, the scene illuminated only by the light of the luminescent rocks in that area.'

Warrinder sniffed. 'Your canvas . . . does it smell . . . peculiar, to you?'

'Not at all.' Stokes smiled. 'It smells, Professor Warrinder, of humanity.'

'. . . all else to do!' Bernice's party finished the song.

During the laughter and cheering, Doran made his way around the fire to where Bernice was sitting, and put his hand on her shoulder. 'Excuse me. Could I have a word? In private?'

Benny felt two terrible urges at the same time: one to scream that no, he couldn't, the other to throw him into a fireman's lift and run off across the dunes with him.

'Of course,' is what she settled on, not without a little lump in her throat. 'The rest of you start packing up the tents. The boat'll be here in twenty minutes.'

They walked across the dunes, in the vague direction of Hettie and Lucinda's barbecue. The trail of smoke from that was the only cloud in the neon-black of the Perfecton night. There was silence, apart from the swish of their feet in the sand and the distant conversation of both camps. Bernice knitted her fingers behind her back, attempting to look old and wise. She and Doran had been smiling at each other over tools and brushing past each other in narrow rock corridors these last two weeks. He'd stopped being shy, and had achieved a sort of gentle confidence around her, which was just the worst sort of thing for Bernice's composure. She no longer felt like the aggressor in their little, held-too-long glances. Something was going to happen here, at some point. If she let it.

'It's about the star,' Doran began.

'Um-hm?'

'I did a course in astrophysics at my last college. Just the basics, but enough to know that this star is a very old, very diffuse red giant. Surely, it could go supernova at any time.'

Bernice nodded. 'Of course. But the ship's sensors would detect the first signs of such a collapse. I've been assured there's a plan to get us away in time.' She took his arm, in a matronly, mentorlike way, and was pleased that the action made him straighten up slightly, nervous. 'But that isn't the most scary bit, Michael.' That was the first time she'd used his first name. 'The climate here is impossible for a planet orbiting a red giant, so, presumably, it's maintained by some remaining piece of Perfecton technology, one which could go wrong at any moment, leaving us all suddenly vulnerable to the chill vacuum of space.' She watched Doran absorb that information. He stopped walking.

'All of a sudden,' he said, 'I feel really cold.'

'Do you?' Bernice let go of his arm. They looked at each other for a moment. He was terrifyingly young. And he was looking at her evenly now, without nerves.

There was a moment in which they just got to know the details of each other's face.

She made a sudden little noise of closure, and slapped him heartily on the shoulder. 'Let's get back to the camp.'

'Yes. Let's.' He seemed almost as relieved as she was.

When they got back to the camp, Bernice was pleased to find that Professor Candy had arrived, carrying his luggage, and that she now had somebody she could naturally talk to without having to look at Doran. The camp was packed up, the tents rolled, and the campfire switched off. Waspo was supervising everybody, pointing to canteens and tools that had escaped the packing, and Arex had already reached his most fearsome level of glower.

'Bernice!' called Professor Candy, waving his chubby hand. 'Ooh, we know where you've been!'

'What?!' Benny flushed. 'What do you mean? I've merely been discussing some important issues with –' She stopped, and forced her face into a chilly smile. 'Ah. Yes. That's me, I never miss a chance to seduce my students. Ha ha ha. Is the boat here yet?'

As if on cue, a moving star grew brighter overhead, and gravitic engines started to wash the dunes flat.

Benny couldn't quite meet Candy's happy glance as the boat descended.

* * *

Menlove Stokes wistfully watched the boat ascend from the archaeologists' camp. Warrinder, Hettie and Lucinda and the other academics had retired to their tents. Candy had got out while the going was good, electing to sleep back on the *Winton*. The night was Stokes's, and the chill of the increasing darkness brought with it a sense of expectation. There was, he felt sure, a key to this planet, a dark heart that could be divined only through the artistic impulse. Perhaps tonight he would glimpse it, absorb it, transfer it to his canvas.

He picked up his artist's materials and his jars, and, with a single Gothic glance over his shoulder, raced off into the night.

The valley of his dreams awaited him.

The boat having docked with the *Winton*, Bernice found that she was very tired. She'd been operating on adrenaline for the last two weeks, and the thought of curling up in a real bunk appealed to her more than anything. She was, for one thing, mentally kicking herself for being so teenagerish over Doran. Like a snake or a spider, he was almost certainly more afraid of her than she was of him. Before she'd got married she hadn't been this much of a wimp. She resolved either to go for it: take him out to dinner, impress him with her wit and depth, shag him like a bunny; or drop it: treat him like any other student and stop being so soppy.

Which of these two options to pursue was an entirely different question.

While pondering this, she popped her head into the tiny flight deck of the ship, and knocked on a bulkhead. 'Hello?'

Captain Balsam glanced up from the desk where he was leafing idly through instrument logs. He was a handsome, athletic, middle-aged man, with a black beard and a receding hairline. At the controls behind him sat a very beautiful young woman with long auburn hair. Both of them wore the uniforms of IAC non-academic staff. 'Good evening, Professor. What can we do for you?'

'Just a small worry before bedtime. One of my students thinks that the star's going to blow up and kill us all.'

'Oh, it's entirely possible.' The captain settled into his chair. 'The blowing-up bit, anyway. That star could detonate right now, or in three hundred years' time. It's impossible to tell.' He nodded over his shoulder. 'Aurum here is my navigator. You've been briefed on this, haven't you, Lieutenant Salvistra?'

The young woman glanced up at Bernice. 'The captain's right about the star. I believe that it was one of the factors that Earth Central took into account when opening the quarantine on Perfecton.'

'You're very well informed. But if it does go boom –'

'We're completely prepared. The automatics are tuned to listen in for the first signs of collapse, and they'll have the whole ship up and about if it starts to happen. We'll have about three hours then before supernova, more than enough time to evacuate everyone and get into hyper-space.'

The captain stroked his beard thoughtfully. 'You know, I have been wondering if anybody told your fellow academics about this.'

'That sounds like the Dean's sense of humour.' Bernice grinned and bade the captain goodnight.

Stokes stood on a ledge above the Great Valley. The whole sweep of the planet, from horizon to horizon, was darkened now, the only source of light being the patches of phosphorescent minerals that lined the valley walls. The bottom lay over two miles below him, obscured slightly by gleaming mists that reflected the light from the walls.

There was something strange about the shape of the valley floor, thought Stokes. He'd expected it to look different at night: he'd chanced across this valley in broad daylight. But . . . there was definitely an unusual shape down there. His artist's eye would pick it out when he started painting, he was certain.

He set up his easel and started to wash his canvas with a silver base. The strangest thing about this planet was the silence. No bird or animal noises, no leaves rustling. The only sound was the continual wash of wind on sand. What with the ozone in the air, it was rather like being at the seaside.

He glanced up at the thin column of smoke that drifted from behind the low hills nearby. They'd put out the barbecue. Good. Human activity seemed wrong here, like bunting at a funeral procession. It was as if they'd brought time to a timeless world, started a clock ticking where previously there had only been forever.

He picked up his palette knife, and made the first slash of paint across the canvas: red on silver. He hadn't got to the bodily fluids yet, but still he shivered slightly at the sight of it.

From the *Informative Record of Recent Grel History*:

(Note by Professor B. S. Summerfield, translator: While the Grel pride themselves on their information-gathering and classification, Grel literature, perversely, tends to emphasize the *emotional* aspects of their story. It's as if the Grel mind can only experience the sensations and excitements of conflict in later contemplation. Their Scribes, working from exact and precise data recordings, transmitted to Grellor on a moment-by-moment basis by teams in the field, feel free to embellish this data with the most heroic details. Presumably, any Grel who wishes to peruse the actual records can access the originals. We could accurately describe the process of writing Grel history as *novelization*.)

Millions of Heights above the heads of the unknowing humans on the planet, the golden shape of the *Winton* swung around the world in its clocklike orbit.

And hundreds of Heights above that, unseen by any of the unsuspecting lesser beings, sat another, smaller craft. Its shape was that of a five-pointed star, with many sensor probes extending from its hull. It was a datarunner of the glorious Grel!

From inside the craft, two handsomely tentacled faces gazed down at the image of the *Winton* on a viewing screen. And laughed a proud and confident laugh.

'Confirmed, Master. That is an *Inman* Class cruiser, withdrawn from military service because of problems with its sensors. Main problem: the inability to sense objects above itself.'

'Good fact, Servitor.' The Master of the Grel dataforce leant back from the screen, the tentacles of its face twiddling themselves into keen knots of anticipation. Above the tentacles sat two particularly gleaming and flat black eyes, and they were filled with excitement also.

(Note: The Grel have humanoid bodies, with thin, tentacular fingers. Their bulbous heads and similarly tentacular faces sit atop thin, muscular torsos. They are so much a human nightmare that it has been speculated that they were created specially by a particularly bloody-minded genetic engineer. Their own creation legends talk of stumbling up from the ocean and being clever enough to make themselves bodies that could walk. That cleverness bit is the central plank of the Grellan psyche as expressed in the *Informative Record*. The Grel are cleverer than everybody else, they know more things, and they like to laugh at the dolts that trouble the planets of other star systems. They think of themselves as the monarchs of information, uncaring that everybody else thinks of them as rather gittish pirates.)

'So they are not aware of us.' The Grel Master turned to his Servitors and clenched his powerful fist. 'Prepare the attack force!'

Extract Ends

Bernice had fallen asleep in the bath, a victim of the lag that, even when the ship's hours have been synchronized with that of the target area on the destination planet, catches up with you in spaceflight. She was woken by the noise of Wolsey, scratching against the door. She sploshed out, staring at her water-wrinkled fingers in shock, threw on her robe, and opened the door for him.

She was surprised to see Doran there as well, in the corridor that ran between the bathroom and the passenger bunkrooms. He was leaning on the bulkhead, dressed in a bathrobe of his own, sound asleep, the towel he was carrying having fallen at his feet.

Bernice picked up Wolsey and breezily tapped Doran on the shoulder. 'Bathroom's free.'

He jumped, and woke up. 'Oh. Right. Thanks.'

'Why ever didn't you knock on the door?'

'I knew it was you in there, from the singing. I thought you deserved a bit of a soak, with all the work you've put in. So I left you for a while –'

'Listening to me sing?'

'"Lullaby of Birdland", isn't that what it's called? It certainly was a lullaby in my case.'

Bernice realized that she was feeling a great deal more stable, having napped and soaked. Her hormones were, at this moment, blissfully under control again. So she made that big decision she'd been sleeping on. She picked up Doran's towel and handed it to him. 'In you go,' she said. 'When you've finished, you can pop in and have a glass of brandy with me. If you want.'

'That would be nice.'

There was a little moment of stillness again. But this

time it was just good. Then he went into the bathroom, and Bernice headed for her room. 'Yippee,' she whispered to Wolsey.

Stokes had slapped the vague shape of the valley on to his canvas. Now, before adding colour and texture, he took a step back from his work and looked down into the chasm again.

Once more, something had changed.

'Oh dear,' he muttered. 'I hope this doesn't turn out to be one of those planets that are actually gigantic living organisms.' He looked quickly between his painting and the valley floor, many times, until he finally worked out what had changed.

Under a particularly dense patch of mist, a new rock outcrop had appeared. At least, that's what he thought it was. He couldn't make out any detail on the shadowy form. It was thin and tall, and – Stokes made a little noise at the realization – it was moving! As if it was alive! The thing was slowly, but surely, turning. Like a plant in a time-lapse film, following the course of the sun.

He glanced upwards, and saw the star that was the *Winton*, sailing smoothly in its orbit overhead. He looked between the outcrop and the ship, and raised a very worried finger.

Bernice dried her hair, and dabbed her wrists, neck and, what the hell, cleavage, with *Ah: A Perfume for an Alien or a Human.* She arranged her robe carefully, to show an accidentally large, but still academically decent, area of herself. She unhitched the catch from the door, so it just hung shut by its own weight. She went to the brandy on the pullout table by the bed, and had a small glass, quietly appalled by what she was contemplating here.

She had worked hard. She deserved this. It had been a very long time. She had love to give, and it had been unfairly boxed up by her ex, shut away with their other shared possessions. He had probably been unfaithful already.

Unfaithful. As if there still was any faith between them. She still felt guilty, felt that he was going to burst in at any moment.

But no. This was hers now. She was free.

She was going to sing this boy a lullaby.

She just hoped that she could stay awake until he'd finished his bath.

Archduke's thesis. Right. That would focus her attention. Bernice went to the lectern on her tiny desk, and brought up the menu from the ship's central computer. There was the manuscript, along with all the other academic source texts.

She put her finger on the button to access it, and paused, while she gave a great yawn.

That was going to put her to sleep, not keep her awake. The central computer's access sprite popped up on the screen after a few moments, and with a flutter of graphic wings and a wave of its virtual wand asked her petulantly if she was actually going to look at the text this time? If not, it would refile it in twenty minutes.

She turned away from the lectern again, and looked around the room nervously. Where should she be when he came in? What should she be doing? Not looking at a textbook, that would set up completely the wrong impression. That would be her being old again, old and unwantable, and just something a student flirted with because he could and he probably laughed with the others about it, and she went to lock her door.

No. No, you must let yourself have this.

She sat down on the edge of the bed, forcefully, and wondered about how she had gone from being a mature professor to an adult seductress to a teenager in the last ten minutes without at any time noticing these vast shifts in age.

Bernice sighed, laughed a little, felt like crying, and arranged herself on the corner of the bed.

From the *Informative Record of Recent Grel History*:

The excitingly coloured Grel ship descended towards the *Winton*, faster and faster, its spines extending and flexing, ready to clip into the other ship's dataports.

At its airlocks, a squad of brave Grel Servitors stood ready, spinning their two-headed dataxes and flicking the security catches off the energy weapons contained therein. They started up an ululating cry as they spun their weapons faster and faster, the harmonics of the chant vibrating the hull that held them until every Grel could feel the purpose of its species in its throat.

Their prey grew bigger beneath them: a shipful of knowledge, an appetizer for the planet below.

Extract Ends

Stokes heard something. It was coming from the valley below, and it was definitely there, not just one of those dream sounds that his ears kept inventing in the silence.

He looked up from his half-completed canvas and stepped as near as he dared to the edge of the cliff. He'd watched the thing on the valley floor track the arc of the *Winton* for a full turn across the sky, after which it had stopped moving. He thought it had fallen back to lie pointing to the opposite horizon, as if waiting for the ship to rise again. The whole business was a major discovery, of course, something to tell the archaeologists on board ship tomorrow. It was probably some sort of robotic antenna. Perhaps it was, even now, sending signals to the ship. For a while, Stokes had been torn between running back to the academics' camp and finishing his painting. In the end, when the thing had stopped moving, he decided that he'd missed the moment for sudden action, and that art was, for now, more important. If he stopped painting, then he'd lose this quality of light, not to mention the quality of his own emotions, and when he returned to the canvas, nothing would be the same.

Besides, if he didn't get a covering of plasti on this thing within a couple of hours, no gallery would be willing to subject its visitors to the smell of it.

But the sound had stopped him again. He glanced at his watch, and did a quick mental calculation. The *Winton* would appear over the horizon in about ten minutes. He got to his knees, and stared down into the valley, trying to make out what was going on beneath an ever more obscuring layer of mist.

The noise was definitely coming from down there. It was a high screeching, gradually increasing in pitch, mechanical rather than biological. It reminded Stokes of . . . now what did it remind him of?

Bernice had nodded off, lying back on the bed in a very unromantic slump, her legs dangling over the edge.

The knock on her door made her sit bolt upright, suddenly in full-on Christmas-morning mode. She made herself take a couple of deep breaths as she adjusted her robe and curled her legs up beneath her. She licked her lips quickly, and pushed her hair back into place. Then she called out, 'Come in!'

The door swung open, and into her room stepped the two men in dark glasses from the Garland College bar. They were still wearing their hats. 'We –' one of them began, stepping forward and pointing at her.

'Who –?' Bernice bellowed, jumping to her feet. 'How –?'

But then a number of things happened all at once.

Stokes had been concentrating on a particular place on the horizon, the vague area where he was sure that the star that was the *Winton* was going to appear. The whine from the canyon had levelled off to a steady pitch, and maintained that volume, an irritating noise that seemed about to continue indefinitely. Stokes couldn't paint while that was going on, so he'd spent his time observing the strange shape in the chasm, putting his fingers in his ears, and wondering if he should tell somebody about all this. The dear ladies and the others at the camp must surely have heard this ear-splitting howl.

The spaceship appeared on the horizon, and Stokes blinked at the shimmering shape for a moment. It looked bigger. Or was that just the effect of the atmosphere? He moved to the edge of the parapet, and looked down into the valley. The moving thing had started to move again. Very fast. And was that just the billowing of the mist, or was it emitting . . . smoke?

Stokes tried to think quickly, but the noise had reached a crescendo. All thought of his painting abandoned, he sketched quickly on his easel, trying to record the shape of the thing in the valley. It was long and thin, pointing upwards, with a rounded top. Right. It was emitting smoke, probably from its rear end. Right. It was making a screeching whine . . . actually, that had changed. It had now become a low rumble. And now a wooshing.

Stokes looked back into the valley and cried out as one end of the object down there flared with brilliant light. The object vibrated for a moment, and then, with a sudden roar, leapt up from the floor of the valley, illuminating every wall with the fire from its tail. Stokes staggered back from the cliff edge, his easel blown aside, as the thing, the . . . missile . . . flashed past him on its way skyward. His ears ringing, peering through the vapour trail that had filled the valley and was billowing out across the sand, Stokes managed to see where it was heading.

It had the tiny star of the ship locked in its sights, and was heading straight for it.

From the *Informative Record of Recent Grel History*:

The Grel ship hit the *Winton* like a predator striking its prey. Its spines slammed into the vessel's dataports, invading them with the usual viruses, which disabled all the cruiser's security systems and blew open every airlock. Tentacles from the Grel ship whipped around the other ship's body, and Grel airlock tubes thrust themselves into each open lock.

The *Winton*, every motion system in disarray, spun on its axis, one thruster firing randomly. This spun the Grel ship underneath the other vessel, putting it, for a moment, between the *Winton* and the planet below.

Which was why, as shrieking Grel Servitors, eager for battle, ran into the other ship, spiralling their axes, the bridge crew, including the Grel Master, were suddenly aware of an imminent danger, one that they had utterly failed to predict.

Extract Ends

Bernice staggered across her cabin as the ship rolled. She grabbed one of the men by the lapels. '– in the name of goodness did you get here?'

'– are on a mission from –'

On Perfecton, Professor Warrinder woke up screaming. 'Oh no!' he squealed. 'It's all coming true!'

From the *Informative Record of Recent Grel History*:

The Grel Master hit a button.

Explosive bolts fired.

The command pod flew clear.

Extract Ends

Doran stepped out of the bathroom.

A screeching squid-faced humanoid with an axe was running down the corridor towards him.

He put up his hands.

The blade slashed down.

Bernice swung her head at a sudden light outside the porthole.

She saw something rushing at the ship.

'God,' said the man.

The missile hit the *Winton*.

And turned it into a vast, expanding blossom of flame.

CHAPTER 3

A COMEDY TONIGHT

Once upon a time . . .

Professor Bernice Surprise Summerfield woke up, stretched, and sang a single pure note. The stretch had brought on the singing. It was all because of the look of the day. Sunlight was dappling through leaves above her. Birds were cheeping. The air smelt of a summer morning.

What had she been doing last night, to end up here?

Absently, she reached out for her glasses. And failed to find them. She rubbed her eyes, slapping all around her for the missing, habitual object as she did so.

She found grass. Roots. The roots of the . . . she looked up . . . old oak tree that she had been sleeping against.

As student pranks went, this wasn't bad at all. If she'd planned it, they would have brought her furniture out into this lovely bit of parkland as well, and probably left her in her nightshirt rather than take the time and trouble to put –

Her boots on. Her boots were on.

She raised a knee to her chin. Not even her boots, actually. These were a pair of green ankle-length jobs, with the tops folded over in a sort of starfish design that Bernice could only describe as a boot cuff.

Strange. But still within the bounds of Garland College mischief. The boots probably implied something in Tashwari culture. As did the golden tunic, rather fabulous puffy-sleeved shirt, which she was keeping, serious tights, zero trousers and tiny tricorn hat. Bernice grinned to herself and settled back against the tree. It could have been far, far worse.

She closed her eyes for a moment, enjoying the sunshine.

Then she opened them again.

She'd remembered the previous night.

'No it couldn't!' she screamed. 'I'm dead!'

She leapt to her feet, and slapped a hand to her mouth. Something had hit the ship. A missile. There had been a moment of impact, of being thrown against something hard.

There had been, and this convinced her with a sudden lurch of her stomach, a moment of ending. A cut off. A dislocation.

It felt like it had been the moment of her death.

And then nothing. Maybe some dreams. She'd woken here.

So . . .

She sniffed the air.

Bernice had never entertained much in the way of religious belief. A bit of arty paganism when her friends had been into it, nothing that involved churches.

There was no smell of burning flesh or brimstone. This place smelt great, in fact. Not hellish, although the costume might be the thin end of a wedge of hellish embarrassment. No, unless the first trick of hell was building up a little hope, this looked much more like heaven. Or reincarnation, there was always that. Maybe this place was as real as it looked, and she had been born again. Except that she still looked like herself, was thirtysomething still, and remembered everything about her previous existence.

Hah! There was a Heaven! And she'd got there without even trying!

She looked up at the gloriously high blue sky, and slapped her hands together, wondering where to begin. 'Hello,' she settled on. 'I just wanted to say thanks very much, whatever sort of god you are. Or the Goddess! Goodness, if it's you, I'm sorry for taking your name in vain all these years. It's very good of you to take me despite everything, and I now believe in you, and will admit to any sins that you want to hear about, and sort of throw myself on the mercy of the court and everything. Thank you for having me.'

She waited, expecting a response.

When it came, it was from the other side of the meadow.

'Hel-lo!' The voice was fruity and jolly, very clubbishly male and English. Bernice turned, rather worried, despite her bright smile, that God had turned out to be an Englishman after all.

But the figure sitting on the stile, his hand on his chin, wasn't God. Or at least, if it was, everybody was completely wrong about every sort of religion.

It was a cat in a hat. A seven-foot-tall, fully clothed cat, in a vast Cavalier hat with a peacock feather. The rest of his clothing comprised a big red coat with tails (that presumably concealed his own), another of those fabulous shirts, a dirty great scabbard, and a pair of big-thighed britches. He was smiling at Bernice and striking a thoughtful pose. 'I say,' he continued, 'I didn't expect you to be awake.'

'No,' muttered Benny, 'neither did I.'

The mancat leapt up from the stile and marched over to the oak tree. He did have a tail, Benny noticed, and it was swinging proudly to and fro. 'Thought I'd leave you to get some kip, while I satisfied myself about breakfast.' He grinned a predator's grin, behind which could be heard distant, echoing twitters.

'Indeed.' Benny brushed down her doublet, wondering why she had come into this story in the middle. If she told this big cat that she wasn't whoever it thought she was, but was actually a dead person, would it still be as friendly? She decided to play it by ear. 'So. What shall we do today?'

'Well,' the cat purred, putting its paw around her shoulder. 'You had some very strange ideas about that last night . . .'

'I did?'

'Oh yes! Before you fell asleep, you said to me, Wolsey –'

'Wolsey!' Bernice was startled. Cat and person heaven at the same time sort of thing, then? In period costume?

But it was him. She could see that now. His colouring was exactly right. He had that little dent on his brow where he'd leapt at a holorecording of one of the Three Pronged Tenors (hoping to carry the little Italian man back to his basket and eat him), but had instead just bashed his head on the player unit.

'Yes, dear, Wolsey. Who were you expecting, Michael Aspel?'

'Who?'

'Oh, you have had a rough night. I'm Wolsey! Wolsey, your oldest, dearest friend! Listen . . .' The cat leant on the tree and picked his teeth with a flourish of his claws. 'I'd do anything for you, you know. Anything.'

Bernice was about to answer that she didn't doubt that when, to her surprise, Wolsey started to sing.

'I'd do anything, for you, dear, anything, for you . . .'

Bernice could only gawp as her former pet swung himself around and about the tree, hopping up into the lower branches, giving sly little waves to birds in their nests, singing all the while. At the end of the song, he dropped on to all fours beside her, rubbed himself against her legs (which was, in the circumstances, thoroughly disturbing), and bounced up into an ornate, hat-doffing bow.

Bernice clapped a little to make him feel appreciated. She wasn't used to her associates launching into production numbers offhandedly. 'I believe you, Wolsey,' she told him, wondering if she could somehow discover just what was going on here. 'So if you'll do anything for me, tell me this: what strange ideas was I entertaining last night?'

'Why, you were ready to give up all thought of becoming Lord Mayor of London!'

Bernice found herself smiling in a rather dangerously giddy way. 'Surely not?'

'You laid your little head down on your little sack, gave a little sigh, and told me your little ambitions. To go back to home and hearth, never more to go a-roving-oh.'

'Little sack?' Bernice glanced at the tree, and saw that there was indeed a little sack, more like a violently spotted handkerchief, attached to the end of a long pole. She unwrapped it, and found a stale sandwich and some sweets. She threw away the sandwich, and threw back the sweets. This was definitely a sugar-comfort disaster moment. 'My packing skills aren't what they used to be, I see. All in all, I am not what I used to be . . .'

'Nonsense, Dick, old chap! That's what I was trying to tell you last night!'

Bernice spat out a sweet. It hit the tree. 'Dick? Chap?'

Wolsey chuckled. 'Listen, when I get together with other cats, usually ones whose owners have done terrible surgical things to them, they tell me that you, Master, are lucky to have a Wolsey. No, I tell them. It's me who's lucky. I'm lucky to have a –'

Bernice interrupted. 'I'm . . . a boy, am I?'

Wolsey laughed, and thumped her on the back. 'More of a man, now, you lively, larkish lad!'

Trying not to look as if she was doing it, Bernice gave an experimental little shake of her hips. Anything was possible, but . . . Thank heavens, no. She leant on Wolsey's shoulder in relief. 'I think you're just a little bit luckier than I am.'

'You seem in higher spirits now, Master. Tell you what: look over there.' He pointed a claw past the tree. At the edge of the meadow stood a white-painted signpost, one of its branches reading TO LONDON. 'Let's give it one more try, eh? Let's turn back on to that road, and prove that the streets of London are paved with gold!'

Bernice looked about her. Her afterlife was as inexplicable as her life had been. She felt somewhat cheated. 'All right.' She shrugged. 'As long as you don't sing.'

Stokes hadn't been able to help but watch as the missile had homed in on the spacecraft above. He was hoping with all his heart that it would miss.

One little star connected with the other.

There was an explosion that lit up the entire sky, causing Stokes to fling up his arm to save his eyes.

When he lowered it again, blinking away the sudden rush of tears, both stars were gone.

Feeling weak at the chest and knees, all he could do was run, tripping across the sands, crying out, until he stumbled into the camp of the academics. Everybody had gone to bed. All the tents were quiet.

'The ship!' he yelled. 'It's gone and got blown up!'

Hettie opened the flap of her tent, and gazed out at him calmly. 'The ship,' she corrected him, 'has exploded.'

'Exploded?!' Professor Otterbland, head of Zero Interest Philosophies, poked his head out of his tent. He was profoundly bald, with three blue lines tattooed around his head, making him a literal target for water bombs thrown from overhead walkways by his bored students. His shout caused the whole camp to wake up, and soon Stokes was surrounded by a gaggle of chattering academics, asking him questions and pointing up at the sky.

'It's definitely not up there,' said Professor Singh,

Theoretical Physics, glancing between the sky and his watch, his hawklike features growing worried. Singh habitually wore a high-collared jade jacket. Now he nervously closed the clip at the collar, as if anticipating future cold.

'If the ship has been destroyed,' Hettie began, 'then what is to become of us?'

'No interstellar communicator,' muttered Professor Epstein. 'No shipboard recycling facilities.' He glanced at the large vegetable on a spit which had been the centre-piece of the barbecue. 'But we have rations.'

'We'll just have to wait it out,' Otterbland agreed. 'The university will realize that the *Winton* hasn't been in touch and send a rescue mission.'

'If the star doesn't blow up,' Professor Owl reminded him. She glanced at Hettie. 'I'm so sorry. I meant explode.'

Lucinda had sat down on the sofa, her hand to her mouth. 'All the crew of the ship . . . that charming Professor Candy . . . and that Bernice woman . . . they've all gone.'

'Yes,' said the ancient Professor A. J. Blandish, History, nodding and sitting down beside Hettie, his white-whiskered face a picture of sadness. He hadn't yet changed from his stained tweeds, with leather patches on the elbows of his jacket. 'I wonder if I shall get her rooms.'

'How dare you?' The ancient Professor A. J. Wagstaff, also History, waved his stick at Blandish. He was similarly whiskered and tweedy, but boasted a vast off-white moustache, witness to decades of snuff abuse. 'I requested those rooms upon the day of my arrival at St Oscar's!'

'Oh dear,' murmured Professor Warrinder, 'I knew this was going to happen.'

'No you didn't,' Singh told him brusquely.

'I did! I saw the whole thing in a dream!'

'Then why didn't you tell us about it?' Singh countered. 'Then we could have done something.'

'I'm shy about revealing certain things . . .' The large

rodent looked at his feet. 'I didn't want anybody to panic if I was wrong.'

'Oh, so it was your fear of ridicule against the deaths of everybody on board the ship . . .' Singh sneered. 'Are there any other dreams that you haven't told us about?'

'Several,' Warrinder squeaked, his little nose curled downwards with worry. 'And you wouldn't believe them, either.'

'Why –' Singh visibly restrained himself from grabbing Warrinder and shaking him.

'Now, wait a moment . . .' Stokes spread his arms wide, attempting to calm everybody down, himself included. 'We're only a week away from Dellah, so we should only have to survive here for about a month at the very most. I gather there's no great likelihood of the star exploding in that time, and we have food and provisions. Assuming that the ship was destroyed by some ancient weapons system, and not a modern aggressor, we are in no danger.' He smiled, feeling rather reassured. 'Besides, look at us! We are the cream of academia, with doctorates in virtually every field of intellectual endeavour! If anybody can survive on a hostile and unknown alien world, it is us!'

'We,' clucked Hettie.

'Something's up there,' noted Otterbland.

The others all looked up, killing off Stokes's last hopes of a round of applause for his oratory. Above them a new, mobile star had appeared, and it was getting brighter every second.

Professor Janes, Space Vehicle Recognition, stepped forward, rubbing his hands together. He was rather younger than many of the other professors, an eager-looking bespectacled boffin, with a messy ginger beard. 'Oh-kay! Now, first the bad news, it isn't the *Winton* . . .'

The crowd mumbled in disappointment.

'It's not a human ship . . . the colour of that exhaust . . .

oh man, that is intriguing! This baby isn't your usual spaceship: this is something special!' Janes, tapping his chin, started to squint and gurn at the descending ship.

Professor Owl took some of the other academics aside. 'Now, I gather it's the case,' she began, 'that the missile that destroyed our ship came from down in the valley. That it was Perfecton technology?'

'That's right.' Stokes nodded.

'Extraordinary,' giggled Professor Blandish. 'The Perfectons did not have, as far as I was aware, any space technology.'

'Indeed,' agreed Professor Wagstaff. 'You may have read my monograph on the subject. The presence of a missile capable of striking down a craft in orbit . . . that is anomalous, to say the least.'

'But there is no life on this planet, not anywhere,' Owl emphasized. 'The first survey orbit made that point clear. So that missile was a working example of Perfecton technology, obeying some ancient order, the nature of which we just don't know. Now, there may well be other Perfecton spacecraft down in that valley. I really don't like the look of the star, and if this thing coming down doesn't turn out to be a rescue craft . . .'

'I see what you mean,' said Stokes.

They all turned back to where Professor Janes was slapping his cheeks, walking in little circles and kneading the air with his fingers. 'I know this! I *know* this! What *is* that spacecraft?' Above the camp, a green, circular vessel was descending, a complex squidlike design on its underbelly, its navigation lights already illuminating the tents as the first draft of its engines started to flutter them. 'It's a pod, yeah, we can see it's been separated from another craft, but what sort of pod is it?'

'Hello!' called Lucinda, waving up to it. 'Here we are!'

Stokes frowned, looking round the expectant faces of his fellow academics. Some of them were waving, some were clapping and cheering. But he'd been part of the cut-throat world of art and design for far too long to take things so much on face value. 'Excuse me,' he began, 'but could I raise the possibility that, rather than wave to this ship, we should be running from it?'

Everybody ignored him.

The ship stopped overhead, and powerful spotlights shone down, catching the nearby spars of rock, and moving across the sand towards the camp. The ship was obviously looking for somewhere to land.

'Got it!' Janes slapped his hands together in glee. 'I knew I'd seen that design before! That's –' His beam froze into a sudden realization of terror. 'Oh my God!'

And he sprinted off towards the towers of the city.

The others looked at each other.

'Well, don't just stand there!' bellowed Stokes. 'He knows something we don't! Run!'

The academics, at varying speeds, and with some grumbling, began to do so.

From the *Informative Record of Recent Grel History*:

The Grel command-deck pod landed on this strange and mysterious world and, following a complete remote-sensor survey, the Grel Master ordered that the ramp be lowered and that he and his Servitors descend to the planet's surface.

'Observation: the beings we observed have departed,' the Grel Master noted, his mouth tentacles flexing as they absorbed and studied the components of the Perfecton atmosphere. 'It is possible that they fired the missile.'

'Possibility receding,' said a Servitor who was walking around what seemed to be the remains of a camp, watching a monitor on his dataxe. 'This is a temporary settlement, designed for exploration. New possibility: these beings were from the ship we attacked.'

'Good possibility,' the Grel Master agreed.

A hoot came from the direction of the valley. Two Servitors were returning to the main party, carrying a macabre, multicoloured sheet of canvas between them.

As they approached, the Grel Master took a step back, swinging his axe up into a protective posture.

'No, Master,' one of the Grel holding the canvas hooted. 'It is not dangerous, despite the smell. Possibility: it is a recording, primitive form, of the appearance of the valley from which the missile came.'

The Grel Master lowered his axe, and put a tentacular finger to a spot on the canvas. 'Good fact. There is the missile. New possibility: that it is an example of the advanced technology of this world. New possibility: the ancient inhabitants of this world have survived and are still aggressive. We will scan for a way into the nearest conurbation and find facts.'

'Find facts!' chorused the Grel.

Extract Ends

Stokes and the others had arrived at the Great Doors of the Perfecton city, to find Professor Janes already there, hiding behind a small rock and gibbering.

'Janes, get a hold of yourself!' Singh told him sternly. 'What is that ship?'

'The Grel!' Janes panted, looking between the others in terror. 'That's the command-deck pod from a Grel data-runner!'

'The Grel!' Stokes gasped. Everybody looked at him. 'Who are they, then?'

'Oh, you don't want to know . . .' Professor Epstein put his hands on his head. 'They appear several times in the Chelonian Chronicles. They're data pirates. They live for information, and they're ravenous about getting it.'

'They carry axes with data monitors,' giggled Blandish, 'and a spike on the end, which they use to break open skulls and suck data straight from the brain.'

'And they have these squiddy faces!' winced Epstein.

'We are sunk!' Janes wailed. 'This sucks! Game over, man!'

'Now, wait.' Stokes was once again surprised, and rather worried, to find himself cast as the voice of rationality amongst this group. If they couldn't do better than he could, then they really were in trouble. 'Why should they want to harm us?'

'For our information,' Epstein told him. 'They've destroyed whole planets in search of the most trivial facts.'

Singh spoke up. 'Does anybody have any guns or other weapons?'

The professors looked amongst each other. There was a shuffling and a silence. 'Well of course we don't,' Lucinda finally murmured. 'And what use would it be if we had? None of us can shoot.'

'I once won a ceramic ornament with an air rifle,' said Wagstaff, hopefully.

Stokes sighed. 'All right, so that isn't an option. If we can get into the Perfecton city, then we can hide there until help arrives. Bernice showed me these doors they were working on. Does anybody have any ideas about how to open them?'

They all gazed up at the doors. They were big and golden, and half concealed by sand. They were covered with incomprehensible hieroglyphs.

'Let us remove the sand,' said Hettie. She took a teaspoon from her pocket, knelt carefully by the doors and started, in a very small way, to dig.

The others dived in and started hauling sand away with their hands. Professor Singh and Professor Farouk, Mathematics, who was a muscular young prodigy in a turban, took a step back as the patterns on the door were revealed, clicking their tongues and rubbing their chins. 'A puzzle in symbolic logic?' murmured Farouk.

'Indeed,' said Singh. 'Those three characters at the top are the first three in a series . . .'

'Of course not. They will be the key codes to a more complex message below.'

'What? Don't be ridiculous! It's as plain as –'

'Ridiculous! You're the one who published that paper on collapsars that made us the laughing stock of –'

'I maintain that my research was utterly valid, you –'

'Stop!' Stokes bellowed. At the bottom of the door, a large circular marking had been revealed, with a depression at its centre. He stepped forward and pressed it.

From deep inside the ground, a vast and ominous chime rang out.

A moment later, shifting sand, the doors ground open.

Stokes ushered the amazed academics inside. 'Let's hope there's nobody home . . .' he muttered.

'There is, you know!' squeaked Warrinder.

'And how would you know?' asked Singh.

'Don't start,' warned Stokes. When the last of the professors had entered, he followed them inside, taking a last look at the night-shrouded landscape before he stepped over the threshold.

To his horror, the great doors rumbled closed behind him.

Dame Candy was putting her washing on the line that fine sunny morning, in front of her cottage on the edge of the woods. Even though she was worried about that useless son of hers, she couldn't help but hum a little song as she went about her work.

'Ooh, look at the size of those!' She held up a vast pair of bloomers to the sunlight. 'It looks like I'm sending a message to sailors.' She pursed her lips and adjusted her hair for a moment. 'Well, perhaps I am.'

From the woods came a sudden commotion, and Dame Candy turned to wag a scolding finger. 'If that's that good-for-nothing son of mine, Jack, then he'd better have my cow with him.'

Out of the trees, however, stepped a party of goblins. They had faces made of tentacles, and carried great axes. They were dressed in black tunics, capes and britches, with gleaming black thigh boots.

'We have no cow,' their leader gurgled. 'We are the Grel!'

'Oh my giddy kippers,' the Dame gasped. 'I haven't seen a sight like that since I popped round the back of the fishmonger's trolley and had a look at his buttered plaice. What do you lot want here, anyway, disturbing a beautiful young woman's underwear?'

One of these Grel stepped towards her, brandishing his axe. 'We must know where we are! What planet is this? Have we travelled through time? How did we come to be here? What are these strange garments that we are wearing?'

The Dame glanced ruefully at the axe that was poised at her throat. 'Put it away, you could do someone a nasty with that. Look over there!'

'Where?' The Grel swung his head.

Dame Candy ducked under the axe, grabbed her basket of washing, and flung it at the other Grel. As they were fighting off a variety of oversized brassieres and bloomers, she scampered past them, only to run straight into another of their kind, emerging from the forest. With a whoop, she raised her hands and ran back the other way, ducking under a chop of the leading Grel's axe.

She ran round and round her little cottage, the Grel running after her.

The Grel leader stopped, and instructed one of the others to stay put and wait for the woman on her next circuit and strike her with his axe. Then he continued his pursuit.

The Grel with the axe stood poised as the old woman

jogged around the cottage towards him, holding up her skirts, the Grel leader and the others in hot pursuit.

With a whoop, the old woman slid under his axe.

Just as he swung it.

The flat of it connected with the face of the Grel leader.

He fell backwards, sending all those behind him falling backwards too.

Dame Candy waved to them and ran off. 'Bye-bye!' she called as she left.

From the *Informative Record of Recent Grel History*:

The new Grel Master, holding his bruised face tentacles gently, turned to his Servitor. 'Question: was I not elected by all of you as the most intelligent Grel present, to be the acting Grel Master until we understand the nature of this situation?'

'Indeed, Master,' said the ashamed-looking Grel with the axe.

'I am becoming aware that the election was not a very close contest.' The Grel Master reached out and squeezed the face tentacles of his errant Servitor until the Grel's eyes boggled and his face went blue. Then he released them. He turned to the others. 'Speculation: the technology here seems limited. It should be easy to conquer this place. Then we will use our knowledge to instruct the natives here in how to make us a spacecraft to return to Grellor. To implement this plan, we need more information about our situation. So find facts!'

'Find facts!' chorused the booted and lace-collared Grel.

Extract Ends

Bernice and Wolsey had been walking along a paved road for some time now, and Bernice was trying to work out just what sort of road this was, archaeologically speaking. It owed something to the Roman, that was certain: it had the greatest camber she had ever seen, nearly a hump in the middle. And there was the medieval way in which the edges were marked by a solid brick border. But it was so clean! It looked as if it had been made that day, which was usually a property of societies advanced enough to employ nanotechnological cleaning agents. That was true of everything. Wolsey's clothes, her own costume, even the soles of her boots, all utterly clean. The colour was the other problem. Every brick of the road was bright yellow. No civilization, in any part of the galaxy that Bernice had heard about, had ever made its ordinary, everyday thoroughfares so . . . garish.

Therefore: this wasn't a place that worked by the laws of the real world. Bernice was dead, she was definitely dead, and, worse than punishment or eternal bliss, she had ended up in a world that wasn't much of either. The Lord Mayor of London thing sounded promising, the pay-off at the end of the game, but even that was nothing to do with spiritual enlightenment or supreme oneness.

Bernice Summerfield had died, and discovered that the afterlife was a theme park.

'Erm,' she said to Wolsey, choosing her words carefully. 'Have you always been . . . like you are?'

'Eh? Oh, absolutely not . . .' Wolsey purred. 'When I was a kitten, I was tremendously gauche and ugly. The runt of the litter, what? To achieve style such as mine requires years of experience, the rough and tumble of the world. But what are you saying, Dick? You knew me when I was young! Is this some sort of clever riddle?'

'No . . .' Bernice sighed, and steeled herself to tell him. 'Wolsey, you, you are my . . . my cat.'

'Well of course I'm your cat, Dick!'

Bernice stopped, and grabbed Wolsey by the cuff. 'I'm not a boy. I'm a woman.'

Wolsey threw his head back and laughed. 'You are

having an identity crisis, aren't you? Well, "Mistress", what would a woman be doing wearing clothes like these? Answer me that! Where are your . . . your . . .'

'They're here. This tunic's just not particularly flattering.'

'Your pointy hat, or your golden eye make-up or your silver slippers?'

Bernice raised an eyebrow. 'What is this, the Land of Disco?'

'No, this is England.'

'England? England on Earth?'

Wolsey dropped down on to one knee beside Bernice. 'Young Master, why are you talking in this dratted strange way? Has the journey made your mind wander? Let's rest: see, there's a cottage just over there.'

He pointed, and Bernice noted that indeed, some way off the road, in a little meadow of its own, there was. The sun was low on the horizon, and she suddenly felt very tired. She stretched and yawned. 'All right. Let's hope it's a B&B.'

From the *Informative Record of Recent Grel History*:

The Grel on the surface of Perfecton had come to the great pair of golden doors. The Grel Master and his lead Servitor took a step back to look at the patterns on them, hooting and gurgling in concentration. 'Question: a puzzle in symbolic logic?' murmured the Grel Master.

'Indeed,' said the Servitor. 'Possibility: those three characters at the top are the first three in a series . . .'

'Bad fact! They will be the key codes to a more complex message below.'

'Bad fact!' the Servitor retorted.

'Bad fact? You cannot say "Bad Fact" to me! I am your Master!'

The other Grel watched as the two of them hotly contested the nature of the symbols on the doors, proud that their comrades should both be so aggressively engaged in their mission to further the cause of the Grel race.

Extract Ends

The cottage appeared to be empty. The door had been unlocked, and Bernice and Wolsey had wandered in, inspecting a scene of general neglect. It looked like squatters had occupied the place and then moved on, trashing the place before they'd left. Or maybe it was a student house. There was a pile of washing-up in the sink, the curtains were still drawn, the air was full of must and damp. Bernice opened the door into what appeared to be a dormitory of some kind, with several beds lined up against the wall. Here there were drawers open everywhere, and the smell was even worse. Shouting out hellos brought no response; the place had definitely been abandoned, seemingly in a hurry.

'I can't sleep here,' Bernice told Wolsey, flopping down at the end of one of the beds. 'Apart from anything else, the smell precludes a comfortable night's kip. I'm going to have to clean up.'

'Are you sure?' The cat was flexing his fingers in a particularly inviting heap of discarded pullovers. 'Sounds too much like hard work to me.'

'Has to be done, though.' Bernice pulled herself to her feet and headed for the kitchen. 'Tidying up is in my blood. I'm the sort of person who does the washing up *during* the dinner party.'

'Suit yourself,' murmured Wolsey, curling up on his woollen bed.

It was only when she was elbow deep in suds in the kitchen sink, sluicing the inside of a teapot in which something was growing, that Bernice realized how utterly untrue that was.

'What?' she cried out, stopping in mid-sluice. 'I'm not the sort of person who does this sort of thing! I live amongst piles of rubbish! Or at least I would do if Joseph didn't clear it all up!' She wiped her hands on a dishcloth and put one to her brow. For a moment there, it had been as if she'd been experiencing the effects of a mind-altering drug. A drudgery drug. She slapped herself a couple of times on the cheek. Then she pulled open the curtains above the sink, and opened the window, intending to let in some fresh twilight air.

Sitting on the window sill was a little blue bird. It whistled gaily at Bernice. Two of its fellows joined it, and they twittered away in tune, seeming to smile at her.

'That's it,' Bernice decided. 'I'm definitely on drugs.'

But before she could shoo them away, the birds flew into the house. Behind them came others, a whole flock of them. And squirrels and mice and voles and shrews and little unidentifiable possum things. Bernice shouted at them to stop, to go back, that the house was in enough of a mess as it was, but they wheeled and rushed about the kitchen, then headed all over the house.

They were chittering and twittering, Bernice realized giddily, in tune.

And then they were opening the curtains, dusting the surfaces, dropping things back into drawers and closing them.

'Hah hah ha!' Bernice held on to a pillar for balance as a group of robins carrying dirty teacups swept by, and an otter bound the discarded newspapers with a recycling ribbon. More birds were dropping squirming goldfish into the sink, which was frothing up as they scrubbed their hard scales against the pots and pans. 'Hah hah ha ha ha ha ha ha ha ha ha ha ah a hah hahh hhahahhhhhh! Waaaaaaaaaah!'

She sank to her knees and started to gently knock her head against the post. Afterlife, dream, psychotic episode, drug fantasy, whatever, this was just bloody out of the question.

When she opened her eyes again, the process was nearly over. The cottage was spick and span, everything was gleaming, and the little creatures were scampering out of windows and doors. A ferret stopped to tie a rather sweet red ribbon into Bernice's hair, then followed.

Shakily, Bernice got to her feet and waved a limp wave to the ferret as it vanished. 'Thank you, my little friend,' she whispered, turning towards the bedroom. 'It's time for bed. I'll wake up back at the exploding ship. Hopefully.'

She managed to slap one shell-shocked foot after the other into the, now gleaming, bedroom, and passed Wolsey, who was still curled up on his pullover, the only item of clothing that was still out of place. 'I had the most wonderful dream,' he mumbled, tiny feathers and bits of fur drifting from his teeth.

Bernice tried to lie in one freshly laundered bed, but found that it was much too short for her. So she pushed three of the beds together and lay across them.

Laundry? She thought as she drifted into the blissful release of sleep. What sort of small creature does laundry? Never mind. I'll wake up, and this will all have been a dream. And I'll be back on the ship, and the explosion will have been a dream too, and I'll not be dead . . .

And soon the only sound in the room was that of two tired and strange creatures sleeping.

Stokes and his fellow academics had wandered for an hour through a maze of tunnels, everybody keeping together by holding one another's hand. That had been difficult to organize in itself, various professors complaining that they ought only to be holding the hands of those of at least equal length of tenure and seniority. Then there was some talk of the relative importance of the arts and science, and where the so-called 'soft sciences' might fit into the hand-holding league table.

Until Stokes had had a screaming fit that startled

everybody into just holding the hand of the person next to them.

There were light sources at intervals along the tunnels, strips of green fluorescence that ran along the ceiling. Stokes led the others through the corridors at random, hoping that nobody was going to stop off to examine anything.

Finally, there was light at the end of the tunnel. Green light. It was coming through a translucent door, and again it was covered in a series of incomprehensible symbols.

Stokes, aware of the weight of the academics who were about to arrive behind him, picked one of the symbols randomly and struck it.

The door swung upwards.

They entered a large, circular chamber. Around its walls were placed a series of screens, and in front of those screens were rows of chairs, and lecterns. The academics filed in and, after the last one had entered, the door once more closed behind them. Stokes was relieved to note that there were many other doors around the room.

'Chairs!' exclaimed Professor Epstein. 'So the Perfectons were humanoid – they needed to sit down!'

'Oh, so do I!' Stokes slumped into the first chair he came across, even though it was made of a translucent green material. A light came on on the screen in front of the chair, and then the whole area suddenly lit up. Stokes leapt out of the chair again and the lights went off. Gingerly, with the professors egging him on, he sat back down and the lights returned.

'Very hospitable,' said Professor Singh. He glanced sidelong at Warrinder. 'Got . . . any particular feelings about this room, have you?'

'No,' squeaked the Pakhar, who was still looking very nervous.

Stokes was about to venture the opinion that the chair/lighting thing was just for convenience when something appeared on the screen in front of him: a fast-moving green dot. He looked at it, and it exploded. Then another appeared, and another, and another. Several of them exploded, several whizzed off the other side of the screen. A series of stable red dots appeared along the top. Stokes suddenly realized what was going on. 'Hey, if I concentrate on these dots, they explode. It's a game. Rather like mental clay-pigeon shooting.'

'I've found something similar . . .' Otterbland had sat down in front of another screen, on the other side of the room. On this one was a single large green dot. It was getting larger all the time. The academics, Stokes included, moved to watch this new game. 'It's like mental wrestling. I'm trying to push this dot back by force of will . . .' He frowned, and the dot got slightly smaller. Then it grew again. Then it grew suddenly much bigger.

Otterbland leapt up out of his seat with a cry and the dot vanished.

'Hey, that one could be dangerous,' said Janes.

'Indeed?' Hettie sat down before anybody could stop her, not that they would have dared. The dot on the screen appeared again, and rushed towards her, increasing in size, as she fumbled for her glasses.

'I really do think –' began Stokes.

'Hush.' Hettie shoved her glasses back on her nose and concentrated on the dot with all her might. The dot halted. Vibrated. Then shrank to a point and vanished with a popping noise. 'An amusement for children,' Hettie concluded, rising.

'It looked so simple,' smiled Lucinda. 'I mean that . . . you made it seem so.'

'So the Perfectons were interested in psychic technology,' mused Warrinder.

'It's probably just an advanced series of body sensors in the chair,' said Singh. 'Nothing that we couldn't have put together in the lab.'

Another argument about the validity of psychic phenomena was about to break out. Stokes didn't have the vast intellectual curiosity that might keep the others here even in the face of impending danger. So he walked away from the group, to calm his nerves, making his way to a table-like green pillar in the centre of the room.

As soon as he touched the table, objects appeared on its surface, scattered there as if left behind by a child after play. They'd faded into vision with no more ceremony than if they'd been thrown there.

One of them was a gun.

Bernice and Wolsey were asleep. The sound of distant singing did not wake them. Neither were they woken as the singing grew louder. The noise of many picks, shovels and sacks being thrown aside in the garden did not rouse them from their slumbers in the slightest.

They were not even disturbed by the sound of a key entering the lock of the cottage door, or by the small, resolute, yet tired, footsteps that made their way towards the bedroom.

Even the little gasps and whispered conversations of those that found them didn't wake the two sleepers.

Their shadows loomed over Bernice's bed. A hand reached out to touch her hair, and then withdrew when another slapped it.

Stokes had always had a problem with guns. They were generally pointed at him by people who didn't understand the power and universality of art, as their particular critique of his work. He had, on two occasions, been driven off a planet by mobs firing guns at him and, once, by a mob firing guns at his paintings.

Still, this was a serious situation and it demanded a serious response.

He picked up the gun. It was shiny and silver, with a

big green bulb at one end. It looked like a toy. It seemed far too light to kill anybody. He supposed that Epstein would say that this meant the Perfectons had had hands and fingers.

On one side of the room, far away from everybody, on a divider between two of the screens, stood a green vase. Without telling anybody, in case he got it spectacularly wrong, Stokes aimed the gun at the vase.

He squeezed the trigger.

The vase vanished in a silent little burst of flame.

The academics noticed that and, with cries of delight, ran over to him. 'Jolly good,' giggled Wagstaff. 'You've found us a weapon!'

'Yes,' said Stokes. 'Sorry.'

They were all startled when another of the screens glowed and was activated, and some of the professors ducked, or dived behind their less-valued colleagues, thinking that retaliation for the vase was in order.

But, instead, on the screen appeared the vase itself. Stokes was certain that it was the same one. It twisted and turned like a schematic from an architectural programme.

'Now that's a bit of a coincidence,' murmured Singh.

Stokes nervously fiddled with the green bulb on the butt of the gun, wondering why it was that the Perfectons had thought it useful to display a picture of the object you'd just destroyed.

On the screen, the vase suddenly elongated, flattened, then seemed to turn itself inside out, changing too fast to follow.

Stokes let go of the bulb. The shape on the screen stayed as it was.

There was a gasp from behind them. Hettie was pointing up at the ceiling. They all turned to look.

From the round ceiling to the floor a thin green line had been drawn. It ran diagonally across the room, and sparkled with a sort of glittering twilight of its own. It stopped just before it hit the floor. It stopped just before it hit the ceiling. It was simply there.

Stokes found himself nervously fiddling with the gun again. The line shrank to a point, a little green star shining in midair.

'Wild,' whispered Janes.

'I do believe that it's a pure point,' said Otterbland. 'We can only see it because of the radiation that it's giving off.'

'A point?' asked Stokes. 'I don't get it.'

'Phrases you never hear,' murmured Epstein.

'A dot,' Singh told him, clapping his hands together. 'A place with no dimensions: no length, width or depth. Such a point should be a singularity, the heart of a black hole. It should collapse and drag us all into it with its vast gravitational pull, but, instead, it just sits there twinkling.'

'Is that because it was made out of a vase?' asked Stokes.

'Made out of –?' Singh frowned at him. 'You mean you think there's some connection between what we saw on the screen and –'

'They're both the same colour. And they're both controlled by this gun. Watch.' Stokes gave the knob a good, solid twist to the right. The dot vanished.

'You . . . dolt!' Singh cried out. 'That was the most important physical discovery in centuries!'

Stokes drew himself up to his full height. 'Perhaps. But I don't think that was what the Perfectons thought. This device isn't made for physics experiments, Professor.' He tapped the gun proudly. 'This device is a tool of art.'

Bernice was dreaming.

She dreamt of when she was very young, in the house of her mother and father, before her world was invaded by aliens and she was sent away to the Academy.

There had been a green vase on a table beside her bed. It had glowed slightly at night, and Bernice had found the glow restful and sweet, a fairy light. She had kept things in the vase: sweets and letters, her first diary.

She was going to be back in the ship when she woke up, that was where she was. Or dead, but you couldn't wake up dead.

She was being shaken awake. Obviously by Doran, ha ha! She laughed, and reached out a finger to touch his face.

The finger closed around a piece of hair.

Bernice curled it, and then playfully tugged.

The resulting bellow made her sit up in shock, wakefulness thumping her head against the wall of the cottage.

She was still in the cottage.

Around her bed stood seven very small people, one of whom was clutching his chin in pain. 'For that,' he snarled, whipping a sword from his belt, 'you die, human scum!'

CHAPTER 4

WHAT KIND OF A–Z WOULD GET YOU HERE?

'Art?' asked Warrinder, his little front teeth sticking out over his lip in concentration.

'Yes, art!' Stokes waved the gun airily, causing everybody in the party to jump aside. 'It's my belief that this gun turns ordinary things into infinitely manipulable objects. The vase wasn't destroyed: it was turned into the picture on the screen, then into the line and the dot. It became, if you will, art.'

'But . . .' Singh opened his mouth, then closed it again. 'No, wait . . .'

'Yes!' Farouk snapped his fingers. 'The gun takes the object from our universe, and reactualizes it a few dimensions up.'

'Eh?' shouted Wagstaff.

'In a world of its own,' explained Lucinda. 'You should know, dear.'

'Such an object could be manipulated across all of timespace.' Singh was now warming to this theory. 'This effect, let us call it the Singh Farouk effect –'

'The Farouk Singh effect.'

'The Singh effect.'

'The Farouk effect.'

'What about the Stokes effect?' asked Stokes, plaintively. 'I discovered it.'

The two scientists turned to look at him for a moment. 'But you didn't understand it,' said Singh. 'This effect – whatever it is to be called – could revolutionize space travel, power generation, the whole of our culture.' Taking a deep breath, he turned to the others. 'Professors, we must take this secret back to human space. It is our duty to survive whatever hazards this planet may offer.'

'Not too hard.' Epstein shrugged. 'We were planning to do that anyhow.'

'You cannot offer a hazard,' said Hettie. 'Hazards are not offered.'

Singh pinched the top of his nose in frustration.

'I said, "For that you die, human scum!" ' The little man brandished his sword again.

Bernice rubbed the sleep out of her eyes, wondering why she'd ever adopted a lifestyle in which she had to deal with death threats at this time in the morning. 'I'll be with you in a moment . . . wait a sec . . .' She blinked as her eyes adjusted to the low light of dawn. 'OK. Right. Human scum, death and all that. Hello.'

Before the little man could say anything more, a great roar caused all seven of the small people to jump in surprise. Something large and fluffy bounced across the beds and landed right on top of their representative with the sword.

'What was that about human scum?' Wolsey purred, running a single claw along the underside of the little man's chin, leaving a smooth, shaved furrow behind it.

'Oh, Moody's always like that, you shouldn't take any notice.' The new speaker was a small woman in a rose-tinted shirt and tie-dyed trousers. 'Underneath, he's absolutely the loveliest small person in the world.'

'I am not a small person!' the boy in the clutches of the

cat spat back at her. 'I'm a dwarf and I'm proud!'

'Yeah, Dwarf Pride!' Another female dwarf raised a fist in salute. She wore long coloured braids in her hair and had on a jerkin with I CAN'T EVEN THINK BIG written on it.

Bernice looked between them all in shock. 'Arex! Rose! Marjorie! What are you all doing in my afterlife?'

'She's crackers,' declared a female dwarf in an elegant dark cape. 'One sequin short of a ballgown.'

'Oh, hush, Bitchy,' said the dwarf that looked like Rose. 'I'm sure she's just confused after waking up. She looks really sweet to me. All tousled and a bit heroic, and with a really fantastic hairdo. Gosh.' She blushed and looked at her pixie boots. 'I'm Gushy. Hi.'

'She?' Wolsey plucked Moody off his feet and threw him on to the nearest bed offhandedly. 'What's all this "she" business? Are you optically as well as vertically disadvantaged?' He pointed at Bernice in puzzlement. 'This is Dick!'

'That's not a very nice way of putting it,' whispered Gushy. 'Besides, I'm sure it's not true.'

'Looks like a girl to me,' muttered a tired-looking dwarf as he stamped off towards his bed. 'As long as she doesn't snore, that's fine by me.'

'That's Lazy,' Gushy told Bernice. 'That's Liberal.'

'Hi.' That was the girl with the slogan jerkin.

'And that's Laddish.'

'Smart.' That was from a fresh-faced boy dwarf with a fringe over his eyes.

Bernice stood up slowly, and looked down at the dwarves. 'But I know you all by other names . . .' she told them. 'You're my tutorial group. Goodness, if this is the afterlife, then you must have done something terrible and karmic involving short people.'

'As I said,' murmured Bitchy. 'She's lost in the enchanted forest and can't find her way to the candy cottage.'

'Perhaps . . .' Bernice walked slowly around the little

people, forming an idea with her hands in the air. 'Perhaps you represent the seven deadly sins. Perhaps this is actually hell.'

'Hell is little people,' said Wolsey. 'But you're mistaken, anyhow, because there are only six of these fellows.'

'So why did I think –?'

'No, there are seven of us,' Gushy piped up. 'The other one is getting you a cup of hot milk. To wake you gently, he said. When he saw you, he could only say –'

The door to the bedroom creaked open and in walked a short boy, gingerly carrying a cup. He looked like he was wearing a long nightshirt that trailed along the ground behind him. He beamed at the sight of Bernice. 'She's beautiful!' he gasped.

Bernice opened her mouth as far as it could go. 'Doran?' she gulped.

'Well, maybe that's what you know him as,' said Gushy. 'But we call him Cute.'

The Professors were trying to get some sleep. It had been a long night already, and many of the older academics were showing signs of serious fatigue. At Stokes's insistence, they had piled everything they could find in the circular room up against the doors. The academics had mostly complained that this was unnecessary, since 1: however ferocious the Grel might be, they were hardly Earth troops; 2: they didn't know the academics were in the city; and 3: they might not even care about their presence. Only Epstein had been as insistent as Stokes. He said that what the Grel prized most was raw data and, in the form of the gun, they were currently sitting on possibly the richest pickings on the planet. That had started Singh off on the business of duty to the human race again, not to mention getting Hettie all grumpy about sitting on pickings, but at least it had motivated everybody towards helping.

While they were distracted moving furniture, Stokes had quietly put the gun in his pocket. He didn't like carrying guns, but he liked other people carrying them even less. Besides, as he'd said, it was no more a weapon than a palette knife was. It really ought to be claimed first and foremost as a means of self-expression. After that it could build a human empire and power the known planets.

He'd lain down, finally, his beret under his head, along a green step and, after much worried shifting of posture, he'd even managed to get to sleep.

He dreamt of the green vase. It was twisting in his mind now, along the corridors of the university, and Bernice was saying something about oh no it wasn't, and he was insisting that, yes, actually, it was.

This continued for some time.

From the *Informative Record of Recent Grel History*:

(Note: Almost uniquely for a sentient species, the Grel do not dream. Dreaming is a method, at its most mechanistic level, of sorting things into boxes, a part of the brain working through all the new information gathered in the day and typing it into deeper memory. Sometimes we achieve a sort of consciousness in the middle of that process and see it all passing by, and make up stories with the stuff. Those stories are what humans call dreams. Like all stories made up of bits flung on to the floor, as in a poetic experiment, for instance, or a history as revealed through archaeology, dreams somehow bring to the surface deep, old, archetypal images: a chance striking of two surreal statements that illuminates something profound; Caligula as icon rather than person; that time Audrey Hepburn wanted your bus fare but you hadn't got any change left. The Grel miss out on all that. They have evolved with another brain behind the one that does their thinking, a brain whose task is to sort out every new piece of information as the individual Grel goes along. The Grel do not have to dream, therefore the Grel do not have to sleep, therefore the Grel roared their way to the top of the evolutionary ladder on Grellor and are now damn near unbeatable in sustained warfare.

Some humans think that the Grel are jealous of dreams, and that their feverish desire for new information is a sign of that pathology at the heart of their culture. But that view is often forgotten by history, because history, as well as being written like a dream is written, is also written by the winning side.)

The Grel Master on the surface of Perfecton had settled the dispute with his Servitor and, through the clever technique of touching every bit of the golden doors, had made them open.

The maze of tunnels beyond took the Grel several hours to explore. The first light source they came to had been greeted with much hooting and gurgling, and the taking apart and understanding of its design was a little party for the Grel, a moment of levity. It was like that every step the glorious troopers took: some new design or device took their fancy. They were in paradise indeed!

It was thus near dawn when they reached the door to a new chamber.

'New fact: this door has been weighed shut with heavy objects,' reported a Servitor. 'Conjecture: the beings we observed when landing have hidden here.'

'Good fact,' the Grel Master decided. 'Your facts have improved since your wasted thoughts about the first door.'

The Servitor's face tentacles wiggled in delight. 'Am I to examine this door for other methods of entrance?'

The Grel Master thought for a moment.

(Note: Perhaps, with the access he had to data concerning all the races of the universe, this Grel Master was aware, somewhere in his back brain, that the people behind the door would be asleep, and dreaming.)

'No,' he said. 'Break it down.'

Extract Ends

Professor Warrinder woke Stokes by grabbing him by the lapels and pulling him to a kneeling position. Thus, the first thing that Stokes saw on waking was a hairy wet nose in front of his eyes. 'They're coming!' shouted Warrinder.

Stokes leapt straight upright. 'Wake up!' he shouted, and started running about. After a moment he turned this into a concerted effort to make sure everybody was awake.

Singh, on the other side of the room, was already on his feet. 'Now, erm, how could Warrinder possibly know that they're coming?' he said, hurriedly starting to pack away his provisions.

Wagstaff pointed to shadows moving behind one of the luminescent doors. One had something raised over its head. 'Look!' he shouted. 'We're doomed!'

The Grel dataxe smashed through the fragile green material, and the door started bulging inward as the Grel outside heaved against it.

The academics screamed, yelled, got to their feet and ran for several of the other doors at once.

'No!' cried Stokes, gaining his balance. 'Wait!' He slapped Warrinder's shoulders, gazing into the eyes of the large rodent. 'Professor, where should we go? Concentrate!'

The Pakhar closed his eyes, and curled up his nose. 'I think . . . oh dear, it's all rather awful, but . . . That one!' He pointed to one of the doors. 'But –'

'No time for buts!' Stokes waved his arms violently and indicated the door that Warrinder had chosen. The professors who were on their feet ran towards it, and it opened as obligingly as the one on the way in had done. Stokes helped Hettie, Lucinda and the two elderly history professors get to their feet and start shuffling towards it and then ran to where Epstein and Farouk were weighing decorative items in their hands and looking grim. 'Come on!' he cried.

'We are going to have to fight them sometime,' Epstein replied. 'They'll be through that door before the older ones are out the other side. We have to buy them time.'

Another axe blow split the door. One more would probably do it. Stokes looked between the exit, which the more elderly academics were being led through by Warrinder, and his two comrades, wringing the air with his hands in panic.

Then he felt the weight in his breast pocket and remembered the gun. He put a hand on it and the panic turned to a cold and heavy fear in his chest, because he now knew just what he was about to do, and it scared him witless.

'You two go on,' he said, plucking his words straight out of a holodrama he'd seen. 'I'll hold them off.' He produced the gun.

There was another crash from the door. Farouk and Epstein didn't argue, which was a bit of a surprise, but sprinted for the far door.

Stokes settled down behind a low, green wall and bit his bottom lip. If he wasn't mistaken, without actually thinking about it very much, he'd just made a heroic sacrifice. He had no idea what thought had driven him to do this. Perhaps it was something to do with not recognizing that missile for what it was. Maybe he could have saved the ship.

One door splintered into pieces just as the last academic vanished through the other. The Grel, now visible on the other side – and, goodness, looking at them, Stokes wished they weren't – started to shove at the remaining objects stacked in front of it. So that business of needing to give the retreating professors covering fire wasn't absolutely correct, then. They could have all got out, and Stokes wouldn't have found himself sitting behind a wall, about to die for no very good reason.

Sod.

This was just such a ridiculous way for an artist to die. Drowning in a big shirt, yes. Taking one's own life as a result of how horrid and arty one's life was, yes – though that one had never appealed to Stokes. Dying in the corner of a gallery opening at an advanced age, yes yes, absolutely. But being shot to bits, and in such a situation that nobody was probably ever going to know of one's heroism? This was just not a situation that Menlove Stokes had ever conceived of as happening to him.

The last object rolled away and the Grel marched into the room, spinning their axes, making cooing sounds and flexing their face tentacles.

Stokes peeped up over the parapet. Perhaps he could negotiate with them.

'Human!' shouted one of them, pointing at Stokes's head.

'Immobilize him!' ordered the Grel Master.

A dozen axes swung up to firing position.

Stokes threw himself to the ground as the wall in front of him thundered with energy blasts.

Remarkably, it stayed absolutely intact.

As bolts of blue neon streaked over his head, Stokes decided that dying like this was, actually, too shameful to contemplate. Though it went against all his principles, including the one about staying alive as long as possible, he was going to fire back.

He hopped into a crouch, poked the top of the gun over the parapet and, without actually showing enough of himself to aim at anything, squeezed the trigger.

From the *Informative Record of Recent Grel History*:

One of the Grel vanished in a puff of fire.

'Vital new fact: the human is armed!' shouted the Grel Master. 'Take cover!'

The Grel ran to various positions about the room, already checking through their huge storehouse of tactical information concerning gunfights in enclosed areas.

When they looked up from their carefully and swiftly chosen locations, they discovered that their quarry, who obviously knew nothing of such tactics, had bolted straight for the exit.

'Fire!' screamed the Grel Master.

Extract Ends

Stokes had a terrible, mortal feeling in his stomach as he ran for the door, clutching the gun to his chest.

Half of it was that he'd shot someone. He didn't like that. He didn't like being full enough of fear and anger to be able to do it. It gave him a fatal sense of deserving the energy bolt in the back that he knew he was about to get. He was a soldier now, and soldiers were killed.

The other half of it was simple, rabbitlike logic. He could see now that there was a long corridor on the other side of the door, that he had bought time for the others after all, because the Grel were going to have a clear aim at him all along that tunnel.

If he had been a rabbit, he would have accepted that immediately and stood still to be shot.

But because he was a human being, he ran anyway.

He just got over the threshold of the door when something far too solid and sudden knocked his feet away from him.

And then he fell into darkness.

Bernice was doing a quick head count of her hosts, who were now sitting around their kitchen table, each at a chair with their name on the back. 'Lazy, Moody, Laddish, Gushy, Bitchy, Liberal and Cute. Seven of you, and I knew that before I was told it. How is that possible?'

Wolsey shrugged a languid cat shrug. He and Bernice

had been given mugs of warm mead and seats with GUEST carved on the back. 'I have ceased to understand much of what you say. What worries me, Dick, is that these seven tadpoles are convinced you're female. Perhaps they've escaped from some travelling show. I hear the King has a new plan to deal with such as they: it's called Care in the Entertainment Community.'

'We have not escaped from a show!' exclaimed Moody. 'We work in our mine, and sell the rubies and diamonds that we find there in the village market.'

Bernice frowned. 'Is there much of a market for precious stones in a small agrarian community?'

The dwarves all looked at her blankly.

'Perhaps they're a little short,' suggested Wolsey.

'Oh, for goodness' sake!' Bernice slapped the table. 'Look, once and for all, where am I? What is this place?'

'The Land of Good King Rupert,' said Gushy.

'Who?' Wolsey laughed. 'Gadzooks, these squibs have never heard of England. Is that possible? Why, I thought there would always be an –'

'Don't sing,' Bernice told him sharply. She rubbed her brow. 'You lot can't even agree on what country we're in. I have memories of being an entirely different person to who you think I am now, and –'

'Was she just as lovely?' asked Cute, in a small, plaintive voice.

Bernice ignored him. She was deeply disturbed by these dwarves. They seemed to be characterizations of her best students, quick sketches of their most basic traits, rather than the whole, albeit young, personalities that she knew. In Cute's case, he was just pretty and gawped at her. That said something about her, surely, that, before all this weird business had happened, she'd been about to bonk the littlest dwarf. She sighed. 'I remember all of you as different people. And, worst of all, I remember the person that I was –' she struggled with the word '– dying. I believe that I remember the moment of my death. So this has to be an afterlife of some sort. But if it is, where's the judgement, or reward, or even punishment? What's the point to all this?' She stood up, looking around the faces at the table, suddenly angry at how incomprehensible this all was. After a moment with no answers, she threw her hands up and headed for the door.

After Bernice had gone, Cute looked at Wolsey and sighed. 'She's so complicated and deep.'
'Yes,' murmured the cat. '*He* is.'

Extract from the Diary of Bernice Summerfield:

I stamped out of the cottage feeling sorry for myself. The afterlife seemed so pointless. I've always been the hero of my own story. The one that does things, the one that things happen to. Now I envisaged an eternity, and I mean an eternity, in this fantasy world, watching odd and mildly pleasant things happening. I doubted that it was ever even going to rain. The fact that Wolsey and the dwarves regarded me as two entirely different people, even down to my gender, disturbed me too. It added up with the way I'd felt compelled to clean the cottage, the way that I knew certain details of things before they happened. If I had been stored by the great celestial Oneness of the universe, my mind preserved for ever in this sublime fantasy, then the great celestial Oneness had buggered up the process and stored me wrongly, scratched the disc that was me as She'd dropped me into my box.

A forever of wrongness, then. An always of knowing that one was askew, an outsider. The only one in this world with the curse of remembering what I'd been before.

Why, this was the end of my marriage, all over again.

Why, this was actually hell.

That thought scared me so much that I went and leant on

one of the perfect oak trees and looked up at the perfect yellow sun in the perfect blue sky, and thought that I was about to throw up. So I tried, hoping to disturb the very green grass with violent, ordinary, human colours. Hoping to make a sound that wasn't sweet.

I couldn't. I couldn't do it. I hadn't been to the toilet since I got here, because I didn't want to. The cottage didn't even have a toilet. Would my hair grow? Would I get older? Would I be infertile now, because I couldn't imagine the blood of childbirth on this perfect grass?

I sat down, and hugged my knees, wishing to wake up in my own bed, wishing for Jason to hold me, wishing that at least I could find some trousers. I was, if truth be told, on the fringes of beginning to consider going a little bit gaga.

So it's a good thing that what happened next did.

From the woods there came the sound of a man crying for help. I rose to my feet, quite pleased, in a guilty sort of way, that something not so nice was happening, and wondering if whatever deity controlled this place had listened to my wishes.

From the bushes burst one of the strangest figures I had ever seen. Dear old Professor Candy, in a dress and very bad make-up, running out of the forest as fast as he could go. He seemed to have taped two melons to his chest, and was wearing a hairnet. 'Help! Help!' he cried. 'They're hot on my tail!' He stopped and leant on my shoulder, panting. 'And let me tell you, that's not as good as it sounds.'

Looking back, my first words to the fleeing man seem to be an index of just how alienated I'd got by this point. 'Tell me,' I said to him. 'Do you think I'm a boy or a girl?'

He looked at me with pursed lips. 'Well, it's so hard to tell these days. But listen –'

And that was when things got so much better for me. Because, at that point, out of the forest ran a group of fearsome Grel Servitors. Of course, they had black doublet and hose on, and carried normal axes instead of their usual dataxes, but I'd know those squiddy faces anywhere. A Grel is a Grel is a Grel, even when he's got tights on.

I actually laughed, which made the Grel step back a bit. Goodness, I must have been more than a little dishevelled at that point. 'The Grel!' I exclaimed, pointing at them as if they were schoolfriends that I'd met by accident at a dinner party. 'The Grel from planet Grellor! You don't think you're gnomes or elves or something, do you?'

'We are the Grel!' confirmed their leader. 'New fact: you know of our true identity. Corollary: you have information concerning our situation. Therefore: you will come with us and tell us all you know!'

My glee hardly faded. This was so exciting! It was almost like being alive again. 'I think not,' I mocked, placing one foot atop a nearby barrel and glancing at my fingernails as I afforded the aliens and Professor Candy the best possible opportunity to gaze at my chubby thighs. (Not that either of them, even in the normal run of things, would have noticed.) 'Do you imagine that this building behind us is a mere cottage?'

The Grel looked at each other and conferred for a moment. Then their leader spoke again. 'Yes,' he said. 'We do.'

Candy looked between the aliens and my now-not-so-cocksure expression, and made the tactical decision for us. 'Scarper!' he cried.

I leapt off the barrel and, together, we ran inside the cottage, slammed the door shut and bolted it. There was a little bit of business with the both of us trying to get through the door at once and getting stuck, but that was so embarrassing that I won't go into it in detail.

Diary Entry Ends

Bernice and Candy stumbled into the dwarves' kitchen, slammed the door behind them, bolted it and leant on it. 'Aliens!' Bernice laughed. 'And they know they're aliens!

All right, so they want to suck all the information out of my brain –'

There was a thump on the door.

'But at least they're from the same universe as me!'

The others looked at her, their mugs halfway to their mouths.

Candy grabbed a nearby chest and shoved it against the door. 'I'm Candy,' she called over her shoulder. 'And I don't know what she's talking about either. But there are some hideous demons out there who've chased me all the way through the woods. And that hasn't happened in a while, let me tell you.'

'Demons?' gasped Cute, wide-eyed.

'Oh sure,' said Bitchy. 'And stepmothers are nice people.'

A Grel appeared at the window and swung back its axe. The dwarves cried out in terror.

Wolsey leapt up and slammed the wooden shutters closed, holding them there against a smash and a tinkling of glass, then fastening them with a bolt. 'Get to the other windows!' he snarled at the panicking dwarves. 'Hurry!'

'OK,' sighed Lazy. 'If we must.'

'We must! We must defend Bernice!' cried Gushy, pulling a short sword from her belt.

'Right,' agreed Moody, doing the same. 'Come on, dwarves, let's reach up high and kick some bottom!'

They ran from the room. Wolsey drew his own sabre and leapt to Bernice's side. 'Who did you say these demons were?' he asked.

'Let's just say that I know them by reputation,' Bernice said, giving him a smile and a quick little hug. 'It's wonderful to see somebody else from home.'

Wolsey looked at her suspiciously, and then glanced at Candy. He indicated Bernice with a claw. 'Male or female?' he asked.

'Erm . . .' Candy stopped piling things against the door and waved her hands in the air distractedly, as if making a decision. 'Male!' she finally settled on.

Wolsey nodded, happier. 'It seems the world is not completely at odds with my opinion.'

There came a crash from the door and Candy was sent flying backwards, her legs going straight up in the air, revealing a pair of bright red bloomers under her skirt.

The Grel ran in through the remains of the door, slashing the air with their axes.

Wolsey leapt forward, pushing Bernice back, and sent the first alien's axe flying with a sweep of his sword. Planting a foot in its chest, he sent it stumbling back into the other Grel, knocking them over.

Bernice pulled Candy to her feet. There was a scream from upstairs. 'Come on!' she yelled. She ran for the stairs, dragging a protesting Candy behind her.

The Grel struggled to their feet, retrieved their weapons, and braced themselves to rush through the door again. Wolsey stood on the threshold, the tip of his sabre twirling before him. 'So, my squidish friends, who's for calamari?'

Bernice and Candy rushed upstairs, to find that a Grel had climbed the outside of the cottage, burst in through one of the windows, and was now standing on one of the beds, holding off a circle of the dwarves with blows from its axe.

'Find facts!' it affirmed, as it struck aside Laddish's sword.

'It doesn't know what it's doing here, and that's the most dangerous situation in which to meet a Grel. Intellectually, it's like a cornered rat,' Bernice muttered to Candy, who was doing a fair impersonation of a cornered rat herself. She called to the alien on the bed. 'Grel! How did you come to be here?'

The alien hooted, fixing the circle of dwarves with its dark eyes. 'We . . . do not know,' it said. 'We boarded the ship. We sought facts. We were suddenly here.'

Bernice pushed through the dwarves and held aside Moody's sword for a moment in order to get close enough to the Grel to see into its eyes. 'Do you remember dying?' she asked.

'I . . . I am alive, therefore: –'

'You do, don't you?' Bernice sighed. 'You're just too literal-minded to appreciate the fact. Tell me, this is important. Do the Grel have an afterlife? What's it supposed to be like?'

'Information: the inner land of Slawcor is inside Grellor. There, none are Servitors. All are Masters. All facts are knowable, nothing is hidden, and the secrets of the universe are available as perfect flowers on the walls.' It fluttered its mouth tentacles angrily. 'There are no dwarves there.'

'But what about if you're evil? Where do bad Grel go?'

The Grel's tentacles bunched up, an expression, Bernice knew, of bemusement. 'There are no bad Grel.'

'Fab.' Bernice smiled to herself. 'So this isn't eternal torment. This is a puzzle. And puzzles are here to be solved.'

The Grel lunged forward. Bernice caught the haft of its axe in her hand and pulled, neatly depriving the beast of its weapon, which she weighed in her hands thoughtfully as she addressed it. 'When whoever your current Master is has given it some thought, he'll realize that you Grel are as much out of your depth here as I am. No dataxes, no comment. Couldn't we join forces?'

'The Grel do not form partnerships with less knowledgeable races,' the Grel gurgled.

'As you wish. All right, Gushy, grab him.' The dwarves pounced on the Grel and, through weight of numbers, pinned him to the bed.

Moody looked up at Bernice. 'We can hold him hostage and get the others to call off the siege.'

'If we do that, we'll be here for ever. The Grel don't like

losing Servitors: they see it as a possible information leak. No . . .' She cautiously went to the window and swung the broken frame open with the axe, glancing to the left and right before looking out. The Grel had surrounded the cottage. With no projectile weapons, all they could do at the sight of her was hoot. She waved to them before turning back to the dwarves. 'This one's too little to bother with. Throw him back.'

The dwarves, all save Moody, started to manhandle the Grel towards the window. Moody just looked at Bernice in amazement. 'Why don't we kill him, then? It'd be one less of the things!'

Bernice frowned, looking down at her boots for a moment. 'I'm a Professor of Archaeology, not a soldier. I don't kill people.'

'Since when are you giving the orders?'

She looked up at him again, biting her bottom lip giddily. 'Do you want your 2:1 or not? Now –' she swung back to the other dwarves before he could argue '– a Grel carapace can quite easily handle a fall from this height. You, you monster, will tell your Master that we should work together, right?'

The Grel opened its mouth orifice into a little circle, the Grel version of a nod, as its eyes fixed on Gushy's blade at its throat.

'Fine,' said Bernice. 'Let him go.'

The dwarves rushed the Grel to the window and threw him out. He landed amongst his peers, to great hooting.

From downstairs, there came a crash. 'Fix that window,' Bernice told the dwarves, meeting Moody's eyeline for a moment. 'I must just see what my cat's getting up to.'

Wolsey, as Bernice got to the bottom of the stairs, was actually doing a cartwheel down the dinner table, at the end of which he leapt off and kicked a Grel in the chest, sending him flying backwards. Half of the many Grel in the room turned to look at Bernice, and she suddenly realized that she was unarmed and almost completely unprepared for this.

Two of them rushed at her.

She grabbed a frying pan that had been hanging on the kitchen wall and pointed it at them like a gun. 'Stop!' she roared. 'Or be atomized!'

The Grel stopped, unsure – as Bernice had bet on – of anything in their environment at that moment.

'But that's just a frying pan . . .' murmured Wolsey.

The Grel looked at him. Then back at Bernice, who glowered at her cat.

'Sorry!' Wolsey slapped his own forehead. 'I see what you were trying to do now . . .'

The Grel leapt at Benny again.

She swiped the first one aside with the frying pan. The other one slashed at her with its axe.

Gashing her across her arm.

The cut swelled with blood. She dropped the frying pan. 'I can be hurt!' she cried in excitement. Then her face froze. 'Bugger, I can be hurt!'

The Grel raised its axe over its head to deliver the knockout blow, but Wolsey leapt at it and chopped the haft of its axe in two with one singing swish of his sword. He shoved the unarmed Grel away into a corner, where it gathered with its fellows for a final rush that would at least drive Bernice and Wolsey back up the stairs, if not overwhelm them altogether.

'Hold on to me, Dick,' muttered Wolsey through clenched teeth.

'I beg your pardon?' said Bernice.

They braced themselves for the onslaught.

And then, from outside the cottage, a trumpet sounded.

The Grel Master poked his head through the doorway of the cottage and shouted to his troops. 'New fact: A large body of troops is approaching! Leave this place and hide!'

Hooting in urgency, and casting dark squiddy glances over their shoulders at Bernice and Wolsey, the Grel gathered up their weapons and injured comrades and ran for the door.

Slowly, the dwarves and Candy trooped down the stairs behind the two friends.

'They stopped trying to get in upstairs,' Moody reported. 'They're running off into the forest.'

They all sat down on the steps, gazing at the wreckage of the kitchen.

'At least the place doesn't look so neat any more,' said Laddish.

'Good cat,' said Bernice, hugging Wolsey's arm. From outside, the trumpet sounded again, this time much closer. 'Come on, let's see who's come to our rescue.'

Outside the cottage stood a small army. Bernice and the others staggered out of the door and stared at it in the morning sunlight, the massed armour of the mounted soldiers reflecting silver and gold. At the head of the column of knights, with their banners and lances, sat a young, square-jawed man with squarely cut, bright blond hair. On top of the hair sat a crown. He stared at Bernice as she stepped into the sunlight, his mouth open in amazement. 'Why –' he breathed. 'She's –'

'Not on top form at the moment, actually. We would invite you in . . .' Bernice gestured to the cottage. 'But the place is such a mess.'

'She's –'

Bernice was trying to pay attention to the young man. For one thing, he looked very familiar, as were a number of his fellow knights, and she was having trouble placing them. But something else was demanding her attention. Namely, that from the column of elegantly groomed and muscular horses, a very different animal, without rider or braid, had detached itself, and had wandered up to her, looking at her expectantly. This horse was small, grey and shabby-looking, totally unlike all the others. It seemed to be trying to communicate something to her in its stare.

Bernice was about to at least find it a sugar lump when the man at the front of the column finished his sentence. '– beautiful!' And leapt off his horse.

He walked straight over to Bernice and hoisted her up into his arms. Which was rather fortunate, as that was the exact moment that Bernice's adrenaline levels dipped and her body informed her that, actually, she was weak from loss of blood. She slumped into his grasp.

'Why – you're wounded!' he gasped. 'Those fiends! I shall hunt them down across the kingdom, I shall not rest until –'

'Brandy!' Bernice hissed as the world started to twist into awful shapes over her head. 'And do put some on the wound as well. Thank you.'

And she fell unconscious.

The man looked at Wolsey and the dwarves. 'You are all her friends?'

'*His* friends, yes . . .' Wolsey muttered, wondering why today had turned out to be so confusing.

'Yes, we certainly are!' chimed in Candy, more loudly. 'And you, if I may say so, look to be a very well-appointed young man.'

'Then you must all come with me,' said the armoured man. 'I am Prince Charming, son of King Rupert. We were out riding when we saw your cottage under attack from those demons and had to intervene. I am taking this unfortunate and beautiful lady to a place where she may receive the best medical attention. We ride to my father's castle!'

With a great trumpeting, the column moved off, separating to allow Wolsey, Candy and the dwarves – once Gushy had locked the door of the cottage – to march in the middle. The Prince walked at the front, carrying the sleeping Bernice, a concerned expression on his face.

Wolsey looked at the strange horse, which had drawn level with him and was keeping pace, an odd, questioning expression on its face. 'I don't know about you,' said the cat, 'but I think that something rather odd is going on around here.'

The horse nodded.

Chapter 5

Beauty and Bernice

From the *Informative Record of Recent Grel History*:

In the chambers of the Perfecton city, the Grel Master smacked the facial tentacles of a Servitor with its own. 'Insult: waste of genetic data!' the Grel Master hooted at its hapless servant. 'I ordered you to immobilize the human, not disintegrate it!'

The Servitor pointed helplessly at the now-empty corridor down which Stokes had fled. 'My dataxe was set on immobilize,' it pleaded. 'Theory: perhaps our weapons act differently in this building?'

The Grel Master glared at him for a moment. 'Weak theory. We shall proceed. We shall find the other beings in the human's party, capture them and extract data from their brains. Forward.'

Extract Ends

Stokes had screamed as he'd fallen down the hole, a noise which probably added, accidentally, to the impression that he had been vaporized. The hole had opened up beneath him at the instant that the Grel had opened fire, and the trapdoor had slammed shut behind him again an instant later. He fell down a glowing green tunnel, rings of light flashing by him at such a speed that he was convinced that, should he ever hit the bottom, the impact would be quite fatal anyway.

But when the bottom of the tube was in sight, and Stokes had put his hands over his eyes, furiously checking off the entry conditions for every religion he had ever heard about, he found that he had started to slow down. His fall became a slower fall, then a drift, then almost a hover, as he touched his feet down on a glowing green surface.

And fell in a heap as whatever field had supported him let go.

'Ah, there you are, Stokes!' called Singh. 'Come and have a look at this!'

The artist clambered to his feet, steadying himself mentally, and made his way into the chamber where the other academics were standing. The floor he had landed on was located under an overhanging roof, and Stokes was initially surprised to see that the others seemed to be standing outdoors. The quality of light, the sky above their heads, the clouds . . . well, some sort of strange spacial curving thing must have happened, if this was a world where you could fall downwards and pop up on the surface again. Singh and Farouk would probably be debating about it already.

But when he stepped from under the roof, he realized where he actually was, and staggered back again.

His friends were standing before him, on a raised, round, green islet at the side of a silver floor. A vast silver floor. A silver floor that he had initially taken to be an ocean. He couldn't see the edge of it for the . . . clouds. He looked at the clouds that were drifting across the other side of the floor, and followed them up. Up, into something that wasn't a sky, but was actually a roof, thousands of feet up. It was glowing with a very skylike golden glow, and one patch, hidden behind the roof overhead, was glowing brighter than the rest. Like a setting sun.

Otterbland saw Stokes's expression and laughed, taking him by the shoulder and leading him to where the academics all sat on their dais. 'We think this chamber would take several days to drive across, and you could fly a pod in here with no trouble, that ceiling's so high. The brightness in the sky is moving, by the way.'

Owl looked up at him. 'At about the speed of apparent motion that Perfecton's sun would have got up to in its younger days. Oh. Thanks for saving our lives, by the way.'

Some of the other academics added their thanks, with varying degrees of affection and volume. Stokes sat down heavily, feeling dwarfed by the sheer scale of things around him. 'Big, isn't it?'

Bernice woke up at the feel of lips kissing hers.

She didn't open her eyes. Were these lips Jason's? No, not enough stubble on the chin. Were they, then, Doran's? Or – her brain persisted with the new information it had for her, even though she could still hardly believe it – that dwarf version of him they called Cute? No. These lips were a bit too sure of themselves for that.

She opened her eyes, and found that she was lying in a vast carved bed in a round room, that her upper arm was bandaged, and that she was being kissed by that man with the army.

She jumped, and pushed him off. 'Erm . . . stop! What are you doing?'

He straightened up, smiling. 'Why, you had been asleep for several days, and that is the traditional method of waking one such as you.'

'Charming,' Bernice muttered.

'At your service.' The man in the cloak and tights bowed. 'I am Prince Charming, son of King Rupert. I woke you because the royal apothecaries assure me that your arm is healed, and I thought that you might wish to attend the King's ball this evening.'

'Ball? But –'

'I shall leave you in peace. You will see me this evening. I hope that you might consider sharing the first dance with me, you beautiful, mysterious stranger.' He gave her what he obviously thought was a smouldering look and left.

The door swung closed behind him to reveal Wolsey hiding there, a set of lock-picks in his claws. 'Dick,' he purred, 'we really do have to talk.'

Bernice flopped back on her pillow, boggled beyond all boggle. 'How long have I been asleep?' she demanded.

'Three days.' Wolsey hopped on to the end of the bed and regarded her, his furry chin on his fist. 'The Prince has made sure that that Candy woman and those deluded dwarves have been given the finest apartments.'

'That Candy woman, as you call her, is a man.'

'Don't you start. I'd heard about noblesse oblige, but that Prince seems to think you're much too obliging and much too –'

'My arm . . . it's healed almost completely . . .' Bernice had gingerly started to touch the skin of her upper arm. 'So we can get injured here, but it's as if this world doesn't like it very much. Are my boots around here?'

Wolsey glanced over the end of the bed. 'No. Dick, what are these strange things of which you speak? We've known each other all our lives. Is it that you have succumbed to madness, or . . .' He cast a glance at the doorway. 'Has the whole world gone mad?'

'I promise that I'll explain,' Bernice told him. 'Turn your back – I'm going to find some clothes.'

'Turn my back?' Wolsey spluttered. 'Dick, you and I have bathed in the same bath when times were hard!'

'And I've seen you poo, but I still think you ought to turn your back, or you'll get a whole new perspective on Dick.'

Reluctantly, Wolsey turned. Bernice headed for the wardrobe and, not finding her jerkin and tights, grabbed everything she could lay her hands on. A few minutes of serious lacing and coughing and she called to the cat to turn round again.

She stood there in a long blue court dress, with a white bodice, silver shoes and a pointy hat with a piece of silk trailing from it.

Wolsey looked her up and down. 'Not very convincing.'

Bernice took his arm and led him towards the door. 'It's time, old friend, to explain to you who I really am.'

'I suppose I always knew,' the cat sighed. 'But behind closed doors is one thing. Are you really going to go out dressed like that?'

'Big, isn't it?' said Stokes.

'You have been saying that for the last hour . . .' murmured Singh.

The party of academics had been walking across the great hall for that last hour, spurred on by the thought that the Grel might have fallen down the same shaft as they had. Initially, they had just set out to cross the vast silver floor, but, after walking for about thirty minutes, they had come to a black line. The line was heading, as the mathematicians agreed, for the centre of the hall, where, in the far distance, a cluster of what must have been rather large buildings stood. Through the clouds in the dome of the hall could be glimpsed some large mass hanging on the ceiling, approximately above the buildings on the ground. It was, they had all agreed, at least something to aim for. The 'sky' was darkening rapidly. The day here was utterly different from that on the surface and everybody was starting to feel lagged. The group of walking professors had become a straggly column as academics paired off or talked in groups, pointing up at some new feature of interest in the ceiling above them.

Stokes had been idly twisting the butt of the gun, hoping to make the vase appear again to please the physicists. In truth, this fiddling also helped to pass the time. Stokes could still feel the sensation of guns trained on his back. He couldn't get it out of his mind. He felt hunted, as if a Grel could appear at any moment.

There was a shout from the front of the party.

Everybody at the back ran forward, colliding with those from the front who were running back, until everybody was milling around in a shouting mass.

Stokes elbowed his way to the front. When he saw what everybody was staring at, he shuddered.

In front of the academics stood a single Grel, just staring at them, spinning its axe threateningly. Those who had made their way to the front made to go back again, but some of their less courageous colleagues pushed them forward, urging them to reason with the alien or attack it.

When the Grel made no move, the group quietened a little, gazing at it uneasily. 'Where did it come from?' asked Stokes.

'It appeared,' said Lucinda. 'One moment it was not there, the next it was.'

Stokes took a deep breath and stepped towards the creature. It turned to look at him, mouth tentacles flexing. There was something different about it . . . a pale green glow that surrounded it. Ah! Stokes bravely strode right up to the Grel and waved a hand in front of its face. His fellow academics oohed and ahed in a most satisfying way. The Grel made little head movements as it followed his hand, but did no more. Stokes turned back to them triumphantly. 'No need to fear,' he said. 'This is the Grel that I shot with the gun. It's been vased. It's not quite here.' He ran a hand through the image of the Grel and was startled to feel textures brush against his skin, as slight as silk or breezes on his hand. The Grel shook and shivered, looking around itself. As Stokes's hand passed out of it, it seemed to see him perfectly for the first time. It took a moment to adjust itself to speaking English. 'New fact: the human that shot me is here,' it said, its voice sounding as if it was echoing down a long corridor. 'A human is in Slawcor.'

'Slawcor?' asked Stokes.

'This is Slawcor, where all facts are known, and there are no queries.'

'Their afterlife,' hissed Epstein. 'The Chelonians boast about sending them there.'

Stokes put a finger to his chin, deep in thought. 'Query –' he began.

'You cannot have queries in Slawcor!'

'I am a foolish human, and am very fortunate to be in Slawcor, so I still have queries, and you must answer them. Query: why did the Grel come to Perfecton?'

'On the trading world of Muss our Master heard stories of the technology of the Perfectons and of how their world was to be soon left unguarded.'

'What did you hope to find?'

'Transdimensional bridge technology that would give us access to all knowledge. It would be like Slawcor while alive, unlimited information. It would be –' The Grel stopped suddenly, its mouth tentacles wriggling fiercely. 'Query –' It stopped again. 'Fact: I can query! Fact: I have need for queries! Fact: humans cannot enter Slawcor!'

'Now, don't start jumping to any conclusions . . .'

'Conclusion: I am not in Slawcor! I have been . . . accessed . . . by this technology! You have interrogated me!'

'More of a quiet chat, really.'

'I must escape!' The Grel looked to its left and right, and then paused, seeming to concentrate. 'There is all time and space here. I must travel. Wherever I go.'

Suddenly, it flipped off backwards, its image spinning over and over, and receding, until it vanished into a point. The green glow faded from that point, but just before it did, the academics started at the sound of a sudden, falling scream.

Stokes fiddled frantically with the bulb on the end of the gun.

'Can't you get it back?' asked Otterbland.

'I don't think so,' sighed Stokes. 'I think he's gone to . . . wherever he was going.'

Wolsey had led Bernice to the battlements of the castle. From there, they looked down on to the sunny expanse of the Kingdom, trees and hills and windmills and rivers and roads, golden under a perfect blue sky. There was no wind. The landscape spoke to Bernice of a golden age, that period every culture has that was just a few generations ago, when everything was great. Only those golden ages were the products of grumpy old folk with selective memories, and this was one she was walking about in.

It was golden, however, apart from the Grel. She wondered what havoc they were causing somewhere in this idyll.

She sat down, her back against the parapet, wrapping her hands around her knees. She needed one person, at least, to understand the truth. 'The thing is, Wols, I remember a life before this one, where I was a completely different person. My name isn't Dick, it's Bernice.'

He scowled. 'Don't be –'

'Bernice,' she emphasized. 'Bernice Summerfield. I'm a professor of archaeology from the year 2593. I get the feeling that something in this place would like me to forget that, so forgive me if I keep repeating it. I'm a woman, not a boy, as you'd have found out if you'd looked round when I was dressing just now.'

'You are as mad as that woman who tried to sell me the magic beans. I don't believe a word of this tale. I leave you to sleep in the forest, and when you wake up, you're a different person. Were you taken by the fairies?'

Bernice frowned in frustration, trying to think of a way to convince him. 'All right, so tell me about Dick, the person that I used to be. What was his surname?'

'Whittington.'

'Richard Whittington?' Bernice was surprised to find the name familiar. 'That's a real person, a historical figure. Three times Lord Mayor of London between 1397 and 1420.'

'Well, that's always been your ambition. You told me that the streets there were paved with gold.'

Bernice glanced over her shoulder at the perfect landscape below. 'Looking at this lot, I may have been right. So I'm him, am I?' She tapped the stone of the parapet as an idea came to her. She pointed at the landscape beyond. 'Wait a minute. You can tell me that I'm Richard Whittington if you want, but you're not telling me that this kingdom . . . with King Rupert and everything, is England in the fourteenth or fifteenth century?'

Wolsey leant back on the parapet, his tail nervously whipping back and forth like a restless snake. He looked around the countryside for a moment, as if searching for a familiar landmark, and an uneasy growling rose from his throat. It was some time before he spoke. 'That has occurred to me. This must be some small kingdom in Surrey or Kent that the real King tolerates.' He still looked uncertain. 'I didn't know that places like this still existed.'

'Oh Wolsey . . .' Bernice stood up, gave him a hug, and began to stroke him behind the ears. 'You can't really believe that.'

The cat gently took her hand away from his head. 'Please, with you dressed like that, that's rather disturbing. Tell me –' he licked his lips with his long tongue, clearly perplexed '– this is important. Where did you acquire your knowledge of those demons you call the Grel? You know every blasted detail about them, yet I, who have been by your side always, have never seen them.'

'Exactly. That's the kind of anomalous detail which I'm talking about. I first met the Grel . . .' She frowned, as if surprised by her own memories. She put a hand to her brow. 'In my bedroom. When I was a child. I thought that it was a nightmare . . . One of them ran through my room, out of the wall and . . . then it fell through the floor. It screamed as it fell . . .' She'd wandered a little distance from the cat now, wondering where these memories had come from. She didn't remember remembering that in the past.

'I see,' said Wolsey, more baffled than ever. 'I assume that I must have been asleep at the time. But the point is: where did you get all these details that you told the dwarves, about how those things live and die? For the past few days, Gushy has been regaling me with stories of your secret knowledge.'

'That's because I've encountered them on several occasions, getting in the way of various archaeological expeditions on various planets. They –'

'Wait, wait!' Wolsey raised his paw. 'Archaeology, this word you've used twice now is . . . well, I know not what. And planets are only those things that determine our fate, as seen by old ladies in tea leaves.'

Bernice suddenly knew that she was absolutely right about the anomalous nature of this world. She grabbed Wolsey by the shoulders. 'Tea?'

The cat looked at her, stunned. 'If you want. Bit early for me.'

'No, no. Tea! You can't drink tea! Not in the England of 1420, you can't! Not in the England of knights and castles, either!' She held on to the cat as he tried to twist from her grasp, not wanting to meet her gaze. 'You've started to see it, haven't you? You've started to see that this world you live in just does not make sense!'

Wolsey took a deep breath and looked at her. 'I might –'

A shadow fell across both of them, as if the sun had suddenly gone into eclipse. Wolsey automatically stepped forward, shielding Bernice with his body.

Beside the door to the stairs stood a strange figure. He was tall and thin, dressed in long, flowing black robes, and a turban with a jewel in it. He had a pair of hawklike, piercing eyes and a vast grin. There was something strange about him, Bernice realized, but she couldn't quite pin down what. 'Oh, 'ere, sorry if I startled you,' he said. His voice was swooping and English. It didn't go with his clothes at all.

'Who are you, then?' asked Bernice, stepping out from behind her cat.

The man bowed. 'I am the King's Vizier, and your humble servant, your highness, your most worthy, your highest upon high, et cetera, et cetera.'

'Your highness?'

He took her hand and planted a kiss on her knuckle, grinning his vast, toothy grin at her. He looked like he was able to take a bite out of the world itself. 'Your beauty is like that of the very stars!'

'Yes, from a distance they seem cold, but get too close and you'll lose your eyebrows.' Bernice smiled politely, shaking her hand loose from his.

'Oh, stop messin' about,' the Vizier giggled indulgently. He suddenly became serious again. 'I come to you with a message from your father.'

'From my father?' Bernice boggled again, and decided to stop boggling and take everything on board. This Vizier had definitely not just popped back from a day trip to the home counties on Earth, where her real father ran a restaurant. 'What did he say?'

'He wishes to see you urgently. He said something about . . . romance?' The Vizier twiddled his eyebrows meaningfully, grinned another vast grin and then, with a sweep of black satin and a high chuckle, left.

Wolsey poked at his ear, looking puzzled. 'Do you hear a hissing sound?' he said.

'Yes,' Bernice nodded. 'I thought it was you. So I'm royalty now, am I?'

Wolsey leant on her shoulder. 'Which means your father is the King, Princess Bernice.'

'Yes, I . . . Hey!' She smiled and gave him a quick tickle on his stomach. 'You called me Bernice!'

'Let's just say that I want to believe,' Wolsey told her, patting her hand. 'Even if it does severely limit my supply of Dick jokes.'

Bernice headed for the King's chamber, feeling quite triumphant. She'd made one person believe her, at least. Sort of. She hadn't felt that nausea of unreality since she'd woken up, but the sleep itself was a worry. Where had she been while she'd slumbered? No dreams, no memory of time passed at all. She had a terrible vision of herself as a stream of data, and an awful feeling that she'd been switched off. At least she hadn't been reprogrammed to fit in.

The castle itself was a delight, a vastly conflicting mess of styles that seemed to be the product of an insane designer. The outside walls were white, with silver spires curling upward like some late Germanic folly. But inside, the banners and flags looked medieval, and the pages and courtiers she passed were dressed in bright colours, jerkins and tights – a sort of horrid collision between the Jacobean era and the Renaissance. On the way to see the King, she had to ask various of them the way, and was surprised that all of them bowed or curtsied to her. Amazing, the difference a frock made. She was suddenly the King's daughter, another handbrake turn of plot, but quite a fun one. Better than being Dick. She vaguely recognized quite a few of those she talked to. But what was an obviously European King doing with a Vizier? And what did a Vizier do, exactly? She had so few answers.

She found the King's chamber at the top of a grand flight

of marble steps, up and down which servants were running as the preparations continued for the ball that evening. The whole castle was in uproar, with food being delivered, entertainers rehearsing, and bunting being hung. Despite Bernice's situation, it was all rather exciting. She stopped outside the door of the chamber. From inside she could hear the sounds of a woman sobbing. Then she heard the King's voice: he sounded mocking and cruel. Oh dear, he was that sort of King, then. This world was about to take a turn for the worse. Taking a deep breath, Bernice knocked on the door and, without waiting to be asked, entered.

The King looked sharply across at her from where he was sitting on his throne, his face set in a scowl. 'Yes?' he growled. 'What is it?'

On the other side of the room stood a beautiful young woman in a green dress, who was crying into her handkerchief, but Bernice's attention was focused completely on King Rupert.

Because she knew exactly who he was.

'Captain Balsam!' she exclaimed.

The King blinked, not knowing quite how to respond.

The girl in the corner threw down her handkerchief and shouted at the King. 'You can't keep me here for ever! My love will come and save me!'

'I'm sure he will, my dear . . .' The King, or Balsam as Bernice knew him, got to his feet, his attention diverted away from Bernice. He went to the table and poured himself a goblet of wine from a flagon. 'And when he does, my men shall be waiting for him. I think I shall give you his head as a keepsake . . .' He threw back the wine and grinned, giving out a little, malicious chuckle.

The girl gathered up her skirts, and ran out, shrieking. She slammed the door behind her.

Bernice glared at the King. 'That wasn't very nice.'

His Majesty slumped back into his throne, suddenly

looking rather sad. 'Oh, I know. Daughters, what can you do with them? Apart from you, of course, my dear.' He gestured for Bernice to take a seat opposite him, and she did so. 'You're the only one of them who doesn't cause me pain. Aurora's asleep in her tower. Marian there . . . well, I just can't understand her choice of boyfriends. I'm a good King, I really am, but I have this terrible blind spot concerning her Robin and that gang of his. Normally, I'm fair and just and actually rather jolly, but whenever I hear about what that lot in the forest are up to it turns me into some sort of . . . evil villain! I just can't help myself!'

'No,' muttered Bernice. 'I'm sure you can't. Tell me, does the name Balsam mean anything to you?'

'Why, of course it does, child! It's our family name, the name of the royal house. You should know that.'

'Oh, of course . . . Dad. I'm just having one of those forgetful days.' Bernice stood up and wandered over to the King, putting a hand on the shoulder of his elegant purple doublet. 'Tell you what, can I do something that I used to do when I was a kid? That old joke of ours?'

'Oh, erm, yes, of course . . .' The King looked at her suspiciously.

She reached out and tugged his beard. Pulled it left and right, all the ways she knew of loosening the bolt that held an android's facial plate in place.

But the King's face stayed on. When she let go, he rubbed his chin and winced.

Bernice shrugged. 'So much for that idea.'

The King, still looking perplexed, picked up a piece of parchment from beside his throne. 'Now, you may be wondering why I called you here today. As you are my eldest and most useful daughter, I have decided that it's time you got married.'

'Oh no.' Bernice raised her hands. 'Been there, done that, painted the spare bedroom.'

The King ignored her. 'Now, there are several eligible

bachelors in the Kingdom. I've prepared a list. These will all be at the ball tonight. There's the Marquis Du Chat, a very rich young man, so I'm told. Young Jack from the village, exactly the opposite, poor but honest. Also, John Wood, who's a woodcutter, will be there. Big and strong, if you like that sort of thing.'

'Thanks for giving me such a wide selection,' Bernice muttered.

'I have a letter here . . .' He took a bottle from beneath his throne, and tipped a rolled-up note out of it. 'From a Mr Crusoe, who, it seems, is marooned on an island. He'd like to be rescued, find his one true love, et cetera. Sounds a nice chap, but perhaps he's more in need of a secretary than a wife.'

'Sort of a Girl Friday?'

'Indeed.' The King nodded. 'He won't be at the ball, of course. Now, we must not discount the interest of young Prince Charming . . .'

Bernice froze. 'Erm, perhaps we'd better. Unless you do things very differently here.'

'Eh?'

'He is, after all, my brother.'

'What?' The King leapt to his feet, aghast.

There was a moment of silence, and Bernice looked at the King in curiosity. His face had glazed over. For a moment, he looked as if he was communing with something divine, deep in meditation. Then, just as suddenly, he relaxed again and his features creased into a booming laugh. 'Ah, my dear daughter, there is something that I have never mentioned to you. The boy you think of as your brother was a foundling, an infant discovered in the forest. He and his sister, the girl you know as your sister Aurora, were found near to a strange cottage made entirely of chocolate and other sweets. I adopted them as my own. Charming has known the truth for years. So you mustn't be disturbed by his admiration for you. Or your love for him!'

Bernice gave this monarch a hard stare, wishing that she had her glasses with her, so that she could glance intimidatingly at him over them. 'Fine. Interesting. So who else is on the list?'

The King turned back to his parchment, his contemplation forgotten. 'Well, this is also, if I may coin a pun, a little incestuous, but my Vizier has been expressing an interest in you lately. He's gone so far as to ask formally for my permission to court you. But if you want to go down that route, I'm afraid you'll have to give up all interest in little Arab boys –'

'Eh?'

'As will he!' The King laughed. 'We'll have no more of that.'

'That's . . . a bit too much to ask.' Bernice was starting to get scared again. She felt as if she was being rushed towards a conclusion, towards being married off, that moment of closure that, in books, was like a little death. Having newly discovered life after marriage, this was an absolute nightmare made flesh. Even worse, she'd found that, during this conversation, she'd wanted to blurt out all manner of strange things. That she loved so-and-so, that she'd never marry another one. Opinions which weren't hers. It was as if this world was forcing her to make a choice, aching for closure. Fortunately, Bernice had had a lifetime of drinking serious ale, and knew how to stop herself blurting out words that would get her into serious trouble, words like 'I'd love to see your judo trophies' or 'Yes, I did snog him in the kitchen, what of it?' But this felt much more serious than that. She had a terrible feeling that, had she made a choice, she might, when next she woke, find that it was a few weeks later, and that she was in some stranger's marriage bed. Very scary.

She needed to learn a lot more about this place. Quickly. The King had come to the end of his list and was looking at her expectantly. 'Um . . .' she said to him.

'Why don't I have a look at them at the ball, and make up my mind then?'

The King clapped his hands together. 'Wonderful! You'll have the opportunity to get to know all of them this evening!' His grin faded as a thought struck him. 'If Marian's going to pine, do you think I should invite this Robin fellow?'

Bernice raised an eyebrow. 'Why change the habit of a lifetime?'

The afternoon turned into a whirl of dress fittings and fashion tips, the ladies of the court attending to putting Bernice into a vast multi-petticoated dress that was, of course, in an Edwardian style. Wolsey watched from a corner of her bedroom, shaking his head every now and then, despite his newfound belief in the feminine nature of his oldest friend. Bernice had managed to get ball invitations for him, Candy, and the dwarves. She'd noticed a certain reticence on the part of the courtiers towards Wolsey, an unwillingness to deal with him. Now, as the ladies busied around her with their lace and tape measures, he would reach out a claw every now and then to snag one of their bustles. They detached themselves from him without anger, but with a little disturbed glance, as though he was in the wrong place, a gatecrasher.

'The dwarves,' Wolsey told Bernice, 'don't know who you are. They're pleased that you've turned out to be a princess, because, I quote, you're so beautiful that you must be one.'

'That's Cute.'

'They should have named him Mawkish. The Vizier is also certain that you're a princess. He – and he seemed to be taking this hissing sound with him wherever he went – insisted that you had always lived here, except when being spirited away by an Arabic boy.'

'If only. What about Charming?'

'He thinks he found you in the forest, a lost princess. He

laughed out loud when I suggested that you were his sister.'

Bernice leant on the wall of her room as she was stitched into her bodice. 'Curious. Ooh, in this thing, it's just as well one doesn't have to attend to any of the biological functions.'

'What are those?'

Bernice laughed, causing a curse and a little howl from one of the ladies as the stitching split. 'There was a time, I recall, when you were quite enthusiastic about all of them.' She held one of the ladies back and straightened up, massaging her lower back. 'So nobody can get their stories straight.' She plucked a flower from a vase by the window and experimented with it as her trousseau. 'Fasten your safety belt, we're in for a bumpy ball.'

Wolsey raised an eyebrow. Then lowered it again.

CHAPTER 6

A WHOLE NEW BALL GAME

Above the stage in the grand hall of the castle there was a huge clock. On every hour, the clock would chime. Exactly as it was chiming eight, two serving men walked down the centre of the hall, up the steps to the great doors, and swung them open.

There waited a great crowd of people. The more ordinary folk, or, to put it less politely, peasants, a select number of whom had been graciously given tickets to the ball, were gossiping and gasping at the decor of the castle. The more fashionable were quieter, and generally further back.

Apart from Bernice and Wolsey, who were at the very front of the crowd. The Master of Ceremonies raised an eyebrow at them as he pulled a roll of parchment from his sleeve and made his way to a little lectern by the doorway, obviously sooner than he'd expected. 'The Princess Bernice,' he announced to the empty room. 'And Wolsey the Cat.'

Bernice and Wolsey marched down the steps, Bernice feeling rather embarrassed. She didn't know the etiquette of such things, and she'd been eager to get the evening started. Enjoying gowns of all kinds as she did, she was still getting used to the scaffolding that was holding her skirts up, not to mention stays so tight that she'd actually developed breasts. The shoes were a bit impractical, too.

They were made of glass, and so Benny was taking tiny steps, aware that putting her foot down too hard, let alone any attempt at disco, could create a horrible ankle-haemorrhaging situation.

She managed to navigate the dress into a sitting position, and she and Wolsey took their places at the head table as commoners filed into the room, obviously cowed by their surroundings.

Wolsey gazed around at the vast number of place settings, the huge dance floor at one end of the room, and the great stage. 'The King's balls get bigger every year,' he purred.

'See? You don't need the Dick jokes,' Bernice whispered back.

The MC cleared his throat. 'Dame Candy,' he called. Then, a moment later, as if under severe duress. 'With nobody. As yet.'

Across the floor glided Candy, in a vastly petticoated dress with polka-dot socks, a huge conical bustier, and a six-foot pile of beehived hair. Her face was pink with make-up. 'What do you think?' she asked Bernice and Wolsey, thumping down into her seat. 'A bit too subtle, maybe? I didn't want anything that said "come and get me".'

'That certainly doesn't.' Wolsey smiled.

'The seven . . .' The MC paused, and made a little cough. Then through clenched teeth, he continued, 'The seven . . . dwarves.'

A ripple of distaste ran through the crowd. In a line, the dwarves marched proudly into the hall, Moody at their head. They were wearing evening dress in very small sizes. Moody had selected a powerful double-breasted jacket. Bernice realized that, now he was a dwarf, he was human, and his arms were in the usual place. Bitchy had the most fabulous black gown, Gushy was wearing a lavender dress with long gloves, and Liberal had chosen a muted fawn trouser suit. Laddish looked like a bouncer, with a silly red bow tie. The only one who hadn't dressed for the occasion was Lazy, who was just wearing his usual dwarfish doublet. Cute was at the back of the group, being the littlest. He waved enthusiastically to Benny. He had had his hair done, and was wearing the cutest little tuxedo . . .

Bernice slapped herself across the face. Hard. This was pathetic. That little being lived for her, adored her, wanted her close to him so completely and utterly . . . If that was what Michael Doran was really like, then how could she ever have considered going to bed with him? In the real world, she was a lonely woman, approaching middle age, who had pathetically grabbed at her first and probably last chance of happiness. An empty boy with a cute smile. Perhaps she should stay here.

Moody glanced around the gathering with a sneer, turned to his fellows and raised his fist in a power salute. 'Hi!' he shouted.

They saluted back. 'Ho!'

Moody spun on his heel, and led the dwarves towards Bernice's table. Gushy took the seat next to Bernice. 'Gosh, you do look pretty in your dress.'

Cute, to Bernice's trepidation, sat down on the other side of her. 'She's beautiful . . .' he sighed.

Bernice concentrated on the doorway.

'The crowd don't seem to be entirely happy with your presence,' Wolsey observed to the dwarves.

'Rumplephobia,' spat Moody.

'There is a lot of post-dwarf and even anti-dwarf feeling,' Liberal explained. 'Even amongst the dwarf community. Some say that we should abandon Dwarf as a social construct altogether, and just get on with being short.'

'Could be because of the Ogre,' Laddish interjected. 'Last year, he was guilty of a number of unnecessary actions which went well beyond the spirit of the game.'

'He went around killing people,' said Bitchy, 'and tried to blame it on us, because he killed each of them in the manner of one of our names. Well, six of them, anyway. He decided that the best way to incriminate Lazy was not to bother.'

'Ogre?' Bernice perked up. 'There's an Ogre in this Kingdom that actually kills people?'

'Ooh, he's a bad sort,' Candy put her hand on Bernice's sleeve. 'But he doesn't exactly live round here.'

'Then where –?'

But Bernice's question was interrupted by another cry from the MC. 'Prince Charming!'

The Prince was dressed in an extraordinary costume. He wore a long military coat, and a pair of britches, with a peacock waistcoat, a red sash, and a cummerbund. He marched down the steps, glancing around the room proudly, aware of the attention and adulation he was getting.

After a moment of feigned uncertainty, doubtless to allow the commoners to gaze on him some more, he spun on his heel and headed for Bernice's table. He hitched one foot up on to a spare chair, slapped his thigh and grinned at her. 'What do you think of the get-up?'

Bernice slid her fan from her sleeve, and tapped his boot with it gently, looking him up and down. 'Ridicule,' she told him, 'is nothing to be scared of.'

He laughed indulgently, and took his seat opposite her, earning a glare from Cute. From the other side of the room there came a fanfare. The majority of the other guests had arrived. Candy pointed out two of them to Bernice, women in huge platform shoes, with extraordinary wigs, garish make-up and vast dresses. They were as well endowed as Candy was. 'Two of my lot. Sisters, if I remember rightly. I must speak to them later.'

'Your lot?'

'Dames. You know. Ladies of a certain age.'

'Yes,' laughed Wolsey, draining his first champagne stem of the night. 'Too old.' Then he stopped in mid-sip, his ears visibly pricking up as his gaze chanced upon one of the new arrivals. 'I say. Hel-lo!'

Bernice followed his eyeline. Through the crowd was moving another humanoid cat. This one wore an elegant lace gown, the same silver as her fur. On her feet were a dainty little pair of boots.

'Puss in Boots . . .' murmured Wolsey.

'I've warned you about your language before,' Liberal told him.

'That's her name.' Wolsey rose to his feet, purring, and adjusted his cravat. 'I'd heard that another of my kind would be coming to this ball, but I could scarcely hope that she would be so . . . soft-furred and silver.' He rubbed his paws together. 'Let's hope she hasn't been neutered, eh?'

Bernice tapped him gently with her fan. 'Hold on. Last time you contemplated romance, it was between two rubbish skips, and resulted in a very angry neighbour and six kittens.'

'I don't know what you're talking about,' said Wolsey, his eyes locked on his target. 'If you'll excuse me . . .' And he slunk off in the direction of the female cat.

Bernice sighed. 'I should have taken him to the vet when I had the chance.'

The MC was announcing some more arrivals. 'Young Jack from the village.'

'Son!' cried Candy, leaping to her feet. She ran across to the tousle-haired boy, enveloped him in her enormous bosom, and then led him, stunned, back to Bernice's table. 'This is my good-for-nothing . . .' She stopped and considered the circumstances. 'My heroic son Jack, who sent that Ogre packing.'

'Oh, Ma!' Jack slapped his rather balletic thigh. 'I only noticed that the murders had all been carried out by someone over nine feet high, and thus couldn't possibly be the work of any individual dwarf. It was nothing.'

Moody slapped palms with the lad. 'Dwarf brother.'

'So.' Jack sat down and turned to Bernice. 'You've met my mother.'

Bernice noticed something very odd about Jack.

He didn't have an Adam's apple.

Oh boy. Or rather, not. This was getting very complicated.

'Yes,' she said. 'She's so feminine. It must be a family trait.'

'Robert of Huntingdon,' the MC announced. This was a dashing young man in green cape and cavalier moustache. He was evidently in charge of the evening's entertainment, because behind him were gathered a group of musicians in hooded capes, carrying large drums, violin cases and other boxed instruments. Robert was pointing out various features of the hall to them. They fell back as Princess Marian ran to greet Robert. To Bernice's relief he wasn't given a place at her table. The King, in cupid mode, had ordered that one be set for him beside Marian. Obviously, the idea was to take her thoughts away from that Robin person.

A great shadow swept over the table, and everybody looked up. The Vizier was standing there, a look of ecstasy on his face, his fingers curled in appreciation. 'My dear, you look wonderful!' he cried, looking right down Bernice's newly created chest. 'Your beauty, Princess, is like the truth itself.'

'Yes.' Bernice smiled sweetly back at him. 'It's hard to get hold of, and you're never going to see all of it.'

The Vizier had a male throat. He still carried that strange hissing sound with him. Bernice suddenly looked around. She could swear that she'd heard somebody shouting something. Boom? Boots? Maybe Puss had admirers other than Wolsey. She'd finally pinned down what was strange about the Vizier, at least. Unlike all the others here, a number of whom were strangely familiar, she was certain that she'd never met him. She would have recognized somebody who looked that unusual instantly. And he looked unusual because . . . because he wasn't quite real. Everybody else had blemishes and wrinkles and all the minor defects of humanity. He was perfect. Stylized. Sketched like an animated character. What was he doing here?

The Vizier, and all the other assembled suitors, glowered as a huge man in a lumberjack shirt, carrying an axe over his shoulder, stamped up to the table and grinned at them. 'Hello!' he cried. 'I'm John Wood the woodsman! Now where can I put my chopper?'

'Over here!' called Candy, patting the seat next to her. She turned to whisper in Bernice's ear. 'Ooh, isn't he bold?'

Bernice ticked another one off her list. Male features on the woodsman.

Wolsey led his new feline acquaintance back to the table, arm in arm with her. 'This vision in feline splendour is Puss. Puss, this is my master, erm, that is, my mistress, the Princess Bernice.'

'Charmed.' Puss curtsied. She indicated a gauche young man, done up in the most expensive finery, but looking as if he was a bad actor playing a part. He stood a little way back, but was gazing at Bernice with that star-struck near-comatose look that she was getting used to from these men. 'This is my master, the Marquis Du Chat.'

'Right pleased. I mean, charmed.' The Marquis stepped forward, slapped his thigh, and bowed deeply, kissing Bernice's knuckle, from which position she got a good look at his throat. And no Adam's apple there, either. As Bernice had now come to expect. He straightened up. 'So, cracking do, I mean ball, tonight, eh?'

He took his place at the table, and Bernice studied the faces of her potential suitors. There was no doubt about it. Two of these lads were decidedly girlish. There had been times in her life when that wouldn't have been too much of a problem, but here such confusions seemed to be more a matter of style than lifestyle.

The fanfare rang out again. 'All rise,' the MC commanded. 'For his Majesty, King Rupert!'

The audience got to their feet. The King, in a smart uniform and garish waistcoat, strode into the middle of the dining area, and spread his arms wide. 'Greetings, my friends. You are welcome to my hospitality. Eat, drink, enjoy yourselves. This ball is for my daughter, Princess Bernice, that she may find a husband!'

Everybody in the room looked at Bernice. And clapped.

Wolsey leant close to her ear and whispered. 'No pressure.'

Extract from the Diary of Bernice Summerfield

Closure, apart from being that point at the end of a Shakespeare play where everybody is either dead or married, is the mind's ability to make conclusions about things that it hasn't directly experienced. For instance, if you throw a rock over a wall, and then you hear a crash, you're not going to stand there thinking, 'I wonder what caused that.' Well, you might, but that's denial, and that's not what I'm talking about here. As they cleared away the food from the tables, and the band that Robert of Huntingdon had brought along began to play, I found myself thinking that I was on my way to being a victim of closure in both senses. Firstly, that the King seemed determined to have me married off, determined to create an ending. For some reason, I was very worried about that, almost afraid of it. I had the instinctive feeling that that closure would somehow be the end of everything. Secondly, that I felt that I was in danger of hopping from one moment to another, much later, something meaningful having happened in between. After all, already I'd fallen asleep as one person, as far as these people were concerned, and woken up as somebody else.

I had thought that the people here were all robots, because they seemed to change their mind to order. But if they were, then whoever or whatever program was controlling them would be able to change all of their minds, to have them come to a unanimous decision about whether I was a man or a woman. And why would female robots disguise themselves as men and vice versa, for no good reason?

I felt that I was missing a very big point.

So I came up with a plan. It employed one of my general rules. These aren't the sort of rules which one makes up deliberately, and sorts one's life out with. These are the sort of rules which govern your behaviour, but which aren't immediately obvious to you. The sort of little behavioural quirk that you look back on and think: 'Yes, that's very like me.' It's very like me, when I have to pick one thing out of a number of different and conflicting options, to try to do all of them. This rule has led to my having a romantic dinner, for instance, whilst proofreading under the table and continually running out to call the drone that I'd left in my ship's cargo bay to pack my dig tools. People tell me it's irritating, but there you are. If I didn't do everything I might miss something.

That's why I, who had become allergic to engagements, decided suddenly, whilst diplomatically having the first dance of the evening with Wolsey, to gorge myself on them. 'I'm going to accept the Prince's hand in marriage,' I told him.

Give the cat credit, he only missed a single step. Around us, the whole enormous dance floor was full of spinning couples and the rustle of taffeta against petticoat. He probably didn't want to make a scene. 'That's . . . a big decision,' he whispered.

'Not really. I want to see what happens if I move so fast that all these intentions and stories and attempts at closure get mixed up. Maybe we'll get to see what's really going on. When I do this –' and I made a chopping motion with my hand '– I want you to distract the Prince.'

He looked rather put out. 'And I was doing so well with Puss.'

'The night is young. I'm sure you'll get to smell each other's bottoms later. Ah, my Prince!' I smiled invitingly as the Prince swished up, and allowed him to cut in, swapping his partner, one of the sisters that Candy had pointed out earlier, with Wolsey. 'You dance so well. Why, I am rather thinking of marrying you.'

'What? You are?' He stopped dancing, there and then, and, this being one of those sorts of ball, everybody else stopped dancing too.

'Please, sir, spare my blushes!' I gasped, fluttering my fan fiercely and taking his shoulder again to lead him back into the dance before he slapped his thigh. Everybody else resumed dancing.

'Sorry. I'm so overwhelmed. This is the happiest day of my life!' He took a ring from his jacket and slipped it on my finger. 'I must tell Father.'

'Just give me a few moments while I prepare myself for the big announcement,' I told him. 'You just keep on dancing, Charming.' And I sped off into the crowd, leaving him smiling.

I headed in the direction of the powder room (which in this world would probably be just that) for a moment, and slipped the ring from my finger and into my corset. Then I changed tack, cutting in on where Candy was dancing with John Wood, knocking him to and fro with swings of her dangerous bosoms. She gave me such a glare as she marched off. 'I like the cut of your jib, axeman,' I told the bearded, muscular man. 'Fancy tying the knot?'

'Why, aye, lady, that I do!' he cried. 'Listen, everybody . . .' He was about to boom his delight out to the crowd, until I slapped a hand across his chops.

'Do not,' I advised. 'For I require a moment to gather myself.' He nodded, and I let go. He produced a ring and tried to get down on one knee, but I sort of jollied him to his feet and accepted the ring on to my finger with a little curtsey. 'Cheers. See you in a bit.'

On the other side of the room I caught sight of the Prince, marching towards his father, his face alight with joy. Luckily, Wolsey was almost beside him. I made the cutting motion, and my cat nodded back to me. If only he was this obedient in ordinary life. I dashed off to find another potential suitor, dropping this ring down to join the other one.

Diary Entry Ends

Wolsey caught the Prince's sleeve as he was heading for the King, and glared at him haughtily. 'I've been meaning to have a few words with you.'

'Later, perhaps.' The Prince smiled.

'This cannot wait.' Wolsey made the hair along his spine stand on end, his tail swishing dangerously beneath his coat tails. 'I have been confused ever since I got here, what with all these strange shifts in personality and point of view. I doubt you'll explain anything to me, no matter how much I ask, so I have come to an important conclusion.'

'What?'

Wolsey paused for a moment, wondering just what he could do to stop the young man from reaching the King. Any accusation or threat could be swiftly countered. It might even result in the King being dragged into the argument, and Wolsey being thrown out of the palace. Then he had an idea. As long as he'd lived, there had always been one way to bring the action around him to a complete halt. 'That I'll never be like human people,' he told the Prince. 'Let me explain.' He turned to the dancers, who had, as he'd expected, all stopped to look at him as he began to sing. The band on the stage struck up a jaunty melody that just happened to fit his words exactly. 'He came along, he saved us at the cottage. He grabbed my mistress for a bit of frottage. That's when I . . . caught his eye . . .'

* * *

Bernice had meanwhile cornered Jack the commoner, and told him that his accent intrigued her, and therefore immediate matrimony was on the cards. He'd given her another ring, which she'd added to the collection before moving on. As Wolsey started to sing, she was accepting the proposal of the Marquis Du Chat, who had rather charmingly confessed to her that he wasn't really a nobleman at all, but a poor boy made good. 'I owe it all,' he told her, 'to my Pussy.'

'I'm glad I've never had cause to say that. Still, in your case, many a true word, eh? Thanks.' She slipped on the proffered ring. 'Don't tell anybody until I'm ready, please. Cheers.'

She left him beaming. Goodness, she thought, so many broken hearts in one day. Hee hee hee.

A shadow fell over her, and a familiar hissing and booing sound filled the air. Bernice quickly whipped off the new ring, added it to the others, and turned round, holding the correct finger out. 'Ah, my dear Vizier. I've heard that you've got a bit of a crush on me. Tell me more.'

'He took the dwarves and me back to his castle,' Wolsey was getting into the swing of it now, leaping about the stage and declaiming at the Prince, who was looking down at his boots and generally affecting not to notice. 'He had his people deal with every hassle. Which was kind. He thought that Dick was actually a woman, a strange position even for a human . . . But in very little time, I thought: I'll never be like human people, I'll never do whatever human people do. I'll never work out human people. I'll never work out human people like you.' He pointed a claw flirtatiously at Puss in the audience, who just shrugged. 'I'll never understand . . . so I just smile and lend a hand . . .'

* * *

Bernice bit her bottom lip and managed a cheery smile as the Vizier kissed her knuckle, admiring the ring that he had placed on it. He paused to wipe a tear from his eye. 'I'm overcome,' he told her. 'Normally, I have to force my brides into marriage through threats to the men they actually love. I've never had this degree of co-operation!' He suddenly turned his head to look over Bernice's shoulder and grinned an insane grin, seemingly in response to one of the strange noises that followed him around. 'Oh shut up, I'm trying to be sincere!' The noises only increased in volume.

Bernice was about to ask him just what he was on about, when there came a shout from the other side of the room.

'Leave her alone!'

Standing on the balcony in front of an open window stood a teenage Arabic boy, his hands on his hips. Even from here, Bernice could spot the by-now-familiar lack of anything masculine in the neck department. 'I've come to rescue you, Princess!'

The crowd gasped and cried out as the boy leapt off the balcony, grasped the great chandelier above the dance floor, and swung himself over their heads, letting go of the light fitting to spin three times before landing right between Bernice and the Vizier.

The band stopped playing, gawping at the intruder. Wolsey put his hands on his hips and sighed in disgust.

The Arabian boy slapped his thigh and thrust his prodigious chest out at the Vizier. 'So you thought you could force her to marry you, eh?'

'Oh no,' purred the Vizier. 'Not this time. She was quite keen. Weren't you?' He nodded at Bernice, seeking confirmation.

The boy grabbed Bernice by the shoulders, as she desperately tried to pull the ring from her finger. 'Is this true?'

'Er, yes, actually, but –' the ring came off, and Bernice dropped it down her bodice to join the others '– I've really gone off the idea now, and want to marry you instead.'

'What?' cried the Vizier, the Prince, the Marquis, Jack, John Wood, and most of the assembled courtiers.

Bernice broke from the boy's grasp, gathered up her skirts and jumped up on stage beside Wolsey. 'In fact –'

'Quick, men!' Robert of Huntingdon leapt to his feet, and gestured to the musicians. 'This is the distraction we've been waiting for!'

The musicians threw aside their hooded cloaks, revealing bright green jerkins and tights. They pulled bows, staves and swords from their instruments.

'So!' The King laughed scornfully, glancing at Marian. 'You have led this vagabond straight into my trap!'

From alcoves all around the roof of the hall appeared men in armour, armed with crossbows. The King drew his sword. Robert drew his sword. They leapt on to the long dining table.

'Stop!' bellowed Bernice.

They stopped. The room fell silent. Everybody was looking at her, including the two swordsmen, poised to fight.

Bernice glanced upwards. Above the stage, the giant clock was indicating twenty seconds to midnight. She had that terrible feeling in the pit of her stomach again. It would be terribly easy to go along with any one of these stories, to give in to one particular suitor, or play along with this sudden, desperate attempt to launch into a new situation. But that would mean The End. And Bernice was certain that, if that happened, nobody was going to live happily ever after. This knotting of stories felt even worse, as if a terrible pressure was on her, the room and everybody in it, as if the world was about to explode. Wolsey was looking around desperately. He was feeling it too, an electric sensation, as if they were all about to be ripped apart by lightning. But she had to go through with it. She didn't belong here – she was Bernice Summerfield, and if this world couldn't accept that, then she was going to pull it down with her.

'Your Majesty!' she shouted. 'I want to marry all of them! Every single one! How's that for closure?'

The King gawped at her, his mouth moving, unable to say anything. 'I . . .'

'Give us your blessing! Bring all these stories to an end!' Bernice held his stare with her own. 'Do it!'

'I give . . . I give . . .' The King stammered, dropping his sword as the table beneath him shuddered. The whole room was shuddering now, as if it was on the verge of some vast, climactic implosion.

Wolsey grabbed Bernice's arm. 'What have you done? What's happening to my world?'

The shuddering became vibration. The courtiers started screaming and throwing themselves to the floor as every piece of glass in the hall shattered into powder. And still the vibration became faster, the walls and floor and ceiling screaming with it.

The second hand on the clock, battering against the body of the clock itself, clicked to midnight.

The clock chimed.

And the room erupted into white light.

A moment of dislocation.

Nothing.

And then something again.

The clock was still chiming. Two. Three. Four chimes and continuing. Bernice stood on the stage, as she had before, and all the courtiers were staring at her. Because her beautiful dress was becoming grey at the edges, the gems in her hair falling and fluttering off as leaves, her bodice unravelling into a slapping spiral of vines.

She felt a wave of emotion rush over her, and she couldn't tell how much of it was what this world expected her to feel, and how much of it was the horror that she actually felt. That she'd failed, that she'd lost, that she was going to be trapped in this insane world for ever.

Howling, she jumped off the stage, and ran for the great doors at the end of the hall, clutching the remains of her dress to her body.

She tripped and rolled down the steps of the castle, sobbing as everything unravelled around her, her elbows and knees bruised on the muddy marble. But what did that matter? They'd be healed in tomorrow's perfect sleep, and then there'd be tomorrow and tomorrow, until she was a perfect grinning inhabitant of this hell.

The slippers slipped from her feet and bounced away. Her body slapped into the mud at the bottom of the steps, and she was not surprised at all when a pair of strong hands helped her to her feet. This world demanded that you play, that you could not even madly sulk in a corner. It kept at you like a –

Weasel. Which was exactly what was helping her into a rather smelly orange carriage: a weasel in a footman's outfit that was unravelling as fast as her own. 'Quickly!' he called.

'I don't care!' Bernice bellowed at him as she fell into the carriage. 'This isn't real!'

The footman leapt on to the front of the carriage, grabbed the reins and thwacked them, causing the horse to bolt forward.

The horse, Bernice observed, on the edge of a laugh that would have consumed her and gone on for ever, was the same strange one as she'd seen in the column of the Prince's soldiers outside the cottage. It looked like it had been sewn together out of two horses, attached at the middle.

Of course. What could you say here but of course? She slapped her hands to her mouth, realizing that she'd begun to hyperventilate. Then she took them away again, enjoying the fast and terrible breaths. The world wouldn't let her die. It needed her to be a character for it.

The coach swept round three bends, down two roads, and into the drive of a large house, throwing mud up with its sudden cornering.

It just about made it up the drive before it transformed into a bouncing collection of fruit. Bernice found herself rolling over and over, her arms wrapped around a pumpkin. She flew through an open door and bounced down a flight of stairs, the rest of the vegetables, plus a collection of chittering small animals, racing down there with her.

She finally thumped to a halt, dressed in rags, all the breath knocked out of her, against a cold fireplace.

The pumpkin hit the wall beside her and exploded into goo, covering her.

The little creatures, including the weasel, slumped beside her.

Bernice put her hands to her face.

She could say something funny.

She could abandon herself to crying, and laughing, and madness.

Or she could try to rip her eyes out. Hit her head against the wall. Anything to escape the hand of certainty that had grabbed her from the ball and thrown her here when she had tried to act against it.

She pulled her hands from her face, on the verge of the decision.

The horse, which was still a horse, made its way down the stairs, and stopped in front of her.

It separated into two sections. A front and a back.

The man in the back section stood up. The man in the front section stood up and took the horse's head off. 'We,' he said, 'are on a mission from God.'

'This time,' Bernice whispered, 'you have my full attention.'

Chapter 7

Fairy Stories

After several hours of walking, Stokes's party had come to the structures in the centre of the hall. The artificial sky above had long since darkened and the only light source for the latter part of the journey had been the lines on the ground, which glowed powerfully green. Indeed, the academics had gasped when they first saw that luminescence, because it became apparent that the pattern of lines stretched across the entire floor, forming a sort of target, with concentric rings around the centre crossed by inward-running lines of the sort they were following.

No thought had been paid to stopping. An hour or so ago, they had heard the first echoes of distant hootings and gurglings. The Grel were somewhere behind them.

In front of them loomed the structures. They were tall, thin, green walls, surrounding a round enclosure with an arched entrance. Nervously, they made their way through it.

On the other side was a large compound, with three similar entrances at the points of the compass. There were many seats, arranged in groups, and machines of unknown purpose scattered between them. In the centre of the compound was a circular area, about the size of one of the university's cricket pitches. On one side of it there stood a spar-shaped object, with wreckage all around it. The floor of the circle was cracked and shattered where it had fallen from above and buried itself, still upright, in the ground.

Looking up, Stokes could see the dark outlines of many vast shapes overhead. Only one spar had fallen. There were many more still up there, with a long way to fall.

Professor Epstein glanced around the seating and the central arena and shrugged. 'Some sort of sporting arena? Not many seats for a crowd that had to come such a long way.'

'The Perfectons could obviously have walked into another dimension and walked out here,' Singh snapped. 'That's why the hall's so big: distance to them was no object.'

'Rubbish!' giggled Blandish. 'Big halls are created to impress, and if you can just hop in and out, then you swiftly cease to be impressed.'

'You're forgetting the issue of functionality,' said Wagstaff, waving the knob of his walking stick in the air. 'What if they needed a big hall to get everybody in here?'

'Ridiculous! A hall this big would take the whole population of the planet to fill!' Singh gestured around him. 'And why, then, would there be so few seats?'

'We did see another encampment across the floor,' said Lucinda. 'There may only be a few seats here.'

'Shoot me down in flames if you like, but you know what this place reminds me of?' Janes was getting excited, kneading the air with his big hands. 'A spaceport departure lounge. This looks just like a boarding gate, and that –' he walked up to one of the machines and gave it a friendly thump '– is a refreshment dispenser.'

'Fascinating,' sighed Singh. 'If only we could find out when the next flight is, we could –' He stopped, noticing that Professor Warrinder had sat down rather heavily in one of the seats, his whiskers wobbling feverishly. 'What's he doing now?'

Stokes went to Warrinder, and found the rodent staring

into the distance, tears welling in his little brown eyes. 'What can you see?' he asked.

'This place . . . We aren't alone here! There's somebody else! Watching us!'

The others, even the more sceptical ones, instantly formed a sort of instinctive protective circle, looking around themselves cautiously.

'What sort of somebody?' Stokes asked. 'A Grel?'

'No. But an alien sort of somebody. I can't see any further – the psionic atmosphere here is so powerful, so much interference.' He squeezed his eyes shut. 'So many minds. It's as if I'm in the middle of . . . a whole world. But they're gone. So long gone.'

'Ghosts!' exclaimed Hettie. 'He's talking about ghosts!'

'No such thing,' said Farouk, and several of the others agreed with him, nodding their heads sagely. But all of them remained standing, on the alert.

Wagstaff settled into one of the seats, laughing. 'Ghosts or no ghosts, my feet are aching. Let's stay here for a couple of hours. Those Grel chappies are going to be too busy with all the things they find to bother us. It'll get a bit lighter. Then we can head for the other side of the floor, find the exit, head back to the surface. The Grel will be too busy down here to follow us.'

Stokes looked around. To his surprise, everybody was nodding. He slapped his hands together. 'Breakthrough! So, who's first for guard duty?'

Everybody started to argue.

Bernice wiped the last traces of pumpkin off her rags, which weren't raggy at all, really, but were quite pretty strips of green and orange – more fashionable slumming than your actual poverty. 'So,' she said to the two men in the hats, trying to gather her composure and put on a brave face despite everything. 'What's going on, then?'

'We can't tell you.'

'Fantastic. Why the golly gosh not?' She slapped a hand over her mouth. That wasn't what she had meant to say. 'What the goodness me? I can't blinking well say what I want to blooming say!'

'That's exactly it.' The stocky man who had been the front part of the horse looked to his left and right, as if he expected to be interrupted at any moment. 'The effect comes and goes, but there is only so much that we are physically able to tell you. This world might seem quite a nice place –'

'Oh no it doesn't.'

'Oh yes it does!' The two men chorused back. Then, to Benny's amazement, they both slapped themselves around the face, quickly, several times, until they had recovered their concentration. 'Never,' the lead man said, 'say those words to us again. If we hadn't broken out of the routine, we'd have been here all night. Now listen, this is vital. You've got to get out of here as soon as possible!'

'I have been trying!' Bernice stepped forward and grabbed the horse's head from the first man. 'You think I like it here?'

'Oh, you will.' The man glared at her seriously. 'You'll come to be part of all this in the end. That's why your speech changes, why you find yourself wanting to do things that you'd never do in real life. We've been using this horse as a kind of disguise, a way to make the stories skip over us, because we're kind of outside them.'

'Stories?'

'Yes. This isn't a dream or an afterlife or a psychotic episode you're having. Start thinking like that, and we're all lost.'

'All?' Bernice frowned. 'Do you mean to say that all of these people here who look like people I know –?'

The thinner man in the back part of the horse piped up for the first time. 'Let's just say that all their lives depend on you. Because of this shield –' he indicated the horse costume '– because of where we come from, and the . . . magic items we carry, we can see both sides of the curtain. And we're all running out of time.'

The first man continued. 'Apart from us, you're the only one who's not completely become part of one or more stories. We don't know why you're so special, but you're the only one who can get us back to . . .' He looked around again. 'Where we came from. So we can complete our mission.'

'So who's this God you're working for? It isn't . . . you know . . .?' She glanced upward.

'You do know him. It would be dangerous for us to refer to him, or to any other concept from outside of . . . where we are.'

Bernice put a hand to her brow, frustrated. 'Can't you give me some clue, at least?'

The second man spoke again. 'Only that there must be a way out. Once you understand the nature of what we're all going through, then . . . it may be obvious. Good luck.' He put his hands to his head, and clenched up his face, visibly concentrating, as the other man was. 'What's going on down here . . .' he whispered. 'No! I mustn't . . .'

Benny stuffed the horse's head back on to the first man's shoulders, then ran to the other, bent him double, and pulled the cloth horse back together.

The horse seemed to relax.

'Just what I need,' Bernice told it. 'More questions than answers.'

The horse stamped its front foot three times, which struck Bernice almost as a gesture of appreciation.

From the stairs there came a great shout. The sisters whom Candy had identified on the dance floor came bustling down them, looking at Bernice aghast.

'What's going on down here?' one of them shrieked, pointing at the horse.

'I knew that you were going to say that,' Benny muttered.

Stokes hugged himself against the cold, wondering how he'd ended up on sentry duty. The other academics were all sleeping again, and the compound was filled with the sounds of snoring, and of Hettie muttering things in her sleep. Things like: 'No, Clive, better to say, "Will you be my wife?" ' Stokes understood how they felt. A lot of them were old and, especially in the case of the two history professors, unable to really comprehend the nature of the danger they were in. The hootings of the Grel were still distant. According to Epstein, they'd want to examine the way stations that Stokes's party had passed by before getting to the centre. Perhaps they'd found some other way down into this great chamber, one which wasn't the result of falling down a hole, and had arrived at some particularly tasty-looking feature on the edge of the floor. Stokes hoped that was the case. The gun hung heavy in his jacket. He felt comforted by it, though he'd sworn to himself that he would never use it again. Even if the Grel hadn't been killed, even if it had enjoyed its newfound access to all sorts of information, there was something cruel about the process it had been through.

He glanced at Warrinder, who was curled up in a little ball on one of the chairs, shivering every now and then. He had produced nothing more of interest, saying only that he felt surrounded by people, that the ghosts were everywhere.

Thankfully, Stokes, who had always been rather blind to all that psychic business, couldn't feel a presence about this place at all. He glanced at his watch, then realized how meaningless that gesture was here. They were even on a different timescale to the surface world. Still, whatever time it was, he felt that it was time for supper.

He reached into his jacket pocket, and found the

sandwiches that he'd prepared to sustain him on his painting trip. He'd ignored them until now, realizing that rations would have to stretch for many days, but now he was really hungry. Besides, they'd go off if he didn't eat them soon, and he didn't want his jacket smelling of stale cheese.

He leant back against one of the luminous green walls, licked his lips and took a bite, luxuriating in the rich taste of Cheddar and pickle. He was determined to make this last – he might not eat so well for a long time. If at all.

As he chewed thoughtfully, he heard the sound for the first time. A sort of low sigh, from just behind him.

He stopped moving, fear racing up his spine and making him take a sharp intake of breath. Perhaps it had been one of the others, stirring in their sleep. Only this had sounded like it was coming from right behind him.

From right behind the wall.

He took the sandwich from his mouth. He put it back in his pocket. He slid his right hand inside his inner breast pocket, finding the stock of the gun.

Then he stopped, actually gritted his teeth, and brought his hand out again. 'Hello?' he whispered, turning his head to look along the short distance to the gateway at the end of the wall.

There was a sound from behind the wall, a sort of high-pitched clicking. Just as Stokes was convincing himself that it was the sound of the wall expanding or contracting or something, there followed a low moan, which echoed eerily around the walls of the enclosure.

Stokes's heart was literally pounding as he made himself inch along the wall. He could hear the sound of the blood rushing in his ears. He could feel everything acutely, every movement that he made. Sheer terror, he thought, absurdly, was a highly artistic experience.

At the end of the wall he stopped and put his palm flat against the surface, wanting desperately to draw the gun again. He had a weapon – why shouldn't he just take it out, as a sign to any potential aggressor? Shouldn't he just shout 'I've got a gun'? Or would that make whatever was on the other side of the wall, if it was armed, willing to shoot him?

He stood there, transfixed, willing himself to look round the corner.

The thing leapt out at him, knocked him off his feet. It was bigger than he was, he realized, as its hands delved straight up his rib cage, into his pockets, the weight of the thing pinning his back to the hard marble of the floor. Stokes lashed an arm out, yelling things he would never remember at the top of his voice, but the thing crumpled the limb under its body weight, and the gun went flying from his coat, skittering across the floor, bouncing off the wall. For one long moment Stokes was sure the beast had a knife and was just going to flip it up and pull his chest open, and he kicked and screamed and snapped his head up to try to bite the powerful forelimb that was holding him down.

If he'd had his gun he would have killed it.

With a shriek, the long fingers grasped something at his chest, and ripped it free. Stokes cried out as the beast held its prize over his head and took its first, immense, bite.

'Sweep, sulk, sweep, sulk . . .' Bernice straightened up from where she was sweeping her broom across the dirty floor of the kitchen, and rubbed her lower back. 'I sound like a faulty windscreen wiper. And look at me: I'm cleaning up again. Bugger!' She threw the broom into a corner and sat down on a barrel, her head on her chin. At least she could say things like that now. She glanced at the horse, which was incongruously standing by the window. Incongruous? That was rich, considering the circumstances.

The two ugly sisters had come back from the ball shrieking with laughter, and had been aghast to discover that Bernice, who was now their sister, apparently, instead of the King's daughter, had let a horse into the pantry and had covered the wall in pumpkin pith. As one of them had put it, 'You just get the kettle on and pith off.' Every instinct that Bernice had had told her to take the broomstick that was sitting in the corner and teach these two harridans a quick lesson in comparative anatomy, but, glancing at the horse, she had instead demurred, and had run about her apparent duties until she could get the sisters out of her hair. She didn't want to cause another upset in the reality around her until she knew what was going on.

The sisters had even made an attempt to sing 'I Could Have Danced All Night', until Bernice cut in, reminding them that it was very late and that beauty sleep was a commodity of which they could never have too much. Finally, they'd gone to bed and left her alone.

Bernice had devoted all her energies to considering her situation. The men in the horse had told her a little more than she'd thought they had initially. For one thing, in some strange way, all the people she'd met who resembled people from her world *were* actually those people. The King was the ship's captain, which made a strange sort of sense. And amongst his court she was sure she'd recognized a number of other people from the ship. Princess Marian, for example, where had she seen . . .? The picture of that face clicked with an image from her memory. Marian handing over the pepper across the table at breakfast on the ship one morning. She'd been in an IAC security uniform. Chief engineer, perhaps? So maybe the royals were all duplicates of the ship's crew. Now she thought about it, she could see Prince Charming in a uniform as well. The only one who didn't fit in with all this was the Vizier. This was so frustrating, what you got for spending too much time with your own gang, and not enough meeting the people who were flying the ship.

Archaeologists: avoid confusion when transported to a

fantasy world populated by duplicates by paying attention to the ship's crew on the way there!

Looking up from her reverie, Bernice was astonished to find that, while her mind had drifted off, her body had started sweeping up and her mouth had begun a sort of jolly monologue directed at nobody in particular. It seemed that concentrating on not tidying up was going to be a major issue in the house of Baron Hardup. Even now, in contemplation, Bernice realized that she was sitting oddly. She jumped up, shook her arms, made herself slouch a bit. Her posture had been extraordinarily good ever since she'd arrived in this world. 'Not only that,' she told the horse, not expecting an answer, 'but why have I got the campest possible body language? My hands hardly stray from my hips or thighs. I'm always striking poses. What with Baron Hardup, who sounds like a character from a cheap porn novel, and the huge amount of cross-dressing and gender confusion in this world, I'm starting to wonder if I'm not living in the Land of One-Handed Entertainment!'

'Don't you wish!' The voice had come from behind her.

Bernice jumped round, her hands raised in surprise. Then she put them on her hips. Then she waggled them in frustration in front of the newcomer and settled for a sort of stiff, attentive posture that was as unselfconsciously non-artificial as she could manage. Then she had a chance to study the figure that had just appeared in the kitchen.

It was a man, and, for once, it was supposed to be a man. But he was dressed in a golden catsuit, with a long golden cape. He wore silver eye make-up and had a little crown on top of his short golden locks. He carried a stick with a star on the end. There was something else strange about him, Bernice realized. He wasn't quite real. Like the Vizier, he looked more like a cartoon than a real person. There was a perfection to the angle of his cheeks and his trim muscular form that was beyond the merely human. He turned away from Bernice and addressed the far wall. 'I thank you.

They couldn't afford special effects, so I've gone without a bang on my entrance. For a long time now, more's the pity.'

'Who are you talking to?' asked Bernice. 'Come to that, who are you?'

He turned to face her. 'I'm your Fairy Godfather. I'm here to make you an offer you can't refuse. I've just returned from the Enchanted Land.'

Bernice frowned. 'Is that yet another dimension?'

'It's a nightclub in Camden. Don't you remember me? You didn't get that ballgown from Vivienne Westwood, dear. And I made that carriage up to some very exacting specifications, with a team of elf mechanics. A man has twenty thousand thoughts every day, they told me, and they showed me a few of them. I told them that I wanted a carriage that spoke my language.' He glanced at the remains of the pumpkin, now dumped on the table. 'So they made me something rude but rather wonderful.' He glanced around the kitchen and sighed. 'You don't seem to have used the first of my wishes to change your situation much. What are you going to do with the other two?'

Bernice was looking at him, tapping her chin. 'Three wishes? That's very familiar. I don't recognize you. I'm sure I don't. But I think my mother told me about you.'

'I very much doubt that.'

'My Fairy Godfather . . .'

The man glanced at the far wall. 'Bit slow, this one. I think she's suffering from PBS – Post Ball Syndrome.'

Bernice wandered up to his shoulder and followed his line of sight. She could only see a wall. 'Who are you talking to when you address the wall like that?'

'I'm talking to –' He pointed, then seemed to decide that he'd better whisper. 'I'm talking to *them*. That lot out there. The punters.'

The question that initially came to Bernice's mind was:

why couldn't *she* see them? But the King's evasions and improvisations had given her a feel for the sort of blunt enquiry that this world had trouble dealing with. She thought for a moment. 'Am I right in thinking that you can do magic? Change the way the world works through supernatural means? Disobey the laws of physics?'

'Of course. But I can only give you two more wishes. Those are the rules.'

'Well then.' Bernice decided. 'Wish number two. Show me who you're talking to.' She glanced at the horse. It raised its front leg and thumped the floor twice with it, approvingly.

'If you wish,' the Fairy Godfather sighed. 'Not very glamorous, but I'm here to serve. As with the bit of palaver with the carriage, there are several things you must do to make your wish come true. Firstly, we need a dirty great big piece of paper.'

Bernice looked around. 'I can't see –' She noticed that the Fairy was making little upward gestures with his head, mutely, as if somebody wasn't supposed to notice.

She looked up. Above her head, hanging from the ceiling, was a roll of paper. A chord hung from it. Bernice reached up and pulled it. The paper unrolled until it hung down behind her. Written on it were the words of a song. She turned back to the Fairy. 'Row Row Row Your Boat? This whole world seems to run on lyrics.'

The Fairy swivelled his wand in the air in a little gesture of approval. 'The next thing we need is a bag of sweets.'

Bernice looked through the kitchen cabinets and found some, a sack of them. 'Got them.'

'Finally, some music.' The Fairy held his finger up in the air, and, from somewhere, a band began to tune up. 'Let your second wish –' he marched up to Bernice and tapped her on the shoulder with the wand '– come true!'

There was a flash and a puff of smoke.

Bernice coughed and waved it away with her hand.

When she managed to see through it, she stood stock still, astonished.

Where the wall had been, there was now an empty space. It was dark, but yet lights shone from it into the kitchen where she and the Fairy Godfather stood.

In the darkness, there were row upon row of dark shapes.

Bernice got the feeling that they were all looking at her.

Professor Ranjit Singh had grabbed the rolling pin from his pack before he knew what he was doing. He'd packed the implement to make dough for unleavened breads, something he'd wanted to cook for the other professors on the campfire. It was the latest in a whole line of friendly gestures that he'd intended to make, but hadn't got round to, having been sidetracked by some argument or other, this time by the attention that Hettie and Lucinda had been giving, over drinks, to that charlatan Warrinder.

Now he rushed from where he'd been woken from his sleep, the makeshift weapon held high, ready to attack the creature that was holding a screaming Menlove Stokes down. It wasn't a Grel, he noted dumbly as he ran at it. And he wasn't any sort of fighter, but the mere fact that he'd been roused by screams, been startled to see one of his . . . one of his colleagues being attacked . . . He bore down on the creature and swung the wooden baton in an arc at its head.

But then he realized that Stokes had stopped screaming, and was shouting at him. 'Stop!'

Singh's would-be blow swished over the creature's head. He stumbled and glared at Stokes, panting. The creature was sitting on Stoke's chest, oblivious to the aborted attack, and it was eating something, but the artist seemed in no pain. 'What's it doing to you?' gasped the physicist.

Stokes craned his neck as best he could to look up at his

fellow academic. 'Eating my sandwiches,' he said. 'I think it likes them.'

From the *Informative Record of Recent Grel History*:

The Grel had found a very tall tree, and had begun to climb it. The plan was to gain a better view of the topography of this strange world that they had found themselves exploring. The climb had taken the best part of a day, which left the Grel Master wondering why they hadn't seen this tree before. It should have been visible from a great distance. It was, however, a very easy climb, with convenient footholds at every point. The suspicion crossed the Grel Master's vast mind that this unnaturally bright and colourful tree had been designed to be climbed.

The Grel climbed up until they were amongst the clouds. Well, one. A fluffy white one that surrounded the higher branches of the tree. They continued through it, and the Grel Master was the first to poke his head out above it.

His face tentacles pursed in a frown, and he ducked his head down again. Strange tree. Ground far below. Cloud.

He popped up once more. And on top of cloud: castle.

The other Grel joined him, hooted in astonishment, and looked to him for guidance.

'Does not comply!' he shouted petulantly. 'Query: the castle does not appear to be supported! Query: it should be visible from the ground! Query . . .' And he sucked in a slow, hooting breath.

(Note: the Grel version of a sob.)

'Where are we?'

'Fe fi fo fum!' roared a voice that made the Grel quiver with its volume. 'I smell the blood of –' The voice paused. 'Hmm. Interesting.'

The enormous gates of the castle swung open and a huge

human, the height of a hundred Grel, marched out. He did not look like other humans in ways other than his size. His features were more stylized than others that the Grel Master had seen, as if he was an illustration brought to life rather than a real person. He looked to his right and left, appearing not to consider the possibility of looking down. He sniffed again. 'Fascinating bouquet. I smell the sea, I smell kippers . . .' He wafted the air towards his nose with his fingers. 'Mm. A pungent blood. Cultivated. Better than common human. Vaguely artificial yet rather pleasing.'

The Grel Master stared up at the giant, and curled his finger tentacles together in glee. 'New data: this big human eats other humans. Inference: he is their enemy. Inference: he would be a useful ally!'

'He desires to eat us,' muttered one of the Servitors.

The Grel Master, nevertheless, approached the big human bravely. 'Greeting!' he called, as loudly as he could. 'We are the Grel! We are here to aid you!'

The giant saw the Grel Master advancing down his cobbled driveway, smiled, reached down, and picked the brave warrior up.

'We have much to discuss,' began the Grel Master.

The giant opened his mouth and threw him in.

The other Grel ran at the giant, attacking his boots with their weapons. But he continued to suck thoughtfully, ignoring them.

Then he yelped with pain, opened his mouth, spat out the Grel Master and stared at him in indignation. The Grel Master had his dataxe raised. 'You will listen,' he said.

'Oh, very well,' the giant sighed. 'I hate food that talks. Come inside.'

He picked up all the Grel and took them inside his castle, into a vast banqueting hall, where he placed them on his table beside the butter. Then he sat down, and glared down at them. 'So what do you want to talk about?'

'We have much knowledge,' the Grel Master began.

'What do you want to know?'

The giant leant back in his huge chair and laughed bitterly, as if not quite understanding why he was dealing with such small and insignificant beings. 'How to revenge myself upon those meddling dwarves, Jack, and all of his politically correct friends at the castle, who suddenly, after all these years, have decided that a giant doesn't have the right to eat whomsoever he chooses when and where he chooses to do so. I used to be in charge of the whole kingdom. Every bit of it. They call me an Ogre now, you know. An Ogre!' He settled a little, having vented his passion. 'As if. I'm just trying to uphold an ancient tradition. Giants eat people! That's all we do. We're not friendly, we're not useful and, if this giant has his way, we're never going to be!'

'You want to harm them, to cause them hurt?' the Grel Master said, proud of his mastery of the giant's mode of speech. 'We want to interrogate a human female, an associate of the dwarves, and of the soldiers from the castle. Abducting her would cause them great sadness.'

The giant thought for a moment, stroking his beard. 'If I agreed to helping you kidnap her, could I eat her afterwards?'

The Grel Master relaxed all his facial tentacles. The deal was about to be made. 'Are you appreciative of the taste of brains?'

'Brains? No. Hate them. Throw 'em away. Don't want to catch Mad Human Disease, do I?'

'Then yes,' the Grel Master concluded triumphantly. 'You may certainly eat her.' He turned to his Servitors and raised one thin finger. They had made their first ally.

Extract Ends

Bernice could hardly believe what she was seeing. She put up a hand to shield her eyes from the powerful lights out there.

'Go on then!' hissed the Fairy Godfather, poking her in the ribs with his wand. 'Get them to sing the song! Throw the sweets! Or they'll get angry!'

'Why –?' said Bernice. Then she decided that this was possibly her only chance to leave this mad world. Not quite as dramatic as finding that somewhere here there was a villain from her past with a big base and a vast cine projector, but if it worked, then what the hell? She clapped her hands together and addressed her new audience. 'I was wondering if you, ah, might be interested in singing a song with me?'

'They won't be, you know,' murmured the Fairy.

'I thought you said –' Bernice began. But her voice was drowned out by a great shout from the audience. 'Oh yes we are!'

'Oh no you're not!' called the Fairy.

'Oh yes we are!' called the audience.

'Well, that's fairly definite,' Bernice tried again. 'They're largely in favour, so –'

'Oh no they're not!' cried the Fairy. He turned back to Bernice as the audience shouted back again. 'Sorry. I love that bit. I could go on like that for days.'

'But you aren't,' Bernice told him. 'Because we're just going to sing this bloody song and then I'm going to hop into that audience –'

'Hop in? You didn't mention hopping anywhere!'

Bernice was silent and still for a moment, containing herself. 'Another wish, then, if that's what it takes.'

'Another wish? It's your last one, you know.'

Bernice looked at him levelly. 'I have to get out of here. Do it.'

With a little glance skywards, he did so, bouncing the wand off her shoulders once more. There was a flash. 'But do take the sweets,' the Fairy advised.

'Yes.' Bernice nodded, eager to get this over with. 'If you want. And then I'm going to find the exit, and I'm going to go home. So. Music, maestro, please!'

From nowhere, a band, a bit heavy on the brass and slightly off key, began to play. Bernice grabbed her broomstick and pointed out each word on the piece of paper as she and the Fairy Godfather sang the song.

Surprisingly, the audience sang too.

Row, row row your boat,
Gently down the stream.
Merrily, merrily, merrily, merrily,
Life is but a dream.

Bernice glanced back to the horse as she started the second verse. She couldn't quite believe that she was doing this.

A crowd of academics, summoned by Stokes's cries, had arrived to encircle him, and watch an alien sit astride his chest, eating a sandwich, utterly ignoring those around him.

'I'm fine,' Stokes assured everyone, though none of them had asked. 'Odd-looking sort, isn't he?'

Stokes's perspective, looking up the creature's nose, wasn't ideal, but even from that angle, he could tell that this wasn't a species that humans had encountered before. Although basically humanoid, the thing was blue, for a start, and had six multi-jointed fingers on each hand. It had no toes, although the pads of its feet looked very flexible and plastic. It wore only a rough loincloth made of rags and its chest showed a slight drift of white fur over a complicated, criss-crossing ribcage. It had high cheekbones, sharp teeth and piercing and intelligent, if feral, green eyes. From the back of its lobed head straggled a long twisted mass of white hair.

It finished the sandwich and licked every spot of it from its fingers. Then it looked around itself, as if suddenly aware of the presence of others. It cried out in a series of guttural syllables, a chain of sounds that moved incredibly fast.

'A highly complex language,' murmured Otterbland. 'Could this be –?'

'A Perfecton!' Wagstaff giggled. 'A living Perfecton!'

'That's impossible!' Owl whispered. 'After all these centuries?'

The academics started to argue again, and several of them produced recording devices, moving to try to get a good holoshot of the creature. 'Excuse me!' called Stokes. 'Hello?'

They ignored both him and the increasingly frantic arm motions and jabberings of the creature.

'If you make it angry,' Stokes hissed, thinking that other people's intellectual curiosity was too low a price for his life, 'it may hurt me.'

But just as he said it, the alien moved.

It moved so fast that the only person that noticed straight away was Farouk, who was sent tumbling aside by its motion. Warrinder, a few seconds previously, had discreetly stepped out of the same path.

The thing skipped across the enclosure, moving in a leaping motion that was too fast for Stokes's eyes to follow, and then skidded to a halt just outside, beside one of the boxes that Janes had taken for refreshments dispensers. Looking at the party with its staring eyes, it slapped both hands to the surface of the green box. There was a sound. An electronic gurgle. The gurgling speeded up, faster and faster, until it became a swift babble of information.

Stokes got to his feet, dusted himself down, and tiptoed with the others towards the being at the box. 'We are absolutely harmless,' he told it, extending his hands in a gesture of friendship.

'Don't tell it that,' hissed Singh.

'Why not?' said Epstein, shrugging. 'Unfortunately, it's true.'

* * *

Bernice and the audience came to the end of the song. 'The sweets!' The Fairy Godfather nudged her. 'Go on!'

So she grabbed the sack and ran to what had once been a wall. She paused on the edge, blinking, trying to see just what sort of people or creatures were out there. She still couldn't make out any details. 'Would you, erm, like some sweets?' she asked.

'Yes!' they cried. They sounded utterly human.

So she grabbed handfuls of the sweets and started throwing them randomly into the audience. There were noises of laughter and applause and wild motion. She looked back to the Fairy. 'Can I – ?'

'Yes.' He nodded urgently. 'As long as you take the sweets with you.'

So Bernice put a foot out into the air.

There was a drop at the edge of this world. She couldn't find the end of the step with her toe. She couldn't see how far down it was.

This was definitely a test of how much she wanted to get out.

She took a deep breath and walked out into space.

A moment of dislocation.

Nothing.

And then Bernice landed in a very quiet place.

She felt like she'd only fallen a short way, a little jump. That was a relief. And there were several things about where she was that were utterly expected. She was in a theatre, with rows and rows of seats, aisles, doors, plush red carpet and gilt-edged balconies, the whole theatrical hoohah.

There were, however, three big surprises.

One: the sheer size of the theatre. It went back row upon row, as far back as the eye could see, towards tiny, distant exits. Luckily, though, there was a side exit right beside where Bernice was standing.

Two: the place was, as she'd immediately noticed when landing, utterly silent. The noise of the crowd had shut off as though a switch had been flicked.

Three: that was because the audience themselves were not a boisterous crowd of humans, but row upon row of silent blue aliens, their eyes closed, their bodies frozen in stillness. They didn't even look like they were breathing.

There was going to be no need for the sweets.

She approached the front row on tiptoe, wondering what would happen if this lot woke up. They were certainly a different audience from the one she'd heard inside the house. The thought crossed her mind that this lot might have set up the whole castle and dwarf business as entertainment. But if they had, why were they asleep? Surely she and her fellows had been more fun than that? Not very flattering. In the right-end seat on the front row sat a particularly large alien, dressed, like all the others, in a white robe and headdress. Unlike those of all the others, the headdress was multicoloured and larger. Bernice reached out and gently touched the blue skin of the thing's face. It was warm. Alive. But the creature didn't react in the slightest. It seemed to be in a coma. It's head was large, a multi-lobed skull. She picked up a slack hand. Six fingers and many joints. Bernice had met thousands of different alien species, but never one of these. 'A Perfecton,' she whispered. 'A living Perfecton. But what's it doing here? Wherever here is . . .'

She looked around and made a decision, letting the hand drop back on to the alien's lap. Intellectual curiosity could wait. The horse had made it clear that she had to get out of here, and in the corner, there was a door marked EXIT.

She trotted over to it and put a palm up against it.

Logic would dictate that, behind this door, there would be the outside of a . . . Bernice glanced back over her shoulder. Yes, of a twentieth-century European Earth theatre. That was something else, she realized. A lot of the people she'd met in this strange world dropped twentieth-century references.

Still. She steeled herself once more. All the answers were through here. Or even if not, at least it was the way home to a hot death or a hot bath.

She pushed the door open.

The Perfecton took his hands off the box, and looked up at the academics clustered around him. 'Aaagh!' he said. Then he frowned, and sucked his teeth for a moment before continuing. 'I'm really scared.'

Stokes laughed in pure relief, and a number of the professors joined in. 'Well, so are we.'

Epstein walked up to the box and stared at it. 'How did you learn our language so quickly?'

'The city's been listening to you. Your words get . . .' The blue alien paused again. 'There's loads here that can't be translated into English.'

'I speak Urdu,' said Singh.

'Not a lot of help. Some of these concepts . . .' He glanced at Warrinder. 'Ah.' He pursed his lips and delivered a fast series of clicks and glottal slurps.

'Oh.' Warrinder nodded and clicked back at him for a few moments. Then he turned to the others. 'Our words were recorded and then – well, I'm sure he's simplifying this for me too – the words were sent into what he calls the Green. In the Green, where there's no time or space, they were . . . interrogated for their meanings, put into boxes. This process has been going on since we arrived here.' The rodent looked down at his boots. 'And, erm . . . also for ever.'

Singh raised an eyebrow. 'You've found a fellow magician. Where is this Green?'

The Perfecton answered him. 'It's inside everything.'

'Another dimension?'

'I'm . . . not quite sure what that means. But . . . oh!'

He laughed. 'This is so fantastic! People! People!' He ran forward and grabbed Stokes by the forearms. 'I love you.'

Stokes frowned. 'I assume that something's been lost in translation.'

'And I loved your sandwich! Do you have any more?'

'No. We haven't got much in the way of food.'

'No food? How?'

Stokes shrugged. 'Erm . . . well, we were attacked on the surface, and couldn't bring much with us, and –'

'But you can get anything you want from the Green!' The alien suddenly drummed the palms of his hands against his head. 'Which you don't get native close with! Of course! How stupid of me!' He took a deep breath, visibly making himself slow down. 'I smelt you and I smelt your sandwich and I grabbed you both because you were different and new. I have not eaten new food for ages! Only the same things, always taken from the Green. And new people. New people. I can't believe my sight. I am Thooo.'

'Menlove Stokes.' Stokes showed the alien how to shake his hand. 'If you've learnt our language, perhaps you've heard of me.'

'No!' laughed Thooo. 'Not at all.'

'I should not be troubled by that gap in your knowledge,' murmured Hettie.

'Are you a Perfecton?' asked Owl.

'A . . . oh, that's what you call my species. Silly. We weren't perfect. We called ourselves . . . well, the closest translation is just "Us". No, we certainly weren't perfect. Oh no.' He sat down on the translator box. 'That was why I rebelled. I wanted to be the only one to –'

There was a sudden sound and a green light from all around them. Thooo jumped to his feet and cried out. The academics shouted and screamed.

All around the enclosure, green circles had appeared in

midair. From each of them stepped a Grel, brandishing its dataxe. The doorways vanished behind them.

The Grel Master pointed at Stokes. 'Information: while you were travelling, we learnt the secrets of this world. Now we will learn more.' He swung the butt of his axe up and a cord shot out, wrapping Stokes's arms. 'Secure them all,' the Grel Master ordered his Servitors.

Chapter 8

Another Break in the Narrative

Bernice pushed the door open and stopped, astonished by what lay beyond.

A grey nothing. Not hard to look at, because your eyes didn't really register it. It was like looking into the sky on a grey day. No cloud shapes, no nothing, just distant grey.

'The budget didn't stretch to doing up the outside of the theatre,' she muttered, remembering the Fairy Godfather's words about his entrance.

She reached out and touched the grey with the tips of her fingers. She could feel something to it. A dreamlike ache, as if she was remembering something beneath the level of her waking mind.

The grey seemed to tug gently at her hand, asking her to come inside. It was the invitation of being sleepy on a Sunday afternoon, the invitation to nod off and dream in front of a warm fire.

And yes, Bernice decided, she would accept that invitation. This was supposed to be the exit, after all. But she wouldn't be sleeping or dreaming. She was going to stay wide awake.

'Yippee ki-yay!' she whispered.

And stepped into the grey.

* * *

A moment of dislocation.

Nothing.

Benny appeared in a corner, turned around and realized with a gasp of shock how ironic her thoughts before stepping into the grey had been.

Because she was sleeping, she was dreaming.

Right in front of her. As a little girl. Snoring. Her little, brown, tousled head lay at an awkward angle, her arms thrown out to the left and right, with her doll stuffed violently under the pillow. Bernice suppressed the urge to just stare at herself as a child and looked around the rest of the bedroom excitedly. It was exactly right. It even smelt right. The dull brown wallpaper, the models of chariots and cars and spacecraft that hung from the ceiling, the glowing green vase on the table by her bed, the Academy poster that Mum had pinned to her wall in an effort to make her enthusiastic about . . .

Glowing green vase?

Bernice paused, tapping her finger on her chin. She remembered the glowing green vase, she knew she did. She remembered it being there. It was just that . . . She shook her head. Thinking about the vase made her feel slightly nervous and emotional, as if it was a religious or romantic thing. Maybe it was just the overwhelming feeling of being back in one's own bedroom, seeing oneself at the age of eight . . . but she was so shellshocked by the things she'd seen and experienced in the last few days that that, horrifyingly enough, was just another distraction in the grand parade. No, it was definitely something about the vase. Like some part of herself beyond the here and now, that part that she would never understand, that cried because of sad songs and laughed because of things her friends said that were so like them . . . that part of her was shouting in her head that the vase was important. Intellectually, even on the ordinary levels of emotion, that just wasn't true. The vase had her everyday childish things inside it, featured in a number of very ordinary memories.

Still. Let's listen to the ghost in the machine, eh?

She tiptoed to the vase, wondering what would happen if her young self woke up and saw the older Bernice. She didn't remember that happening. She realized that the sheer reality of all this, particularly the familiarity of the smell, had just thoroughly convinced her that this was real, that this wasn't an illusion like the world of cats and castles. She knew in her heart that she was really standing by her bed, that, in the next room, were her parents. That this was another time.

It would be good to go into their bedroom, to tell Dad not to go off to war, to tell Mum not to run back out of the attack shelter to pick up the doll, which her screaming daughter had dropped. Remember to duck, Mum, she'd say. Dodge that energy beam, OK?

Of course not. They'd never listen, the time stream would get messed up, all the stodge of time travel would get in the way.

But . . .

Bernice realized that she'd been standing, looking between the vase and the door, for several minutes, locked in indecision.

The men in the horse had said that time was running out, that everybody's lives depended on her.

She picked up the vase and put her hand inside, rustling around amongst the notes and the marker pens and the hairslides and the brooches and the badges . . . And seeing each of these old things, she realized that the immortal feeling she'd had about the vase was a very ordinary thing to feel, really.

The I DIG ARCHAEOLOGY badge she'd got from a club she'd written off to.

Magic.

Merrily, merrily, merrily, merrily, life is but a dream.

Her hand closed over something different. She took it

from the vase. It had always been in there. As a girl, she'd never known what it was. A piece of space junk that Dad had brought back, maybe. She hadn't thought about it for years.

It was a small black box, absurdly functional, with a big green bulb on top of it. The bulb glowed with the same soft green light as the vase. The muted childhood light of Christmas and Hallowe'en.

Bernice put the box in her pocket.

She turned back to the corner and saw that the grey was still there, slapped across the wallpaper like a cloud, seen better from the corner of her eye.

She walked to it.

Then she stopped, and turned around, and walked back to the bed, for a long final look at herself, sleeping there.

'Aren't you young?' she whispered. She bent down and kissed the girl, very gently, on her hair. 'Don't worry,' she told her softly. 'It's all going to be all right.'

Then she turned back to the corner, pinched her nose between her fingers and ran at the grey.

From the *Informative Record of Recent Grel History*:

The giant had carried the new Grel Master and his Servitors to the steps of a forbidding castle, set atop a dark and stormy mountain. Then he stepped back and left them to negotiate the rest of the way alone, through a pair of ominous black doors, down shady corridors, deep into the catacombs under the castle.

Finally, they came to a door marked: DANGER, WICKED QUEEN AT WORK. POINTY HAT AREA.

'Do we knock?' asked the unfortunate Servitor who had previously incurred his Master's righteous wrath.

The Grel Master spared him not a glance, but bravely pushed the door open and marched inside.

Extract Ends

The Wicked Queen stood before her magic mirror, dark-nailed fingers raised high above her head, eyes blazing from beneath her cropped, dark hair. 'Mirror, mirror, on the wall,' she cried, 'who is the fairest of them all?'

A lugubrious face swam into view in the mirror. 'Michael Howard?' it suggested.

'Dolt!' The Wicked Queen spat.

'I agree completely.' The face in the mirror shrugged, as much as a face could shrug. 'But it looks like we're stuck with him.'

'I mean you, dolt! Where is the one I seek, the woman called . . . Snow White?'

'She's . . .' The face frowned. 'She's . . . actually, at the moment I can't see her anywhere.' He glanced over the Wicked Queen's shoulder and swallowed nervously. 'Erm . . . behind you!'

'Don't try to distract me! I want her image here, and I want it now!'

But the strange voices that often echoed around the catacombs, the ones that hissed and occasionally booed when the Wicked Queen was about her work, were agreeing with the doltish mirror. Sighing, she looked over one shoulder, then turned back to the mirror, inclining her head in a dangerous smile. 'Oh mirror, you should really know better. There is nothing behind me.'

But again, the voices insisted there was. She looked over the other shoulder. Nothing there, either. She put her hands on her hips and swung right round.

And found herself face to face with a party of squid-faced demons.

'Well,' she said, swiftly recovering her composure. 'We are not used to visitors in the castle. May I get you something? Some wine? Champagne?' That dangerous smile played around her lips again. 'A nice, juicy apple?'

The leader of the demons ignored her. 'You are similar in nature to the giant, animated.'

'Very animated, as I think you'll find if you don't get to the point.'

'We have ascertained that this land has a King. Query: are you his marriage partner, or does he also have a Queen?'

The Wicked Queen regarded them for a moment. 'As I once told that pettifogging imbecile, there's only room for one Wicked Queen in this fairy kingdom. Now, before I lose my temper. What brings you here?'

'We have come,' the demon said, 'to make an alliance with you.'

'An alliance? How . . . interesting.' The Wicked Queen went to a couch and swept into a reclining posture, plucking up a tall glass and indicating other couches for her guests. 'Tell me more.'

The leader of the creatures turned to his fellows and raised two of his squiddy fingers.

A moment of dislocation.

Nothing.

Bernice landed in a crouch on a hard marble floor.

She looked up, and swore profoundly and repeatedly, but it all came out so harmlessly that it left her feeling more frustrated than ever. She was only back in the scullery of Baron blooming Hardup! She straightened up and stamped her foot. So much for escape. There was no sign of the Fairy Godfather either. The horse was still standing in the corner, and it looked as upset as she was – if it could be said to express emotions – to see her back.

'Language . . .' purred a familiar voice.

Bernice spun round. Standing at the top of the stairs was Wolsey. He held a glass slipper in his paws. 'I'd ask if this belongs to you, but I'm starting to realize that that isn't a simple question.' He slid down the banister nonchalantly and accepted her hug, not without a trace of a shudder.

'Oh Wols, I thought I'd made it out of here,' sighed

Bernice. 'How did you find me?'

'Quite simply, as it turned out. I didn't see you leave the ball, since I'd slipped out for a moment and was otherwise occupied . . .'

'Oh yes?'

'Let's just say I've been to London to see the Queen.' Wolsey licked his lips. 'Anyhow, by the time Puss and I had got down from the roof of the palace and returned to the ball, you were long gone. I thought that you'd been spirited off by one of your many fiancés, but they were all still present.'

Bernice perked up. 'So you remember all that.'

'I remember being rudely interrupted in the middle of a rather wonderful production number.' The cat raised an eyebrow. 'But I'll get to that in a moment. The only one of your chaps who still seemed interested was Prince Charming. He was holding this slipper up to the light and making twee little noises about searching the whole land for you.'

'He's not here, is he?'

'No,' Wolsey chuckled. 'Because I crept into his chambers that night and nicked the slipper. He'd put it on a little red pillow, the utter fetishist. I did have some slight help in that regard . . .' He gestured towards the stairs. 'Are you quite finished up there?'

A small face poked around the door. It was Gushy. 'It took longer than we thought. They put up quite a struggle.' She beamed at Bernice. 'I'm really glad that we've found you.' She glanced over her shoulder. 'Are we ready? All right.'

She held open the door and the rest of the dwarves trooped down the stairs. Over their shoulders, they carried the two ugly sisters, bound up tightly in the laces from their bodices. Behind them hopped Dame Candy, trying to hold their heads up and failing utterly, so that they bashed against every step on the way down. The sisters were trying to shout incensed orders, but they were prevented from doing so by a pair of bright, polka-dotted gags.

The dwarves dropped them in a pile at the bottom of the stairs. Candy threw up her hands. 'I'm such a butterfingers. And I should have done better for these two. We're members of the same union, you know. USDOR: the Union of Silly Dames Overacting Rigorously. We strike every spring for higher wages and better bloomers. But we're always prepared to go to arbitration.' She sucked in her cheeks. 'We like a bit of arbitration.'

'There was really no need.' Bernice patted the dwarves on the head, even Cute. 'I'm still amazed that you all got here at all.'

'The slipper did it for us.' Wolsey hopped on top of the cooker and resumed his story. 'We just went with it, from cottage to cottage, house to house, and the third place we visited turned out to be this one. As soon as these two old harridans –' he indicated the ugly sisters '– started denying frantically that they had a sister, we knew we were on to something.'

'How clever of you!' Bernice smiled, glad that, even if she had been dropped back into this insane world, she had her cat for company. 'You're starting to use the way this world works to get things done.'

'Exactly.' Moody stepped forward and nodded to Bernice. 'We had a talk about the way things are and the way they should be, and we're all agreed, something ain't right.'

'None of our stories match,' added Gushy. 'It's as if Dame Candy and us and Wolsey . . . we all come from different worlds.'

'Which is taking multiculturalism a little too far,' said Liberal. 'The thing is, we can only see that these strange things of which the cat has been speaking might be true. We can't actually see the joins, feel how things should be. Wolsey can.'

'Can you?' Bernice turned to Wolsey, amazed.

'I'm beginning to . . .' the cat murmured, looking away

in contemplation. 'It seems like the more I'm around you, the more I realize that there's something profoundly wrong with the nature of who I am. That, apart from a certain nostalgia concerning Dick Whittington –' he grinned a quick and sharp-toothed grin '– was why I had to find you again. I've been listening to the voices that one hears in dreams. They seem to be saying to me . . .' He concentrated, closing his eyes ferociously hard. Then he relaxed again and sighed. 'I don't know what they're saying to me. Whatever it is, it's disturbing.'

Bernice marched back and forth in a little line, aware of the anticipatory gaze of the dwarves, thinking. 'I've been wondering why I was the only one who didn't take this world at face value. I still don't know the answer to that, but it's nice to know that somebody else is starting to feel the same way . . .' She stopped and clicked her fingers. 'You were the only non-sentient life form aboard the ship! Maybe that's why!'

Wolsey frowned at her. 'Non-sentient? What does that mean, exactly? It doesn't sound terribly flattering.'

'It means . . .' Benny couldn't think of a nice way to put it, so she changed tack. 'In my world, you were a cat, a household pet. Don't you have cats here? Real ones, I mean, about this big?' She indicated the size of a normal feline.

'Of course we do, but they're not . . . cats like I'm a cat.' He stopped. 'Oh my gleaming boots, there are only two of us, aren't there?' He looked away into the distance again, profoundly disturbed. 'Me and Puss. All the others are the size you describe, and are without manners, conversation or dress sense. I had never even considered that strange before. Still, could be worse.' He glanced at her with false brightness. 'I could have been a big goose. There's only one of those.'

Bernice went to him and tickled him behind the ears. 'There is something we could try, to free your memories of what you used to be like. You'd be a lot more help to me that way. You might even be aware of a way out of this mess.'

Wolsey shrugged a long cat shrug, flicking his ears at the tickling. 'What have I got to lose?'

Extract from the Diary of Bernice Summerfield:

If any of my future biographers are, by this point, in any doubt as to the veracity of my account of this particular adventure, I would like to point out now that I have not (recently) taken any sort of illegal chemical compound. You may accept my word for it that we all trooped up to one of the bedrooms, and that I, surrounded by a fellow professor in drag and seven miniature duplicates of the brightest students from my tutorial group, proceeded to attempt hypnotic regression on a giant humanoid version of my pet cat.

Listen, at one point it was a toss-up as to whether I wrote this up as a diary, or attempted to create a classic of children's literature.

Anyhow, Wolsey kicked off his boots and lay down on the bed in the darkened room, while the rest of us sat down all around him.

'Ooh,' muttered Candy. 'Dark, isn't it?'

I looked around for something small that might glitter, and found, in my pocket, the box that I'd recovered from my old bedroom. (Yes, that bit's true as well.) Only now it had changed shape completely, as if reacting to the new world that I'd brought it into. It had become a ring. The glowing green bulb was now the jewel set in its collet. Fair enough. I instructed Wolsey to relax and began to circle the ring in front of his nose, trying to remember everything that Professor Laight, the University Counsellor, had told me about various forms of therapy. (When we happened to meet over coffee one day in the Senior Common Room, that is. Yes, it was quite a long coffee, to learn so many of his professional techniques, but I was very interested, all right? He'd done so much for me, made me feel so much more . . . Look, what's it to you, anyway? Bloody biographers. It's your job to paint me in a good light, remember? Just avoid all psychological speculation, that's my advice.) Wolsey put his hands down beside him, tail twitching violently beneath him. But he did his best to concentrate on the warm green light that I was waving in front of him. 'You're relaxing. And as you're relaxing, you can feel your breathing slowing, and as your breathing's slowing you can feel yourself relaxing . . .' I repeated the mantra over and over, emphasizing the sounds in my own breathing that would send a human being into a trance, rounding and shaping my vowel sounds as Laight had taught me to do in front of a mirror. Of course, this was assuming that Wolsey was now like a human being, but, since he was in so many other ways, it seemed a fair bet. Wolsey kept his eyes open, but I felt sure I was succeeding when I heard a gentle snore.

But then Gushy tapped me on the shoulder.

Candy was slumped against the far wall, out cold. Trust a dame always to go for the oldest joke in the book. (Not that that's the oldest joke in *this* book. Ahem.) While Moody gently slapped Candy awake once more, Wolsey smiled gently.

'Do go on,' he murmured. 'It may not be working, but it's very relaxing.'

I redoubled my efforts, however, and gradually a look of peaceful contemplation came over the cat's features. I attempted to use the regression therapy I'd learnt from Professor Laight to take him back to his earliest memory, but when we went back more than a few days, he started to twitch and shake and make disturbing mewling noises deep in his throat. There was obviously some sort of barrier at work. I settled back in my chair, thinking that here was another possible exit being denied to me, and fiddled absently with the jewel on top of the ring, considering what to do next. Good thing I did, too, because the green gemstone suddenly shone and Wolsey let out a long groan.

'My first memory,' he whispered. 'Saying hello to you. Sitting on the stile. My hand on my furry chin.'

'That's when I first met you,' I told him. 'What's before that? What were you like before?'

The green gem pulsed some more and Wolsey shook, his eyes flickering to the left and right as if watching a parade of images whip past. 'Before!' he gasped. 'I'm . . . so small! I have no hands, only feet. To have words for these things is so strange. There's darkness outside. How hard I have to push to leap is different and that worries me a little.'

I realized that Wolsey was talking about his time aboard the *Winton*.

'I'm lying on a bed, only I don't know it as a bed. I know it as Soft Warm Thing that Smells of Servant Woman.'

Good to know that all one's suspicions about the nature of human/cat relationships are correct. 'Is Servant Woman there?'

'Servant Woman is asleep. She's making loud and bad sounds. Her legs are hanging over the edge of the Soft Warm Thing.'

'That was the night when –' I glanced at Cute. 'My last night on the ship.'

'I can see a soft yellow light,' Wolsey continued. 'From the Window to Pictures.'

'Window to Pictures? Pictures and words, perhaps? Is that my computer lectern you're looking at?'

'Words? Yes, there are words. I was interested in why they were shining. I didn't know what they were then, but I can read them now.'

'What do they say?'

'They say: "*English Pantomime: A Critical Study*, by Prof. F. Archduke".'

'English . . . pantomime!' I jumped to my feet and slapped my thigh. 'Panto! That's what this is!'

I looked at the others expectantly. Perhaps unsurprisingly, none of them seemed to know what I was talking about.

Diary Entry Ends

Panto was a genre that Bernice knew only vaguely, mainly through references she'd found in her studies of twentieth-century Earth. But now that she saw the connection, it all made perfect sense. What she didn't understand was how the matter of a thesis had become the matter of her lifestyle.

'You say we're all part of . . . of a kind of story!' Gushy squealed. 'I won't believe it! I feel real!'

'It's true . . .' Wolsey surprised everybody by sitting up, rubbing his chops with the back of his paw. 'And you are real, we all are, if transformed. Some more than others.'

There was something new about him, Bernice realized, a look of repressed horror. The way his hair was bristling made her feel nervous too. She put her hand on his shoulder. 'Wols, how are you –'

'It's not important.' He shrugged it off. 'None of us are as we should be. Therefore . . .' He took a deep breath and managed a knifey grin. 'We must return to what we were. Tell us more about this . . . panto.'

Bernice frowned, trying to remember the few details about the form that she'd learnt. 'It's a sort of mutant offshoot of the *commedia dell'arte*, developed in Britain in the early eighteenth century. Originally, it featured Columbine and Harlequin, characters like that, but then the British, being, erm, British, started to add comedy characters who'd take the mickey out of the leads. Eventually, it became the most popular form of theatre, a genre which featured celebrities from other media and, uniquely, depended on audience interaction for its impact. I'm told that a lot of pantomimes were set in a curious netherworld, half a land of kings and princes, half a satire on the age that made them or the place where they were performed. Which seems apt for where we are. Certainly, all the other details fit. The hero was often a woman playing the part of a boy, though the girl he married at the end was also played by a woman. And a whole class of male comedians arose who specialized in dressing up as busty old ladies to play "the dame".'

'Really?' said Candy. 'How peculiar.'

'There are audience interaction traditions too. There are certain phrases that, over the years, have achieved significance simply through repetition – '

'Oh no there aren't,' began Bitchy, with a puzzled look on her face that suggested she wasn't entirely sure why she'd said it.

'Exactly,' said Bernice. 'There's even the tradition of a pantomime horse or cow, played by two people bending over in a single costume.' She slapped her thigh in frustration. 'If I'd ever seen one, or read one of the stories, other than those that are nursery tales, then I might have recognized all this.'

From the *Informative Record of Recent Grel History*:

The giant and the Wicked Queen waited at the corner of the street discussing politics while the Grel Master led his squad down into the sewers of the great city of London. The Wicked Queen had given the giant a sweet which allowed him to shrink for a short period of time, so, with the Grel in their cloaks, the whole party was as stealthy and inconspicuous as it could be. Which, admittedly, wasn't very.

The Grel Master was pleased by the darkness and the smells of the wet sewer. It reminded him of the glorious saline mines of Grellor. The Grel had come here to keep an appointment, one which they had made with a shady figure in the corner of a bar. As instructed, they walked one hundred human paces to the north, then turned right. Two hundred paces later, they found themselves in a round chamber, with a single shaft of light shining down from above.

In the shaft of light stood a dark figure.

It was a rodent, the Grel Master realized, as its name had indicated. But it was a rodent the size of a Grel, clothed in the manner of a rather dowdy human, in a messy business suit and cravat. On its head sat a shiny crown, covered in extravagant jewels. 'Are you the Rat King?' asked the Grel Master.

'I am,' said the figure. 'And you are these demons that have been contacting villains all over London and the Home Kingdoms. Tell me, can you offer me help in exterminating those two dratted cats: Wolsey and Puss In Boots?'

'I believe that we can do business,' said the Grel Master. He turned to his fellows and raised three fingers. 'And that,' he concluded, 'shall be all we need to conquer this strange world. We have found our allies!'

'Found allies!' chorused the proud Servitors of the Grel.

Extract Ends

An hour or so later, Bernice and her companions marched out of the house of Baron Hardup and into the forest. The horse trotted along behind them. They'd untied the ugly sisters before they left, and thus had to endure a barrage of things being thrown at them and various comedy insults. Bernice had dressed herself in a hooded doublet of moss green, with a brown belt and some truly hideous green tights. The idea that this somehow made her look like a boy was quite beyond her: while her legs weren't everything she'd asked for, they hardly looked masculine.

'Dick,' Wolsey had breathed when he first saw her. But Bernice had told him not to start that again. She'd realized, while she was dressing, that the vast majority of people she'd met in this strange world were actually people who'd been on the *Winton*. People like Menlove Stokes or Hettie and Lucinda weren't represented. That was a pity, really. The joint holders of the Chair of Etiquette would have made fab dames, had they been men, of course. Now she was thinking that the characters that she didn't recognize were probably based on people on the ship that she'd never, or only barely, met. Everybody looked quite ordinary, despite their grand clothes. The exceptions were –

She suddenly stopped and the dwarves collided into her from behind. She spun on her heel, possessed by an idea. 'The people who don't look normal are the ones who can do magic! Like the Fairy Godfather and the Vizier!'

'Really?' murmured Wolsey, glancing back over the party behind him.

'Yes! People who do magic are all angular and cartoony.' She put a hand to her chin. 'I think we should go back to the castle, find the Vizier and find out what that means . . .'

'Beloved!' The voice came from the other side of the glade. Bernice turned around and saw Prince Charming, carrying another glass slipper. He was beaming with delight. Behind him were a detachment of his guards.

'I knew we should have taken the other slipper as well,' whispered Moody.

The Prince stepped forward. 'I've searched on high, I've searched on low, I did not know where else to go. And then by chance, I stumbled here, to take you back from pain and fear!' Getting close to her, however, he looked her up and down, his face filled with a sudden confusion. 'Oh, excuse me, my dear young sir, I do confess I'd no idea. My sight has gone, from all this searching, for in your tights there's something lurking.'

Bernice remembered that in many pantomimes the courtiers spoke in rhyme, while the commoners spoke prose. That was going to make life at the castle much more difficult, but if she was going to get anywhere . . . She took a deep breath. 'Don't get het up about my gender; I'm sent a message quick to render. In your palace lives a –' she screwed up her eyes, trying to think of a rhyme for Vizier '– man. And to meet him is my plan. Hooray, you've come, let's go to the castle; I'll pretend you're nice and not an –'

'This is going to take some getting used to,' Wolsey muttered as Bernice took the Prince's arm and the joint party headed off into the woods.

CHAPTER 9

JUST DESERTS AND DEEPER PLOTS, AND DEADLY DANGER LOOMING . . . LOTS!

Bernice and the others had walked silently beside the Prince and his cohorts all the way to the castle. Messengers weren't important to the plot of a panto, so they didn't get much in the way of dialogue. When they arrived, however, and had left the Prince's retinue, Bernice left the others to get some food and made her way straight to the door of the King's chamber.

'Boy,' she told herself. 'I'm a boy. Right.' Then she knocked and entered.

The King was standing by the wall, his hands behind his back, examining an illustrated family tree that hung over his fireplace. He turned and glanced at her rather crossly. 'What ails you boy? Go, get you hence! If you go I'll give you twenty pence.'

Bernice frowned, interested in the family tree, which she could see, rather alarmingly, still had a picture of her on it, as a Princess. She stumbled to formulate a reply that might fit in with one of the plots of panto and lead her to the Vizier. 'Hello your Highness, I'm an Arab, from the land of sand and scarab. I've come to work here, talking courtly, for a master thin or portly.' She had an idea, and restraining the urge to slap her thigh, turned to the wall behind which the audience was hidden and put her hand to her mouth, as if she could whisper to them without the King hearing. 'Maybe this way I'll get to see the Princess that I love, and steal her away from under the gaze of that evil Vizier.'

The King pondered for a moment, looking Bernice up and down. It gave her the chance to hop forward and take a long look at the illustrated genealogy. The King had three daughters and one son, as represented on this chart. There was Marian, pictured in a Lincoln-green outfit and a little hat with a feather in it. Somebody had been rather angrily and hastily cut from the painting behind her. There was Aurora, painted asleep, her head on her pillow. There was Charming, teeth gleaming. And there was Bernice, in courtly garb. She had now become, according to this story, the boy who had arrived to sweep herself off her own feet. Very masturbatory. Looking at them like this, Bernice's suspicions solidified. These were definitely all members of the ship's crew. The King was definitely the captain. Marian was . . . possibly one of the senior officers – she certainly remembered her in uniform. And Prince Charming had the look of a spacefarer about him too. She thought that she'd seen him about, in uniform. What had Aurora's position been?

The King made up his mind. 'Enough with all dramatic padding. What's your name, my boy?'

'Aladdin.'

'Well go and find my aide the Vizier; he'll fill your head with tasks much dizzier. Go down the steps, take second right, and I'll have cook send some broth tonight.'

Bernice smiled at him. 'My King is just, my King is kind, that magic person I'll now find. Your poetry does fair astound me – that Vizier rhyme always confounds me.'

And with a bow and a bit of a headache she left.

* * *

The Vizier of all the Realm rubbed his fingers together in glee as he stood over his magic cauldron in his dank dungeon, deep in the bowels of the castle. He was delighting, as he always did, in the sibilant sounds that wafted around whatever room he was in. The noise of hissing, and the occasional loud boo, were music to his ears. Now he looked deep into the depths of the cauldron and intoned. 'Paratha, Aloo Saag, Peshwari Naan . . .'

'Are you summoning a demon, great master?' asked the spirit of the cauldron, its eerie voice echoing around the slimy walls.

'No, you great fool, I'm ordering a curry.' There was a bubbling noise from within the cauldron and a puff of green smoke rose from the surface of the magical waters as a face formed there. This caused an ooh, which the Vizier liked even more than a boo, because, while a boo indicated that he was being evil, an ooh meant that he was being spectacular with it. He wafted the smoke away and wrinkled his nose, then shouted down into the cauldron. 'Better make it a mild one, then!' He glanced over his shoulder and saw the subject of one of his plots hesitantly descending down the stairs. He rubbed his hands together in glee. 'Aha! The one I seek! The boy Aladdin! I should have ordered an extra portion of rice . . .'

Bernice had found the cellars of the castle quite easily, but had had trouble finding just which of the many cavernous magical workshops and dungeons was actually the one she was after. They really ought to have produced some kind of directory. When she'd found the one she wanted, she'd tiptoed down the stairs, hoping to catch the Vizier unawares. But he'd seen her as soon as she'd entered. Now he ran over to her, and swept down into a regal bow. 'Ah, Aladdin, my favourite boy! May the bounties of the heavens rain down upon your lands.'

Bernice bowed back. 'And on yours.'

'May the wealth of all nations be carried in your barges.'

'And in yours.'

'May the goodness of the oceans flow up your rivers.'

Bernice looked up. 'Erm, let's get down to business, shall we?'

The Vizier grinned a vast, toothy grin and wrinkled his nose at her. 'Oh, stop messin' about.' A moment later, he was serious once more. 'It is as well you have found me, dear Aladdin, for I have a small favour to ask of you. It is a minor task, but the reward will be whopping great riches.'

Bernice tapped her chin. 'Let me guess, you want me to go down into a cave somewhere and get a dirty old lamp for you?'

The Vizier looked downcast. 'How'd you know? Yes, that's exactly it. What do you think?'

Bernice had been watching the way the man moved. Unlike everybody else she'd met in this weird place, both the Vizier and her Fairy Godfather were strangely animated. Literally so. It was as if they were very advanced animations, distinguishable from people only in that they were stylized. She reached out a hand and touched the Vizier's robe. He was solid enough. She decided to try something. 'Let me guess: you want me to go down into a cave somewhere and get a dirty old lamp for you?' she repeated.

The Vizier looked downcast in exactly the same way. 'How'd you know? Yes, that's exactly it. What do you think?'

Bernice uttered her phrase a third time, and his response was, again, exactly the same. A slow smile spread across her features. She felt like she was getting the hang of panto now. 'Let me ask you something first,' she replied. 'You can do magic, correct?'

'It's . . . a kind of magic,' the Vizier began.

Bernice stopped him. 'No, no, I haven't got time for the

musical version. Can you or can you not perform feats beyond the bounds of the physical sciences?'

'Yes.' He nodded eagerly.

Bernice considered her next move carefully. He might, therefore, be able to get them all out of this strange place. But she had to find the right pantomime way to make him do it. That, for the moment, eluded her. She still didn't have enough information. There was only one way to learn more. 'Then I'm your man,' she told him. 'Where do I find this lamp?'

'I've got a map.' The Vizier grinned and scuttled off to find it. He glanced back at her over his shoulder. 'It's going to be a great adventure!'

'A great adventure?' Bernice shrugged. In the world of pantomime, it was more likely going to be something like . . .

CHAPTER 10

RAIDERS OF THE SEVEN DWARVES

'A desert? There's a desert just outside the King's palace?' Wolsey raised his sunglasses and looked slowly from one horizon to the other. He was standing astride a line. On one side of the line, there were verdant fields, cottages and fluffy grazing sheep. On the other side there was a rolling golden desert, oases and tethered camels calmly chewing. The corner of the palace that intruded into the desert had developed a minaret in sympathy. 'Why don't I ever notice things like this?'

Bernice patted him on the shoulder and took out the map that the Vizier had given her. 'Life is but a dream, Wols. Or this one is, at least.' Beside them stood the seven dwarves, in desert kit, with oversized packs and Arab headscarves. Candy, on the other hand, had brought a parasol and was painted entirely white with sunblock. The horse was still a horse. Sort of. 'Now, do we go that way, towards that oasis –' she pointed at a clearly defined landmark on the horizon '– or that way, towards that one?' She swung her finger to a more distant oasis, its image flickering in the heat haze.

'Oh, the second one,' Candy offered, putting a hand up to shade her eyes. 'I've always preferred blur to oasis.'

They all turned to look at her. A tumbleweed rolled

lazily across the desert sands. 'So,' said Bernice finally. 'Let's get going, shall we?'

The map took them into the heart of what it called the Empty Quarter. Then into a quarter of that that was known only as the Empty Sixteenth. In the very centre of this dusty wilderness lay a cluster of sandblasted shrubs, clinging to a gash in the ground, a pothole eroded over ages, half concealed by the ever-shifting, whispering sands.

Beside this monolith to the vastness of existence and the passage of time stood the Spice Girls. They were carrying huge jars, from which they offered the party their exotic spices.

'Look at the size of those jugs!' gasped Laddish. Until Liberal slapped him.

'No thank you, dears.' Wolsey waved the scantily clad maidens away. 'Thanks for appearing. That'll help the box office a bit.'

Bernice looked at him as the girls wandered off into the sandstorms, throwing their urns aside with petulant gestures. 'You're becoming quite cynical, aren't you?'

'My life –' Wolsey looked at her seriously '– has been revealed to be a pantomime. How seriously am I supposed to take it?'

'You had a good life, you know, as you were before.'

'And I'm sure you kept my litter tray fresh and maintained a supply of wool mice.' Wolsey suddenly waved aside her protest. 'It doesn't matter. Let's see what's down this hole.'

Bernice bit her lip for a moment, then could only follow his lead as he turned and slid down into the lip of the cave. There was really nothing she could say.

The dwarves and Candy followed them down, their careful feet finding ledges and holds in the sand, while Bernice fell several times, supported only by the weight of Candy beside her. The overhanging cave mouth became a long, dark tunnel, dripping with condensation, and the temperature soared. Bernice was grateful that she'd elected to stay with the short green jerkin, but the tights were starting to be a problem. Still, she wasn't likely to get an opportunity to change down here. She was trying to remember the exact plot of the pantomime *Aladdin*. She'd seen a couple of animated versions when she was a child, but they had differed from each other on vital details. It was probably fortunate that they were trapped in such a flexible genre. If this world had been based on Shakespeare's sonnets, for example, they'd have been theeing and thussing for ever, without any leg room at all. Wolsey forged ahead of the party. He turned around. 'It's getting dark in here.'

'That's all right,' Candy called, fishing in her pockets. 'I'm carrying a torch.'

'No surprises there,' muttered Bitchy.

The dame pulled a thick piece of wood from her voluminous dress and slapped it in the palm of her hand. 'Wait a moment. Ah. There!' She flicked a piece of bark from one position to another, and the torch burst into flame.

The party carried on down the tunnel. Bernice was certain that Wolsey was trying to ignore her, until he slowed down slightly and murmured to her. 'Bernice . . . I'm new at seeing this strange world of mine from the outside, as you do, but doesn't it occur to you that this is somehow a . . . strange experience?'

'Strange? In what way?'

'Not sure. I thought you would know. Forget it.'

He moved on. Bernice was considering his words when he stopped suddenly. 'Oh my . . .' he purred. 'I think you'd better all come and have a look at this.'

The others pushed forward. They'd come to the edge of a large cavern. A narrow pathway led across it to a door on the far side. On all sides of the cavern, however, were strewn piles of glittering jewels, gems and valuable baubles of all kinds. There were many fortunes of them, lying in heaps, apparently discarded, glittering in the flickering light of the torch.

'Bagsee the tiara,' said Bitchy, diving forward.

'Stop.' Bernice caught the dwarf by her collar and pulled her back into the group. 'So this little lot has been sitting around, unguarded, at the end of a short tunnel, for a very long time without anybody ever taking it?'

'Stranger things have happened,' said Lazy, shrugging. 'Like that business with the transvestite wolf.'

'He was a cross-dressing wolf who was only expressing himself as a predator,' muttered Liberal.

'It wasn't your granny that he ate!' huffed Laddish. 'OK, so it wasn't mine either, but –'

'Quiet!' snapped Bernice. 'The long and the short of it . . .' She caught Moody's eye. 'I mean, the *point* of it is: we cross the bridge without touching any of the easily accessible riches. Agreed?'

They all mumbled terse agreement. Wolsey stepped aside and Bernice led them across.

Surprisingly, they made it to the other side. A short stretch of darker corridor followed and then they found themselves suddenly . . .

Outside.

No, Bernice realized, they weren't outside. They were in an area where ruddy stormclouds appeared to sweep overhead, purple ones below, billowing about their feet. Firestorms and streaks of lightning split the air with fearsome flashes. The effect was quite disorientating, and Wolsey instinctively fell on to all fours. Bernice half expected him to vanish into the clouds around their feet, but thankfully he found support. He was standing on a series of piled stones, arranged like stepping stones across a river. Bernice glanced over her shoulder. The others were bravely standing at the entrance, waiting to see what happened to the two of them. 'It's all right,' she called. 'These are just illusions, designed to scare us away or make us fall. Keep to the stone pathway and you'll be fine.' Through the clouds ahead, she could just about glimpse an archway in the far wall.

'Illusions, eh?' Wolsey murmured. He pulled up an object from beneath the clouds, something he'd obviously found on the walkway, and pointed it at Bernice. 'So what's this, and where did it come from?'

Bernice raised her hands. 'Wolsey, that is what we call a dirty great gun. Please don't press or squeeze anything.'

Wolsey turned it away from her, gazing at it, an intense expression on his face. 'It speaks to me of my former life.'

Bernice relaxed. 'Well, it is one of those objects that we have in the outside world, and you don't have here. Thank goodness. There must be something genuinely magical about these special effects . . .' She clicked her fingers a few times, putting a theory together. 'Magic equals . . . a door between the worlds, between this place and where we come from. That's how the gun got here. Hmm . . .' She put her hands on her hips and inspected the room, a rueful expression on her face.

Wolsey looked around the cave to his right, leaning his weight on his right front paw, holding the gun in his other hand.

They stood like that for a moment.

Then a great tremor rocked the cave. Wolsey dropped the gun, and it fell away into the infinite depths beneath the stones.

'It doesn't want us to stay here too long!' Bernice shouted, hopping from stone to stone almost as nimbly as Wolsey did. 'Come on!'

Behind them, screaming and shouting at each other to form a chain, came the dwarves and Candy.

The horse came to the edge of the stone path, regarded it for a moment, then turned around and headed for the exit.

* * *

Bernice counted all the dwarves in through the entrance into the next room. It was thankfully quite normal in appearance. It was full of urns, gilded boxes and big square metal containers with locks.

Bernice put a finger to Laddish's lips. 'Yes, they are chests, and neither are they small. Let's leave it at that, shall we?' She turned back to the room. Sitting atop one of the urns, at the back of the room, illuminated by a shaft of glittering light, sat a rather dowdy and messy-looking old lamp. Bernice rubbed her fingers together, experiencing again that delicious feeling of discovery that had always accompanied her archaeological adventures. There remained a short stretch of rather too smooth, untroubled sand between her party and the nearest urn. The others were quiet. She realized that they were waiting for her word. She turned to Laddish. 'You couldn't just go and get that lamp for me, could you?' She stopped him as he took a step forward. 'No! Joke, joke! Give me a moment to think . . .' She swung back and regarded the lamp. If only she could remember what it did in this particular panto, what its function in the plot was. It looked rather grotty to be a big and groovy MacGuffin object. She dropped into a crouch, pursed her lips and gently blew at the sand. It swirled into ripples. She blew harder.

There was a thunk of impact. A dart had landed, its shaft still vibrating, vertically on the spot where the swirl had formed. She looked up at the dwarves. 'When I say blow . . . blow like it's your hundredth birthday.'

'Some of us are used to that, dear,' murmured Candy, adjusting her hair.

Bernice counted down from ten and they all blew together. The sand swept aside, revealing a complicated mosaic on the floor.

A hail of darts pelted down, turning the floor into a garden of hard, upright stalks. Bernice stood and carefully examined the pattern of where they'd fallen. 'I think that's all of them,' she whispered. 'Oh well, here goes nothing. I do not want to find out what a funeral in this world would be like . . .'

And she hopped into the middle of the mosaic.

Nothing happened. She let out a breath and grinned back at the dwarves. 'Fine so far. Now, I'm assuming that all this jiggery-pokery on the floor actually just comes down to "Don't step on the white tiles". Second puzzle's usually a deceptively simple one.' She met the worried eyes of the dwarves. 'See, you're getting that archaeology field trip after all.'

She suddenly realized that their mouths were open in terror.

Her body picked a direction and hopped in it.

The swinging blade swept across the room where she'd been standing, the flat of it smoothing the sleeve on her forearm as it went.

She raised a finger. 'As I said: it all comes down to "Don't step on the black tiles". Now, what's the third problem? The law of threes, in traps as well as in comedy, is near universal . . .' She took a series of quick little hops from white tile to white tile, making her way across the floor until she was standing against the bulk of the urn atop which the lamp sat. She thought for a moment and then intuitively reached up and just touched the shabby-looking ornament. Nothing happened. She took off her belt and made it into a loop, then glanced back over her shoulder at her transformed students. She'd rather wanted to get into a situation like this with them, if truth be told, but she'd imagined that it would be on the sands of Perfecton, rather than amongst the sands of some sort of bargain-basement Arabia. 'I'd like my epitaph to be "Back in a mo",' she told them, and winked.

Then she flipped the belt up on to the top of the urn, lassoed the lamp with it, and hooked it off into her hands. She paused for a moment, looked around, shrugged and then hopped happily back to the others. 'Maybe the law of threes doesn't always hold true,' she told them, relooping her belt and hanging the lamp from it.

Laddish had spotted a pair of large, gilded nesting birds painted on one of the urns. He pointed at them. 'Look at the size of those –'

'Quiet!' snapped Wolsey. 'I can hear something... something very faint. But it's coming closer.'

Bernice looked uneasily at him. 'It wouldn't be a sort of rumble, would it?'

'Well, more a sort of –'

'Only, I've just noticed those.' She pointed at two broad channels, one of which ran down either side of the room. 'And I've been struck by a sudden and rather frightening mental image. Those urns remind me of something.'

'Yes, it is a rumble.' Wolsey nodded. 'Definitely a rumble.'

Bernice shooed the dwarves and Candy back the way they'd come. 'Then I think we'd better –'

The smooth, perfectly polished boulder smashed right through the urns, knocking them spinning to the left and right. The dwarves yelled and ran for their lives, leaving Bernice and Wolsey to grab the gawping Candy and, in one movement, throw her through the door.

The party dashed across the strange storm-filled room as lightning cracked around them, the boulder inexplicably bouncing from one pile of stones to the next as the dwarves sprinted as fast as their little legs could carry them, the taller humanoids swiftly catching them up.

The whole party thus sprawled neck and neck out on to the walkway which ran across the room full of jewels. The boulder was going to fit neatly through both doors, Bernice realized with horror, and run right up the tunnel after them. They got to their feet and rushed across the walkway as fast as they could go, and had just about got to the other side when, out of the corner of her eye,

Bernice saw something very scary.

She saw Bitchy reach out a hand from the yelling party of careering dwarves and snatch a tiara from the piles of valuables as they fled past.

Which was probably why that huge metal door immediately fell across the entrance, blocking their way.

They slammed against it, panting. Then, as one, they spun round. 'You . . . absolute . . . .' Bernice began, snatching the tiara away from Bitchy and tossing it back into the pile.

'It's just what you did yourself, with the lamp!' the dark-haired dwarf complained.

'When I do it, it's archaeology. When you do it, it's shoplifting. That's the rule.' Bernice looked up and sucked in a terrified breath. 'Oh my Goddess.'

The boulder rushed through the far door and straight at them.

Bernice closed her eyes and whispered, 'Jason.'

Stokes, the other academics and Thooo had been tied to chairs in the enclosure, secured by the taut, thick wire that the Grel had fired from their dataxes. Epstein had been trying to reason with the Grel Master for several hours, which was a rather trying process as, unlike the villains in holodramas that Stokes had seen, the Grel seemed entirely open to the idea of talking away with their captives and listening to their point of view. Not that they actually did anything merciful or generous as a result. They just liked to listen.

'So, you see, we ought to join forces,' Epstein concluded, looking up at the Grel Master hopefully.

The Grel hooted amongst themselves. Then the Grel Master, the only one of them, it seemed, who could speak English, turned back to Epstein. 'Information: your reasoning is inaccurate, if informative. We must take all the information here, and it is incorrect to say that you must have the information also. We will take the information from you and from these machines, with your cooperation or by force.'

'But you're missing my point,' sighed Epstein.

'Enough words,' the Grel Master concluded, at which point Stokes realized that the Grel had something in common with those holodrama villains after all. 'Your philosophy is of no more interest.'

'One for you, then,' said Epstein, glancing at Otterbland, who made a face back.

'Oh, and you were doing so well,' murmured Hettie consolingly.

Thooo, who was tied beside Stokes, had been staring at the Grel since they first appeared. 'They're different to you as well! At first I was afraid . . . I was petrified! But now I'm enjoying myself.'

'Whatever turns you on,' Stokes muttered. 'Try not to tell them anything about your technology.'

'Oh?' Thooo looked disappointed. 'Why not?'

Stokes frowned. 'Well. Because.'

The Grel Master approached the alien carrying a piece of equipment in each of its tentacular hands. 'Conclusion: you are a native of this planet. We have tested the use of what you call the Green for short-range travel. We do not, however, know what these are. We have found many.' He opened his gelatinous palms. In one sat a gun, similar to the one that the Grel had taken from Stokes's jacket. In the other, a smaller device. It was a black box, with a big green bulb on top of it that glowed. It was obviously a companion piece to the gun, and Stokes wondered, a little enviously, why he hadn't got one of those. 'These weapons are present at many places on the upper level,' said the Grel. 'Places where weapons should not be stowed. The boxes are all concealed within green vases. We know the weapon disintegrates its target. Query: what is the nature of the box?'

Thooo, to Stokes's horror, began to chuckle happily.

'Explain!' snapped the Grel Master, swinging his dataxe so that the beam weapon pointed straight into the alien's face.

Thooo didn't stop laughing. He just smiled a simple smile. 'The box and the . . . gun, as you'd call it, are both parts of one thing. The gun isn't a weapon. It's . . . what's the word . . . it's a . . .' He found the word he was after and clicked his tongue triumphantly against his palate. 'A children's toy!'

Stokes and the Grel Master, despite themselves, exchanged a worried look.

The boulder roared into the room. Bernice made herself open her eyes to look at it. She could see the details, the fine lines on its polished black surface. In a second –

And then, with a crash, the walkway collapsed beneath it.

And with another crash, the cavern floor collapsed too.

And then the boulder was gone, down to the depths below, leaving only a big hole and a little gust of wind.

The party of adventurers hesitantly stepped forward, and ventured as far back along the walkway as they dared. Bernice lay flat on her stomach and crawled to the end, gazing down into the pitch dark of the pit into which the boulder had fallen.

'That floor must have been like balsa wood,' muttered Moody. 'What sort of cave is this?'

'A pantomime cave,' whispered Bernice, grinning all over her face. 'A very badly made set. Which is odd, really, because –' A sudden thought came to her. 'Wols, what you were saying about this being an odd experience. Well, it's true, isn't it?' She leapt to her feet, and as the end of the walkway creaked and bent towards the hole, nervously jumped back to where the others were standing.

At that moment, from far below, there was a very distant, very tiny, splash.

Bernice gulped, but continued, her enthusiasm unabated.

'This has been a rather non-generic adventure, don't you think? Well, I mean, all right, it's got a genre, the genre of adventure and perilous exploration which generally constitutes my life, but it's not really panto, is it?' Wolsey and the others nodded slowly, trying to understand her words. 'Where are the men dressed as women and the other way round? Where are the stupid tricks and the audience interaction and the songs? No, ever since we set foot in this cave, it's been deadly danger all the way. Odd, don't you think?'

The others all nodded again.

Bernice slumped. 'Now, if only we knew what it meant . . . What do you reckon we should do with this lamp before we give it to the Vizier?'

Cute tugged at her sleeve. 'I'll give it a rub if you want. Clean it up a bit for him.'

Bernice wagged a finger at him. 'Absolutely not. That's the first rule of archaeology. Don't go rubbing your artefacts. He'll probably want to clean it himself. Oh well, come on then. If nobody else has any suggestions we'll just have to hand it to him and see what happens.'

Bernice headed for the tunnel, and the others followed her – all except Wolsey, who stayed behind for a moment, an expression of intense concentration on his face.

'I can't help but think,' he whispered to himself, 'that we're all missing something rather fundamental.' He tried to understand just what was bothering him, but it wouldn't reveal itself. Finally, he just shrugged his shoulders and, still uneasy, followed his friends.

Bernice was thinking frantically as her party made its way along the corridor. The lamp had a real significance in this particular pantomime, she was certain. But what was it? What did it do? She felt a tugging on her sleeve once again and looked down to see Cute, walking beside her, struggling to keep up.

'I was afraid,' he said, 'when the blade swung down. I

thought you were going to be killed. If you had been I'd have been . . . really sad.'

'Would you?' was all Bernice could say. 'Why? How do you feel about me?'

'I . . .' The small figure seemed to marshall all his courage. 'Well, I love you.'

'Oh,' was all Bernice could say.

'I think you're wonderful,' Cute continued. 'I want to learn all I can from you, and be like you. You're not like all the dwarf girls.'

Bernice winced. So this was what motivated her potential lover in the real world. She felt a great wave of sadness rise in her chest. Probably a reaction to the boulder, and that little image she'd had of Jason, of lying against him as if they were moulded into each other, his arms curled round her. Secure and warm. She'd seen all that she'd thrown away and had just wished for him to be there at the moment of her death. It didn't change how she felt about him, she thought. It was just a recognition that what he'd represented, real love, matching halves, wholeness and connection . . . it was still a dream she had.

It wasn't really fair to judge Doran by what Cute did. All of the dwarves were extraordinarily exaggerated versions of just one particular trait of the real student's personality. But was this what love was going to be for her as she got older? Somebody who didn't know, but who wanted to? Somebody who just wanted to get inside and see? He didn't love her: he loved the world that she represented. He loved her learning and age and experience. Once he'd grown a little, he would leave her.

She reached out and touched Cute's face, gently. He looked at her with imploring eyes, because she knew the touch must instantly feel like a departing one. 'Sometimes,' she said, 'life isn't a dream. Sometimes it's a bloody nightmare.'

* * *

'Query: a toy? The artefact of most interest on this world is . . . a toy?' The Grel Master leant closer to Thooo. 'Query: is your mental functioning impaired?'

'Of course!' laughed the alien. 'I've been alone for centuries. You'd be crazy too. Actually, sorry,' he giggled. 'You'd be dead. But we Us are a long-lived race. Unfortunately.'

'About the toys . . .' Stokes prompted him, not wanting to see how the Grel Master would react to this provocation. 'I hope they're not valuable. I fired the gun at one of the vases. I suppose it might have contained one of those boxes.'

'You fired a gun at a vase?' Thooo's head snapped round, as far as it could with him in his bonds, and he gazed at Stokes attentively. 'I wonder if anybody's ever done that before. The Green in the Green. What a puzzle!' And he started to giggle maniacally again.

'I'm afraid,' Singh muttered to Warrinder, 'that I have encountered someone more annoying than you.'

'Oh.' The rodent smiled. 'Good.'

'Query?' screamed the Grel Master. 'Query: Query?'

'I think, dear,' said Lucinda to Thooo, 'that, in a very ungrammatical fashion, he's asking what you mean.'

'Oh. Ah . . .' Thooo made an effort to stop laughing. 'All so interesting, after all these years, hard to take anything seriously. Fine. I'll stop.' He looked up at the Grel, soberly, sniggered again, and then, taking a deep breath to steady himself, resumed his story. 'The gun and the box are used by children to send things into the Green. The gun has a control on the end so that small adjustments in position can be made instantly. The box does the big all-over-the-place-control-of-Greened-object stuff. If a box was sent into the Green, and somebody found it there . . . Woo! They could invade! We might all be in deadly danger!' He looked around the group seriously, then his face flopped and he shrugged. 'No, actually. Probably not. But it'd be fun.'

'What is this Green?' asked Singh, despite Stokes's imploring look that he should restrain his intellectual curiosity in front of the Grel. 'Is it a higher dimension, or a sort of virtual reality?'

'Virtual reality?' Thooo frowned. 'What's that? This is real reality. An . . . area that accesses all the dimensions, a playground in time and space. The children send things into the Green and stick them out into places and times where they want to put them, or manipulate their pets so that they can enjoy the sensations of dimension nine, the Skyful of Dreams, the sleeping feelings of suns, stuff like that. Silly, eh?'

Stokes frowned. The scientists amongst the party, and the Grel, and even some of the Humanities staff, were staring at Thooo open-mouthed, awestruck. 'Sorry,' he said. 'But what does that mean, exactly?'

It was Farouk who broke the silence. 'Limitless, instantaneous information transfer across time and space. Access to higher dimensions. All knowledge and power accessible at the flick of a switch.'

'Yes . . .' Thooo mused. 'Not that you can use the Green to travel anywhere. It . . . stitches other times, places and dimensions to itself and you can take quick steps through, look around. But it's like a bad coat or a good injury. The stitches don't last. So you can see why I got bored. Our species can't leave home like all yours can, lucky things. We got . . . allergic to being without our technology, our plants, our civilization, centuries ago. It's a physical need. If we were to go into space, we would require taking this world here with us, all of it.'

'I'm a bit like that,' said Professor Wagstaff. 'I don't like to leave my study very often.'

'And all the others of us, too. That's why I've been so lonely, because I thought I could be alone. I didn't go with the others when they left.'

'They left?' Stokes said. 'I thought you said that they couldn't go into space.'

'They did not,' replied Thooo, showing his first sign of impatience. 'They went into the Green.'

The first thing that Bernice's party noticed when they emerged from the cave was the horse. It ran up to them and nudged Bernice on the hip, urgently.

'Are you after the lamp?' she asked. 'Because, I have to say, it's going to be difficult for you to use it.'

'But not for me!' Atop a high sand dune, looking down at them, stood the Vizier. He was rubbing his hands together in glee. 'Just toss it up to me and I'll shower you with gold. Oh, go on!'

The horse once more nudged at Bernice's hip. 'Erm,' she called up to the Vizier, 'we were just wondering, what do you want it for, exactly?'

'Well what do you think I want it for? As an ornament! I've got a plinth put aside for it. It'll go right between the china cats and that picture of the crying boy.'

Wolsey put his hand on the horse's head. 'Is he telling the truth?'

To everybody's surprise, the horse nodded emphatically.

'So what's the problem?' asked Bernice.

The horse stood rigid for a moment, as if its occupants were desperately trying to think of a way to convey their information. Then it quickly nodded. It raised a front hoof and lifted it towards the Vizier.

'The Vizier . . .' Benny followed.

The horse shook its head.

'Is not the problem?'

The horse nodded. Then it turned, lolloped a few feet away and then turned to look at her again.

'The problem's farther away?' suggested Gushy.

The horse nodded again. It reared up on its hind legs, which, frankly, astonished Bernice, and described a little circle. Then it rolled on its back, shook its legs in the air, stiffened, and fell over on to its side.

Bernice and the others looked at each other, then back to the horse. 'Sorry. No idea.'

The horse leapt up again and looked all around itself frantically. It shivered and shook.

'I can see you're trying really hard,' Bernice told it, 'but I'm afraid we're none the wiser.' If it had made any sense, she would have glanced at her watch at this point. This was hardly the time for charades.

The horse ripped itself in two.

The dwarves cried out and Candy screamed. 'An exploding horse!' she whimpered. 'We're in an art movie! No wonder I'm confused: my eyesight's so bad I can't read the subtitles.'

'That is so gross . . .' whispered Bitchy, hiding her eyes.

The man in the front part of the horse pulled his equine head off, to more screams of disgust. 'Listen!' he shouted. 'What we're trying to tell you is –'

'Yes,' the Vizier called. 'What are you trying to tell us? I'm freezing up here. The toes of my slippers have gone all droopy.' His grin hadn't faded, nor did it when a hand tapped him on the shoulder. 'Not now.' He glanced around and then turned back to Bernice's party. Then all the blood seemed to drain from his face and a look of horror overtook him. He spun back round and raised his hands in shock. ' 'Ere,' he said, 'I thought *I* was the villain in this story? Eh? Ooh!' A hand shoved him and he fell over backwards, rolling down the dune until he collided with Benny's ankles. He crawled swiftly round to hide behind them.

Bernice and her party looked up at the edge of the dune. Over it, framed by the moon, stood a line of imposing figures. Grel Servitors, spinning their axes.

Behind them, sand dropping from his vast body as he raised himself from his hiding place, there was a giant. He eclipsed the moon as he stood to his full height.

The man standing at the front of the horse costume slapped his forehead with his palm. 'We're surrounded,' he finished.

'Information: you are completely surrounded!' The call came from the other side of the little depression where the cave mouth stood. The party of adventurers spun round. Standing on that escarpment, with their leader, were a line of man-sized, hissing rats, dressed in rags. Beside them were the Grel Master and, oddly, a woman in a rather fabulous black cocktail dress. 'Operation Dessert Spoon has been a complete success!' the Grel Master continued.

'Dessert spoon?' murmured Wolsey.

'That's probably what they intend to do with our brains,' Benny whispered to him.

Moody pointed at the giant. 'That's the Ogre! The one who tried to frame us!'

The Grel Master made a gargling sound, the Grel version of laughter. 'He is now employed as our stealth giant.'

'And that's the Wicked Queen,' gasped Gushy.

'And the Rat King!' Wolsey drew his sword and snarled, the fur along his spine rising into a vicious plume. 'I swear, Bernice, if this comes to a battle, I shall have his gizzard for my supper!'

'Save a piece for me!' Moody pulled his short sword and the other dwarves followed suit. The giant took a step forward, his shadow falling across them.

'We could go back down the cave,' whispered Cute.

'No,' said Bernice. 'There's that hole, remember? We'd be trapped.' She grabbed the Vizier by the collar and hauled him to his feet. 'Have you got any magic that might help?'

'Well if I'd known I was going to be attacked by a giant, I'd have brought my potions, wouldn't I? Besides –' he glanced scathingly up at the Wicked Queen '– she'd keep me busy while the others . . .' He drew a line with his finger across his throat.

Bernice turned to the Grel Master. 'What do you want with us, exactly?'

'Your brains. Your knowledge of what this world is. But most of all –' he stuck out a squiddy finger '– we want that.'

Bernice's hand went to her belt. 'You want the lamp? Why?'

'It glows with power. It radiates energy. Information: my retinal sensors report it to be the most powerful artefact we have encountered since arriving . . . wherever we are.'

Bernice took the lamp from her belt and squinted at it. It didn't look like it was glowing to her. Neither did it look powerful.

The man from the front of the horse waddled closer to Bernice and whispered sidelong to her. 'Just don't let him rub it. I remember this story if nobody else does.'

'Rub it?' Candy enquired loudly. 'Why should he want to rub it?' She glanced up at the suddenly interested Grel and then back to Bernice's stormy expression. 'Oh dear. Sorry I spoke.'

A line shot out from one of the Grel's axes and wrapped itself around the handle of the lamp. Before Bernice could tug back or even react it had flown off. It landed in the hands of the Grel Master. He gurgled in triumph.

Bernice put her hands on her hips and looked down at her boots. 'I'm just having one of those genres,' she muttered.

From the *Informative Record of Recent Grel History*:

The newly elected and, so far, rather successful Grel Master could not resist a gurgle of delight as he thrust the glowing lamp skywards in his hands. 'Information: the lamp is mine! Mine!' he shouted, regarding himself, of course, as a representative of the might of Grellor.

Watching the reactions of the cluster of humanoids gathered below, he lowered the lamp again and paused before placing his fingers against the shining but burnished metal of the ornament. 'Information: they do not wish me to rub this lamp. Conclusion: I will do that.'

Ignoring the cries and implorings of those he had conquered, he began to rub some of the must of centuries from the lamp.

After a moment, the lamp began to tingle with power. The colour of the glow changed from gold to a verdant green. Then, with a thump, the lid of the lamp burst skywards and a plume of green smoke whooshed upwards. The smoke coalesced in the air, thickening and gaining structure, until above the Grel stood another giant. This one was blue, with a bare chest covered in white fur, as was its head. It had six multi-jointed fingers on each hand. It had blazing green eyes and a mouth full of sharp teeth, a mouth which was opened in a roar. It had no legs: its torso faded into a wisp of gas. It lowered its head and looked down at the Grel Master.

The Grel Master turned to his Servitors and hooted with excitement. 'Information: with the aid of this being, we will conquer this world!'

(Note: This particular narrative ends here. Obviously, the original Grel editor thought that, from his species' point of view, this was the best possible ending . . .)

Extract Ends

The vast genie's eyes glowed a brighter shade of green. Wolsey put a hand on Bernice's shoulder. 'Come on! We can't stand against that!'

Bernice shook her head, staring at the creature that

floated above the Grel Master. 'It's a Perfecton, like the ones I saw in the audience . . .'

'Nevertheless –' the cat began. But then he spun his head at the sound of an explosion.

A beam of green fire had flashed out from the genie's eyes, incinerating a row of the Rat King's subjects.

The Grel Master froze, still in the posture of a gloating conqueror. 'Query . . .' he began, haltingly. 'Is this being not . . . on our side?'

The Perfecton genie threw its head back and roared like a dinosaur.

The Wicked Queen raised her arms in an attacking posture, red light sparkling around her fingers –

And the genie swung its hand like a mace, sending her flying high into the air, off into the distance.

The Grel were running away from the monster now, as Bernice continued to watch, unable to take her eyes off the slaughter. One or two of the aliens turned to fire at the genie, but the energy bolts went straight through it, doing no visible harm. The Rat King vanished, stamped into the soil by a boot that suddenly formed out of the smoke of the genie's lower body.

'Giant!' called the Grel Master. 'Engage this being in combat!'

Rather bravely, Bernice thought, the giant actually did so. He stepped forward, his hands outstretched in a wrestling posture, and grabbed the genie by the shoulders. The genie grabbed the giant back, flexing its muscular arms around his back, and the two huge figures twisted this way and that, tottering around the landscape, their roars and footfalls making the ground vibrate.

'That's not something you see every day, is it?' the Vizier grinned nervously.

The man from the horse glanced at his fellow equine impersonator and with one movement they ducked back into their costume.

'Bernice, we must go,' muttered Wolsey, his hand now clamped on her shoulder. 'What if they fall? Come now, or I shall pick you up and carry you.'

'Where is there to go?' Bernice took his hand. 'If we try to run –' She broke off as the genie looked up, aware that, while he fought the giant, others were getting away. The beam flashed from his eyes again, and the running Grel blazed into gas, the Grel Master caught in the act of turning his weapon back towards the creature. 'See?' She glanced around her group quickly. 'We need a way out of here that won't bring us to the attention of that thing.'

'Eh? Say no more!' The Vizier closed his eyes and held out his hands. 'Form a circle and take my hands while I concentrate on my conjugations.'

'I've heard that before,' muttered Candy as the group formed a circle. The horse raised one hoof, then another, then finally settled for standing in the middle of the others.

Bernice looked over her shoulder as the Vizier started to mutter under his breath. Behind her, the genie had managed to destroy all other opposition and had turned all of its attention back to the giant, whom it was trying to overpower through sheer grappling strength.

She looked down at Cute, who was holding her hand and gazing up at her, a certain and brave expression on his face. He was, she realized with a sigh, convinced that she was going to save them all.

With a sudden roar, the genie pushed the giant from its clutches. It grabbed him again before the large humanoid could react, and swung him, with limitless strength, above its head. It began to spin the vast mass around and around, faster and faster.

The Vizier opened his eyes for a moment, faltered over his words, and then closed them again.

With a cry of triumph, the genie let the giant go. He flew into the air.

His shadow swept over Bernice and her friends.
He hung in the air above them.
Cute gulped.
'Vizier!' Bernice shouted. 'Now!'
A puff of smoke engulfed the group.
And was snuffed out as the giant body slammed into the sand.

CHAPTER 11

'SCUSE ME WHILE I RIP THE SKY

'Repeat of information owing to surprise: they went into the Green?' The Grel Master stared at Thooo, its facial tentacles flickering with glee. 'They left this world by way of this transport mechanism?'

'You could say that, yes!' said the friendly alien, smiling and shaking his head vigorously.

The Grel Master turned to the other Grel. 'Conference,' it said.

Stokes raised an eyebrow. He gathered that the Grel were unfamiliar with human body language, but he wondered if Thooo was, too. 'Excuse me,' he whispered to the Perfecton. 'But when humans want to express agreement, we usually nod.'

'I know.' Thooo nodded, as if to show that he could. 'That was an attempt at telling a lie. How did I do?'

'Oh, fine,' Stokes sighed. 'So your people didn't leave this world using the Green?'

'Using . . . no. I said to you, quite clearly, that you can only go to other places using the Green for a short walk. My people developed the Green thinking of travel, but could not travel using it. That is why it became a toy. So they didn't go somewhere in it, like the Green was a spaceship. They went to it. They may still remain there, if the plan didn't work out.'

'The plan?' Epstein prompted. 'What plan is this?'

Thooo made a low whistling noise, which, from the context, Stokes took to be the Perfecton equivalent of a sigh. 'Any of you hear of a spaceship vanishing from its course? A mystery vessel that disappeared, didn't show up where it was supposed to?'

'Oh, there have been thousands!' Wagstaff chuckled. 'Why, the subject has a pedigree as ancient as mankind itself. To begin with, we may examine the missing-vessel legends of ancient Sumeria . . .'

'Wagstaff, you old fool, he's talking about spaceships!' Blandish whispered urgently.

'Yes, yes, yes.' Wagstaff giggled. 'But the context, the nature of the tales, is exactly the same . . .'

'What these two are trying to say,' Singh cut in, 'is: yes. Lots. Thooo here could be referring to any one of them.'

'We were even on one such ship ourselves,' sighed Stokes.

'What?' asked Thooo.

'Our ship was destroyed by one of your missiles. That's going to go down in the history books as a mysterious loss, unless we get back home to talk about it.' He realized that Thooo was looking at him strangely. 'What? Have I missed something again?'

'Your ship? A missile? After all these centuries, was yours the first ship to come to our planet?'

'Yes, dear,' Hettie told him comfortingly. 'There was a blockade. Nobody was allowed near.'

Thooo laughed again, though, already, Stokes had begun to recognize the signs of sadness in the being's voice. 'Isn't that . . . ironic? I have been here for so many years, and my people were . . . nearby.'

'What do you mean?' Singh hissed. 'Do get around to telling us before the heat death of the universe, won't you?'

'Very well,' Thooo decided. 'Many centuries ago . . .'

Bernice's party appeared back in the Vizier's dungeons.

Several feet above the floor.

With a shout, they fell in an awkward heap.

The Vizier, his turban at an odd angle, crawled from the wreckage, and Bernice struggled free behind him. 'Well, what do you expect?' he asked her. 'I didn't have time to sort out my vertical hold.'

'It'll do,' Bernice told him, brushing herself down and making sure that the others were all right as they clambered to their feet. 'Is there any way that we can find out what that genie's doing right now?'

'Yes,' said the Vizier, trotting over to a mirror mounted on the wall. 'PNN – the Pantoland News Network. Watch!' He waved a hand before the mirror, and a picture appeared, the genie advancing on a tiny hamlet of thatched cottages. Jolly peasants in colourful costumes ran from the buildings as the genie's eyes blazed, setting fire to the buildings. A caption read: LIVE FROM RABBITSVILLE.

'That's inside the Kingdom,' Moody muttered. 'That thing moves fast.'

'The creature seems unstoppable,' a commentator was crying out. 'A royal decree has gone out to all the points of the Kingdom, seeking a hero, woodchopper, or boy with something puny given to him by an old woman, who will save us all from this terrible threat. This genie –' the commentator paused for dramatic effect '– is not here to grant us three wishes.'

Gushy pushed her way to the front of the crowd and stared at the screen. 'What's it doing?' she whispered.

The genie floated past the village, and had paused on the horizon. It spread its arms wide, curled its fingers.

And gripped the sky with its fingertips.

The dwarves gawped. The sky was creasing against the pressure of the genie's hands.

Then, with one mighty rip, the genie pulled the sky down.

'The sky is falling!' gasped Cute.

Indeed it was. Bernice watched as lumps of painted backdrop fell everywhere, crushing buildings, thundering into lakes, sending shockwaves across the countryside. Where the sky had been, there was now only darkness, illuminated by vast, distant lights that were too bright to look at directly. Bernice recognized that environment.

'The fourth wall has officially been broken,' she announced. 'I think we can expect visitors.'

'Visitors?' asked Gushy. 'What do you mean?'

From the stairs came the sound of somebody running down into the dungeons. Running with great haste. It was Prince Charming. He stopped when he saw Bernice and the others, but his message was too urgent for surprise. 'The audience!' he cried to the Vizier. 'The audience is revolting!'

Bernice slapped a hand over Candy's mouth and nodded grimly to the Prince. 'We know.'

Thooo was looking into the distance, as if his eyes could see back in time. The academics waited in silence. The Grel were still gurgling amongst themselves on the other side of the enclosure. Typical of them, thought Stokes, to focus on the first fact that revealed itself, and so miss the complete picture.

'Many centuries ago, my people realized that, at some point within the next few hundred years, our sun would become a supernova. They couldn't, for reasons I've already mentioned, leave. By spacecraft or by the Green. So they developed another plan, making use of the Green indirectly. They wanted, remember, a way to take the whole population of my world, and all its culture, all its words and art and lifestyle, away at once. They knew that the Green was infinite, that they could all stay there. The Green isn't a world in itself – its not a place to live. But it could be a shelter. So they came up with a big plan. Every member of our race was to meet together, in this big hall.' He gestured at the distant ceiling above. 'All three billion of them. They marched, and this took days, with entertainment and refreshment along the way, until, group by group, they were under this central projector, a giant gateway into the Green. Being the sort of race that liked parades and music and lining up, and long-lived enough to worry about stuff like supernovae, they really got into it. Day after day, I watched them pass, week after week, until, after about an Earth year, only the Greater One was left. The Greater One and me.'

'Greater one?' asked Wagstaff.

'The leader of our people. He decided on this silly plan after his coup toppled our last leader, the Great One. The Great One wanted to stay, have a party and die with our sun. Maybe he was right.'

'Why didn't you go?' Stokes asked. 'Why would you want to stay behind?'

'Because I had lived far too long a time, so I thought. Because I was a rebel. I wanted to see what life was like without all of my people around me. If one of us could survive alone.' Thooo's blue tongue flicked out and licked the tips of his sharp teeth. 'I remember the Greater One telling me that I would enjoy it for about a week. He was wrong. I enjoyed it for about a year. Then I wanted to see my friends and family and species again. I was so foolish.'

'Well,' murmured Farouk, 'if your people are in the Green, and these toy guns send things into the Green, why didn't you just –?'

'Yes, I did think of that!' Thooo's tone verged on the angry for a moment. 'But if I shot myself with one, I couldn't control my path through the Green. I would be lost, with no guarantee of finding them. To navigate through the Green using the toys, somebody has to be outside, using a control box. I was going to ask you to shoot me. Wish I'd got around to it now.'

'Yes,' Singh nodded excitedly. 'That Grel who got shot didn't really seem to know where he was going. He might have ended up anywhere, or anywhen. But what about the big version, up above us?' He indicated the vast machinery overhead with a flick of his head.

Thooo lowered his gaze slowly. 'I was . . . an artist. A poet. I don't know how to use it. It was the most advanced part of our technology. Even with centuries here on my hands, I couldn't learn.'

Stokes had been alone many times in his life, and, secretly, had never been comfortable with it. Centuries of solitude sounded like torture to him. He spoke softly. 'I'm very sorry.'

'Him!' The Grel Master marched across the enclosure and pointed at Stokes. 'Information: he will be the subject of the experiment.'

'Experiment?' Stokes squeaked.

'I'm the expert at anything scientific,' babbled Singh. 'He's just an artist, you should take me instead.'

Two Grel Servitors released Stokes from his bonds as the Grel Master turned to his fellows. 'It is because he is recorded in our databanks as an artist, and thus useless, that he is a suitable experimental subject.'

'What are you going to do to me?' asked Stokes, feeling both indignant and pleased at the same time. Indignant that art was regarded as useless by the Grel, pleased that, for once, it was all art that was at fault, and not his particular contribution.

'We are going to send you on an expedition into the Green,' said the Grel Master, raising the gun and the control box. 'You will gather data, and, if you return, report.'

'Oh.' Stokes looked at the others, considering Thooo's words. If the Green was good enough for a whole species, it was good enough for him. 'Well, that's not so bad.'

The Grel Master's face tentacles thrashed in consternation. 'Information: "report" may be the wrong word. "Be dissected" is a closer translation.'

'Ah,' said Stokes. 'Have I mentioned that my brain has several major structural flaws?'

'The experiment begins now,' said the Grel Master, as his Servitors stepped back from Stokes. He raised the gun.

Stokes looked to his left and right as the Servitors stepped away from him, remembering Thooo's terrifying words about being lost in the Green.

Suddenly, he thought of a very clever plan.

Which was a pity, because at that moment the Grel Master fired.

Menlove Stokes vanished in a burst of flame.

'Right!' Bernice and her party strode into the King's chambers, the Vizier and the Prince scampering behind her. 'How many men do we have?'

King Rupert looked up from where several advisers had gathered around his table, pointing at locations on large maps. 'Who's this young whippersnapper?' he growled. 'And why does he think to advise us on military policy?'

Bernice put a hand to her brow. She'd forgotten. If her theory was right, she was going to have to fight a war against a massive, well-armed, highly advanced army with a force consisting of ten soldiers in cardboard armour, an Arab boy with a flying carpet, a troupe of comedy outlaws, seven dwarves and a pantomime horse. At least they weren't all speaking in rhyme at the moment. She slapped her thigh, which always seemed to impress people, and forced a jaunty smile. 'Do not be fooled by my simple garb, sire. I am your long-lost son, the Prince abandoned in the woods. I was saved by a kindly woodcutter, a sweet old woman, a wolf, and –' Bernice tried to remember her pantomimes '– a family of bears who fed me on porridge.'

'Son!' The King ran to Bernice and embraced her. 'You

come to us at the most opportune time. A great genie has come upon us.'

The dwarves all looked at Candy. 'You're making up your own jokes,' she muttered.

'Nobody else?' Bernice asked, surprised. 'It's just genie grief you're having at the moment?'

'Well, behind him there marches an army. But surely the genie is more important.'

'The genie is just a servant of the army.' Bernice glared sternly at the characters around her. 'And if we're going to win this battle, you're going to have to give up that habit of withholding vital tactical information if it gets in the way of a bad joke.'

'I didn't even get to make the joke,' Candy sulked.

'Is this army really the Audience?' asked Wolsey.

'We think so.' King Rupert lifted up one of the maps and pointed to a dark line, the path of the invading army. 'They come from the fabled land beyond the sky, where the big lights shine.'

'You know about the audience?' The world of pantomime continued to surprise Bernice.

'Oh yes.' The Vizier nodded. 'They loom large in our legends. They're the ones who – oh.' He looked a little disappointed. ' 'Ere, they're not hissing me any more!'

'So that was where that sound was coming from.' Bernice resisted the temptation to slap her thigh again. It was going to end up bruised at this rate.

'In our great myths,' the King continued, 'the Audience appear only infrequently. One or two of them sometimes appear and help us to sing a song. We are told that, if they are angry, sweets will appease them. When this threat to our land first became apparent, I ordered an aerial bombardment of the enemy.'

Despite the grim nature of the threat facing them, the idea appalled Bernice. 'You dropped bombs on them?'

'No.' The King frowned. 'Liquorice toffees. But if their

aggression persists, I can see no option but to deploy our most terrible weapon.'

A hush fell over the room. Bernice folded her arms and tapped her foot. It was finally Gushy who realized that nobody else was going to say the cue line. 'You don't mean –?'

'Yes.' The King walked to an alcove where a large shape was covered with a black cloth. He pulled the cloth away. Revealed was a shiny, black, egg-shaped object. There was a gasp from everybody present except Bernice. The King nodded grimly. 'The A-bonbon. The most terrifying sugared confectionery ever developed by mankind.'

Laddish raised his hand, looking like he was salivating over the prospect of the bomb's use. 'What does the A stand for?'

The King paused dramatically. 'Aniseed.'

Before everybody could make more horrified noises, Bernice grabbed the cloth from the King and dropped it back over the big sweet. 'All right.' She started to tick off the possibilities on her fingers. 'I don't want to hear about how the scientists developing the bomb caught aniseed poisoning. I don't want to hear about the potential threat of an Aniseed Winter. I don't want to hear speculation about what sort of goose could drop this thing, or whether or not the enemy have developed a cruise gobstopper. There are to be no calculations of how much an ounce of aniseed would cost in a "black sweetshop", and if I hear so much as a single mention of aniseed fallout, I shall scream.'

The assembled inhabitants of pantoland looked at each other and said: 'awwwww . . .'

Bernice remained stern. 'In short –'

'Stop messin' about?' volunteered the Vizier.

'Exactly. Now let's get up on to the battlements and have a look at the enemy.'

* * *

Having 'a look at the enemy' was frighteningly easy, as it turned out. From the topmost battlement of the topmost tower of the castle, Bernice and her friends gazed out over the Kingdom, and saw a huge black line on the horizon.

The King raised a spyglass to his eye and exclaimed. 'By all my horses and all my men! There are –'

'Many, many millions of them,' Bernice finished. 'Enough to overwhelm the entire Kingdom. If that's what they want to do.' She glanced at Wolsey. 'That's the biggest audience we'll ever see.'

'But how can we hope to stop them?' Prince Charming wrung his hands together. 'I should take my cavalry and –'

'Absolutely not,' said Bernice. 'That would be sheer folly. And considering the state of your cavalry, not even magnificent folly. No, we need to find out what's caused this to happen. Why the genie was so aggressive. What the purpose of the lamp was. Why the caves where it was hidden were so very un-panto.' She stopped, and pointed at the Vizier. 'You're our lamp expert. You said that you had a plinth put aside for it. Where is that, exactly?'

'Well where do you think it is?' the Vizier snapped. 'Where else would I put a lamp? In the master bedroom that the King here has reserved for his daughter and her future husband, of course!'

The King was nodding along with him. 'Where else would you put an ancient and mysterious lamp?'

Bernice turned to Wolsey and the dwarves. 'Now, can you spot the single flaw in this argument?'

The master bedroom was decorated in an extraordinary style. As the Vizier had mentioned, the plinth was, indeed, situated between a shelf of china cats and the picture of the crying boy. Bernice and her party approached the plinth, while Prince Charming looked uncomfortable. 'I don't know how this is going to help us win the war,' he muttered.

Wolsey popped a claw and idly scratched his chin with it. The Prince fell silent.

Bernice automatically dropped to one knee in front of the plinth. The thing was at the focus of the whole room, the kind of object that, in archaeological terms, added up to spear traps and falling weights. It was made of the same, rather battered, material as the lamp. There was an indentation in its surface that was exactly the shape of the lamp's base. It so cried out 'Put lamp here' that there ought to have been a sign to that effect. She gently rested her fingertips on the top of the plinth, estimated how much the lamp had weighed, and pressed.

A moment of dislocation.

Nothing.

And then everything was back as it had been.

Except the room was rolling, and everybody was staggering to and fro.

'Terrible things!' Lazy was screaming.

Candy was huddled in a corner, clutching her breasts.

Wolsey was in a foetal position on the bed, shivering.

Bernice stepped up and away from the plinth, and shouted that she wasn't going to do it again, that everything was fine. She remembered a timeless time during the blankness, a little moment of fizzing haze, like she'd experienced when making those jumps between stage and audience.

She went to Wolsey.

He opened his eyes, and was almost glaring at her with his bravery. 'You . . . were correct.' He hissed from clenched teeth. 'I am a thoughtless thing. I function as if in a dream, propelled here and there by instinct and base desire. When I return to my usual form, I shall lose . . . all this. I shall lose . . . the Wolsey I am. It is worse than death.' He suddenly roared and sprang up into a standing position. 'Never! I will fall in this war if this is the victory we aim to achieve!'

Bernice took him in her arms. 'You're loved, Wols. In your other form. I take care of you. You feel that emotion, I'm certain.'

After a moment, his stiff muscles relaxed in her embrace. 'I cannot do it,' he said. 'I cannot go back to that.'

Bernice looked around the others. They all seemed deeply shaken. 'Did you all see?' she asked. 'Did you all experience what you once were?'

Candy had got to her feet, not quite able to look at anybody. 'I did,' she confirmed. Then she looked up suddenly and winked. 'I may not have a lot upstairs, but I've got a bit more than I thought I had downstairs.'

They had all resumed their usual body language. The rules of pantomime had swept back into the room and changed them again.

'What do you mean?' asked the Vizier, grinning maniacally as ever. 'What you once were? What are you talking about?'

Bernice patted him on the shoulder. 'Don't worry. You didn't go through it, because you're just a simple computer program, with a single goal in mind, to take part in a story about the lamp. Either you would have taken it from me and put it here, or I, as either Aladdin or the Princess, would have beaten you and ended up here, happily ever after. My spouse and I would also, presumably, have put the lamp there. So our friendly genie could attend to us.'

'And then?' asked Wolsey, obviously still shaken.

'I think the phrase is: game over. But there's been a major change to the script.' She started to laugh at the irony of it all. 'Through some extraordinary circumstances, we managed to do something with that lamp that this world didn't expect us to. We managed to give it to an alien invader with the head of a squid.'

There was a sudden shout outside.

And then an impact.

Bernice and the others were blown off their feet.

They were just struggling upright as a messenger ran into the room. 'The army with the genie! They are upon us!'

'Already?' yelled the King.

'They're magic, they can do what they like.' Bernice was hauled to her feet by the dwarves. 'Now, I have to think . . .'

'Thinking,' cried Prince Charming, 'is a luxury for which we have no time! Only force of arms can –'

With a hiss of impatience, Wolsey grabbed the Prince by the collar and threw him out of the door. 'Bernice,' he said, 'tell us what we must do.'

Bernice looked at the expectant faces around her, and considered the options left to her. While she was doing that, she became aware that, in the corner, the pantomime horse was doing a little dance to attract her attention.

She raised a finger. 'Excuse me.'

'You're trying to tell me something again, aren't you?' Bernice said to the horse, having hustled it out into the corridor. 'Rather than go through several more rounds of charades, couldn't you just take your head off for a second and tell me?'

The horse stamped its hoof several times, as if in protest.

'You're still afraid that the pantomime will overwhelm you. But why? It hasn't managed to take me over.'

The horse reared up, as if chastising her for something obvious.

'It's a long message, not something you can just shout out like you did at the caves?'

The horse nodded.

Bernice thought for a moment. 'If I do something completely un-panto, will that upset the conditions enough for you to be yourselves for a bit?'

The horse nodded again.

So Bernice ran back into the King's chambers, grabbed the Vizier, pulled him out into the corridor, spun him round twice and gave him the most passionate of all possible kisses.

' 'Ere!' he cried when she released him. 'I'll have you know I've never been so molested in my life.' He glanced a wry glance in the direction of the wall, and then slapped himself, remembering. 'Sorry, I don't half miss having the audience there.'

'So do we all,' murmured Bernice, watching as the horse split open once more. She gently pushed the Vizier back into the room.

'We –' began the man in the front.

'From God, mission, I know.' Bernice hurried him. 'It's your catchphrase. Go on from there.'

The man took a deep breath. 'You have, in your previous travels, encountered a very advanced species from outside the Milky Way galaxy, a species known as the People?'

'The People?' Bernice was surprised to hear them referred to in these circumstances. It took her a while to get her mental bearings. The People were humanoids, basically, who lived in a Dyson Sphere, the material of their entire solar system formed into a globe which entirely encircled their sun. The People, being as far up the evolutionary ladder from humans as humans were from cacti, had abandoned all hierarchical government, and lived an idyllic existence, their only form of organization being Interest Groups, which were sort of like clubs devoted to a particular hobby. The fact that a couple of the more bloody-minded of these groups had fought an interstellar war on behalf of the People and won it gave some indication of the level of technology involved. Apart from being liberated from absolutes concerning their gender, race, shape and sentience, the People also lived in tandem with the drones – sentient robots who enjoyed working with them, some of whom liked being houses.

Bernice had spent a few days on the Dyson Sphere once, making her one of only a handful of humans who were even aware of the People's existence. That time had passed in a blur of intoxication and intrigue. The best sort of adventure, that, where you could stop at any point for home-baked bread and a casual snog. She'd always wanted to go back. The People were looked after by a vast, omnipotent central computer that they called 'God'. She pinched the top of her nose in amazement at her own stupidity. 'You were being absolutely literal. You are on a mission from God.'

'And he says to say Hi,' the man said. 'We're not of the People ourselves. We're both human beings. One of a choice few who have been picked to represent the People, or rather the Tiny But Interesting Interest Group, in the Milky Way.'

Bernice frowned. 'But the People are forbidden to interfere in the Milky Way. The greater powers of the universe agreed that, strategically –'

'The People,' the man interrupted her, 'aren't here. We are.'

'Which is within the letter of the law,' the second man chimed in. 'If not the spirit.'

'Tiny But Interesting are a group devoted to collecting information concerning trivia,' the first man said. 'Mostly trivia about the Milky Way. They need more agents, and you're particularly well placed to deal with some of the things they're interested in. Dellah lies in the same sector as several things with which TBIIG are very concerned.'

The second man chimed in. 'God's been awfully cagey about what precisely he's so interested in, but then you know God. The smart money's on some ancient –'

'But this is idle banter,' the first man cut in, giving his equine partner a stern look. 'We were sent to make you an offer. The job would involve occasional missions across space, some unusual travel. Basically, we'd like you to poke around interesting places every now and then. We'd pay you well for your services.'

Bernice folded her arms. 'So why all this panto business?'

The men shrugged. 'Nothing to do with us,' said the second one. 'We just came to visit you on your ship when it was hit by that missile. Changed the place a bit.'

'Changed the place? You mean –?'

'This whole world is created out of quantum particle fluctuations, or "magic", if you're primitive enough to want to call it that. As we tried to tell you, we've all been moved up a couple of dimensions but, geographically, we're all still on the *Winton*. And – and this is the important bit – if that ship doesn't get moving soon, the business of panto will be the least of our worries, because we'll all be dead.'

CHAPTER 12

IMMINENT DESTRUCTION GRIEF

Bernice trotted back into the King's chambers somewhat galvanized. She clapped her hands together to get everybody's attention. 'I've just had a message from God, and he says that, unless we do something really, really useful very soon, we're all going to die. Now does anybody have any good ideas?'

Silence.

They were all still, unfortunately, relying on her. What panto options hadn't she explored? Her gaze floated aimlessly across the dwarves. Cute was gazing up at her in expectation. Moody was slapping one tiny fist into one tiny palm. Lazy had gone to sleep in a chair . . .

'Asleep!' She turned to the King. 'Why is your daughter Aurora always asleep?'

The King looked as if he rather doubted that this was important, but he went along with it. 'She was cursed by a witch. She pricked her finger and, unless we can find a way to wake her, is doomed to sleep for a thousand years.'

'Take me to her.'

As they ran up the stairs of a particularly isolated and gloomy tower, Wolsey patted Bernice's shoulder. 'Why are you interested in this sleeping princess?'

'The royalty here are the crew of the ship. If we're still on the ship, it strikes me as odd that one of that crew is permanently asleep.'

They came to the door of the turret room, and the King put a finger to his lips. He took a key from his belt, unlocked the door, and shepherded them in.

The Princess Aurora was very beautiful, her hair flung back over her pillows, her face relaxed in sleep, but, as Bernice swiftly realized, this was a real person, not one of those characters she'd started to think of as computer programs. Indeed, now she was this close, Bernice knew that she recognized her.

Aurora was Aurum Salvistra, the ship's navigator.

Her situation at that moment was very strange indeed.

She lay in a huge, round bed with a red bedspread. The bed was at the centre of a round tower room, with, and this was appropriate for a navigator, Bernice thought, a starscape painted on the roof above. At its centre was a large red orb. But the strangest thing about the room was what was wrong with it.

It had a missile sticking through the wall.

There had been, of course, no sign of this sudden bit of interior decorating from outside the castle. The nosecone of the missile had gone straight through a shelf of books along one wall. Its thin, tapering nose spar had punctured right through the spine of one book, and from there led across the room to where Aurora slept. Her hand was flopped out over one side of the bed, her ring finger hanging limply. Its tip was pierced by the very end of the missile's spar, an old wound, long healed.

'That,' purred Wolsey, 'is one extraordinarily well-armed witch.'

Bernice went to the bookshelf, and inspected the book that the missile's nose spar had burst its way through. The title along its damaged spine was *English Pantomime: A*

Critical Study, by Prof. F. Archduke. Bernice put her hand on the volume, thinking about snapping the spar to get it out of both the book and the princess. But then she started to get that feeling. That Nancy Drew, Scooby Doo feeling that had so enlivened her reading under the covers when she was a girl.

She thought that she'd got the solution to this one before the author had given it away.

She let go of the book, and marched to the bed. 'Have you ever done anything to try to make her wake up?'

The King looked rather abashed. 'Charming offered to kiss her a couple of times, but the consensus was that, since we didn't understand the magic involved, it was best not to interfere.'

'I see.' Bernice nodded. 'Oh well, then, here goes nothing.' Before anybody could stop her, she took Aurora's finger and gently plucked it from the end of the missile.

The Princess gave a sudden, deep breath.

'She's beautiful!' exclaimed Cute.

'Do you have to do that?' Bernice asked him.

'I can't help it,' said the dwarf.

The Princess Aurora tossed her head, as if waking from a nightmare, and then opened her eyes.

'My beloved daughter!' cried the King, and embraced her.

But the navigator's wide eyes fixed on something terrible past her father's shoulder. The red sphere at the centre of her ceiling mural.

She pointed at it, and screamed at the top of her voice.

'What is it?' asked Bernice, taking her by the shoulders. 'What's wrong?'

'I . . . I don't know. Just a bad dream. Something . . .' The woman looked around, blinking, as if adjusting to the life she'd found in the waking world. 'Something magical.'

Bernice restrained herself from slapping her. 'Red giant!'

she shouted at the struggling Princess. 'Navigator! *Winton*! Concentrate!' The matrix of pantomime, all the beliefs and expectations of this world, seemed to be weakest at the edges of sleep. This life was, indeed, a dream. Maybe all life was. Whatever, Bernice wasn't going to lose the insight the navigator had had when she first woke.

She stared right into Bernice's eyes, as if looking at any of the others in the room would make her lose the thought, and she said, 'The star. Perfecton's star. That size . . . on my screens. She's going to go supernova. We have hours. Less.'

Bernice let her go, and she collapsed into the arms of the man she would now think of as her father. He glared at Bernice. 'What did that mean? Why were you so rough with her?'

'Because all of us, that Perfecton army included, are running out of time. Can we get PNN in here?'

The King gently eased Aurora into the arms of Candy, and went to a brass plate mounted on the wall behind the bed. He waved a hand. The plate swam into life. The view it showed made Bernice hold back a little shriek of panic. It was a close-up of the marching line at the front of the enemy army. A row of literally thousands of Perfectons, male and female, stretching as far as the eye could see. At their head, the genie floating beside him, strode the individual that Bernice had examined in the front row of the audience, his headdress larger than all the others.

He carried the lamp before him.

It was obvious now that it was glowing with energy. Bernice nodded to herself. 'Vizier, with your magic –'

'Oh, so I'm more than just a simple whatever-it-was now, am I?' moaned the magician.

'A computer program, but quite a sweet one.'

'As long as you don't try to kiss me again. Go on. I'm all ears.'

Bernice looked determined. 'You're going to kaboom

me from here to right in front of that big bugger with the lamp.'

'Us too!' cried the dwarves, Candy and Wolsey.

Bernice sighed, and caught the eye of her cat. He was looking like he looked on a wet morning when he'd just come home, that same lost mixture of sadness and anger. 'Just Wols,' she said.

'Indeed,' Wolsey drew his sword.

'Come on then,' said the Vizier. He looked around, as if struck by a sudden thought. ' 'Ere, anybody got any chalk?'

Bernice and Wolsey stood at the edge of a chalk pentagram drawn by the Vizier on the floor of his dungeon. 'Now, once I start my incantations, don't step over the lines, or you'll lose your extremities,' he told them, straightening up. 'When you want to come back, just say the magic words: "Open Sesame".'

They stepped inside. Wolsey looked at Bernice seriously. 'Do you know exactly what your objective is?'

'Well, sort of.' She grinned. 'I am, to a degree, improvising, but I'm really after two things. One, I want that lamp back. Two, I'd really like to compare notes with that big Perfecton about just what's going on here.'

'You're going to *chat* to the vanguard of an invading army?'

Bernice gently punched his arm. 'Ah, but I have an absolutely guaranteed panto-related trick worked out. It can't fail.'

Wolsey was silent for a moment. 'What do you want the lamp for?'

'Because if I put it on the plinth, I think . . . Oh, Wolsey.'

'Finish your sentence. You think that doing that will bring this life to an end, and take us all back to where we came from. That it will transform us into our previous selves.'

'Yes,' said Bernice, unable to meet his gaze. 'I don't know why, but yes.'

Wolsey nodded slowly. 'Thank you for your honesty.'

'I won't use it . . . Not unless –'

'Don't be so foolish.' He reached out, and gently touched her chin with the pad of his paw. The first time he'd touched her, Bernice realized, since his transformation. 'Let us see the way the world goes, and act accordingly.'

Bernice took a deep breath, took the paw in her hand, and turned to the Vizier. 'Go on then,' she told him. 'Carry on spellcasting.'

The Vizier cleared his throat. 'Pilau Aloo Sang . . .'

The Greater One surveyed the land before him, and shook his head in disgust. He turned to one of the others of his race who marched beside him and expressed, as he had several times that day, his general dissatisfaction. 'It is astonishing. Where has this land come from? Who are these individuals? I would understand if there were simply chaos, if there had been decay in the program. But . . . Why has it become like this?'

'This state will not persist,' said his lieutenant purposefully.

'Correct,' buzzed the genie floating beside them. 'I will correct all anomalies and bring the program back under our control. I will find the underlying code and shape it back into our plan. I will destroy all anomalous beings.'

'Good to know,' said the Greater One. 'Continue with that.'

The army, or rather the entire species, that followed the Greater One had covered a great deal of ground through this anomalous mass of programming, and were finally approaching what appeared to be the centre – a structure with turrets and a large gateway. Perhaps the solution to the Greater One's problem would be there. He certainly hoped so. The current situation was baffling, not one of the many possibilities he had envisaged when implementing this project.

The line of marching figures passed, one by one, and rather awkwardly, over a stile that led into a small meadow. The genie offered to erase the feature, but the Greater One enjoyed the feeling of exercising his muscles. It was the only thing that kept him certain that this was not all a dream.

As the three hundred and twenty-eighth of the three billion or so was climbing over the stile, the Greater One's lieutenant indicated that he should observe something that was happening in the centre of the meadow. A purple cloud of smoke had appeared, and out of it wandered two figures, coughing and waving smoke away with their hands.

'I will –' began the genie.

'Wait, wait.' The Greater One raised a hand. 'Let's try to learn something at least. Let me have a quick word, see what they know. Then you can erase them.'

Bernice stared at the vanguard of the vast army that had so far hopped over the stile into the meadow. 'The one with the lamp is looking at me in a funny way,' she murmured.

'Well, three billion's a crowd,' purred Wolsey. 'If you don't want me to play gooseberry, just ask.'

Woman and cat looked at each other, then girded their loins and stepped forward. 'We come in peace,' declared Bernice, raising both her hands.

Wolsey quickly sheathed his sword. 'I do wish you'd told me you were going to do that.'

'As I said,' Bernice whispered as the larger Perfecton stepped forward, 'I'm making this up as I go along.'

'You speak our language!' chuckled the Perfecton leader as he approached. 'How charming. Doubtless a function of our existence here.'

'Doubtless,' agreed Bernice, a little disturbed by the fruity and jovial English accent that the large alien had turned out to have. She'd expected to have to cross cultural barriers slowly at this point, delay the army by a lengthy process of translation and diplomacy. It sounded like this chap was ready to wave aside her objections and devastate anything he wanted to devastate. Which meant that she'd probably have to play her exceedingly dodgy trick. 'So.' She waved her arms vaguely. 'Tell me about this army of yours. Who are they? Where do they come from?'

The large alien puffed his oddly shaped chest out proudly. 'We are Us.'

Bernice thanked goodness that Hettie and Lucinda weren't there, and adopted her best interested-listener pose, aware that, moment by moment, the meadow was filling up with impatient and very well-armed Perfectons. 'Hello, Us. And who are you?'

'Is he one of Us, or is he one of them?' murmured Wolsey, who had obviously not entirely rid himself of the habits of panto.

'I am the Greater One,' sniffed the large alien. 'The leader of my species. We once enjoyed a technologically advanced, perfect civilization, having achieved powers which lesser races such as yours would describe as god-like. We elected not to pursue the physics of interstellar travel, but instead made ours the best of all possible worlds. Then we realized that, with cruel irony, in a scant few decades our planet would become uninhabitable, owing to changes in our sun.' A number of the other Perfectons were nodding along, sighing and looking sad.

'So.' Bernice couldn't resist trying her own theory for size. 'You preserved your entire culture as a computer matrix, and downloaded all your secrets, technology, and finally, good selves, into a single missile.'

'Erm . . .' The Greater One looked rather put out. 'Yes. Got it in one.'

'The missile was programmed to launch itself at any suitable spaceship that came near to your planet. Through the power of quantum particle fluctuations –'

'Eh?' asked Wolsey.

'Magic,' Bernice whispered. She addressed the Greater One once more. 'Through them, you planned to reactualize that ship into a vessel for the whole Perfecton culture, a vessel that would actually be bigger on the inside than the outside –' She stopped and glanced at Wolsey, as if to make sure that everything was OK.

He nodded impatiently. 'I think you got away with it. Go on.'

She did. 'A vessel that would carry your entire world and people. The original crew would become Perfectons – sorry, would become Us – and everything about the ship would become a thing of your world. That ship would be free to take your race out into the universe, leaving your dying star to expire.'

The Greater One inclined his head in a shallow bow. 'You are correct in all respects. Is it not a majestic plan?'

'Well, it would be,' Benny smiled, 'if it hadn't been royally buggered up. That missile hit our ship, many many centuries after the automatic systems you left to launch it were supposed to have been activated. Through what seems to me to be a billion-to-one chance, it hit smack dab in the middle of our computer mainframe. Actually pierced it. The quantum particle fluctuation warhead activated, but instead of accessing the databanks you'd stored in the rest of the missile, it used as its source material my colleague Professor Archduke's thesis: *English Pantomime: A Critical Study*. Hence all this.' She gestured around her. 'Until I popped down into those caves and the Grel rubbed the lamp, thus breaking the panto ambience decisively, the only role in the pantomime for you lot was as the audience.' Her smile slowly faded as she realized that there was a whole area of this experience that her theory utterly failed to explain. 'But . . . that doesn't explain why . . .'

The Greater One slapped himself on the forehead, and

turned to his people, his arms spread wide. 'Why . . . of course! This makes so much sense! We're living in the wrong world!'

Bernice and Wolsey laughed along with him. 'So there's something we can do to work this out, right?' Benny asked.

'Oh, of course,' the Greater One grinned. 'Our master program here, storehouse of all our technological knowledge, and sprite for running the quantum particle fluctuations, who now rather wonderfully looks like a – what does he look like?'

'A genie,' said Wolsey.

'– who now looks like a genie, will move through this invalid data and delete it all. We'll take this world by force, and transform your ship into what we wanted in the first place. Thank you so much for clearing up those few little queries for us.'

'Ah,' Bernice said. And, 'Oh.' And, 'Well . . .'

Wolsey put a hand on her shoulder. 'I rather think it's time for that party piece you mentioned.'

Bernice calmed herself. 'I think you're right.' She looked up at the towering ethereal presence of the genie and took a deep breath. 'Oi! Genie!'

The genie looked down at her. 'Yes?'

'You think you're very powerful, correct?'

'Yes.'

'More powerful than the Fairy Godfather, who I'm certain was the personification of the central computer access sprite on my shipboard lectern? More powerful than the Wicked Queen and the Rat King, other programs on the ship's computer?'

'Yes.'

'More powerful even than the ship's mainframe itself, the intelligence that, in the world of panto, became the giant?'

'Yes.'

Bernice snorted. 'Rubbish. I thoroughly disagree. You can't be such a powerful genie, because there's one particular feat that you're completely incapable of doing.'

'Oh no there isn't,' said the genie.

A slow grin spread across Bernice's face. 'Oh yes there is.'

'Oh no there isn't.'

'Oh yes there is.'

This continued for some time, until the genie looked ready to explode and many of the Perfectons were tapping their feet and looking at their metaphorical watches.

'Oh . . . no . . . there . . . isn't!' he bellowed.

The Greater One raised a finger. 'Let me settle this. What is this feat of which you speak?'

'Simple,' Bernice said. 'It's easy to spout out of a lamp like that, but it's incredibly hard to get back in. I don't believe he can do it.

'Do you seriously expect –' began the Greater One.

Just a second too late. Because in that time, the genie had roared, reduced itself to a speck and vanished back into the lamp. This panto business, as Bernice had realized, was really rather catching.

Wolsey leapt forward and grabbed it off the Greater One. Holding the lid on tight, he rolled back to Bernice and yelled. 'I've got it! Say the magic words!'

Bernice blinked very slowly. 'The . . . magic words?'

'Yes, the magic words that will get us back to the castle!'

'Why don't you say them?'

'Because I've forgotten them.'

Bernice felt a horror rising in her stomach, and clenched her buttocks very tightly. 'Oh sod. So have I.'

The large and messy click of over a thousand safety catches being released echoed across the meadow.

'Give us back the lamp,' said the Greater One, 'and we will let you live . . . a little longer than everybody else.'

'Try to think of the magic words,' Wolsey purred.

Bernice closed her eyes, half to help her think, half in anticipation of being horribly shot. She reached inside her mind, trying to remember all those absolute memory tricks that Professor Laight had taught her. Blank. She breathed deeply and slowly, searching for her hidden depths. She realized that there was a lumpy thing in her jerkin pocket.

She put her hand on it. Slipped her finger into it.

And opened her eyes smiling.

She swung the finger with the green gem on it into the Greater One's line of sight. 'Ah-ha!' she said. 'You didn't bet on me having this, did you?'

The Greater One adopted the tone of voice one uses to address infants who've brought home half a bat. 'No. What is it?'

'It's a ring which . . . does all sorts of dangerous things.' Bernice wondered if laughter meant the same thing for Perfectons as it did for humans. She hoped not. 'It can summon a powerful genie of my own.'

'Really?' said the Greater One. 'Then show us.'

Bernice glared at him, and rubbed the gem. She was really only killing time, hoping that the magic words would pop into her head, or that Wolsey would remember them.

So she was quite surprised when there was a burst of flame in front of her.

Between her and Wolsey and the mass of the Perfecton army appeared Menlove Stokes.

CHAPTER 13

A CAT IN HELL'S CHANCE

Stokes looked at Bernice and smiled. Then he looked at the Perfectons and screamed.

He ran straight to Bernice and Wolsey and hid behind them.

'Most impressive,' the Greater One gestured to the two humans and the cat. 'Now destroy them. Take care not to harm the lamp.'

'No!' shouted Bernice, grabbing Wolsey before he could throw himself between her and the alien guns.

'Cowards!' Wolsey was shouting at them. 'Which of you will face me with a sword?'

The aliens aimed carefully.

'Erm . . .' Menlove Stokes cleared his throat apologetically. 'What about going that way?'

'What?' Wolsey and Bernice looked in the direction he was gesturing. There was a hole in the side of a bush only a few feet away. It had obviously been caused by a piece of the scenery landing there. Through the hole was the blackness and glaring light sources of the theatre area. Bernice was certain that she hadn't been able to see it before Stokes had pointed it out.

'Those are all over the place,' Stokes whispered. 'What are they?'

'Escape routes,' purred Wolsey. 'One . . . two . . .'

They leapt into the hole before he got to three.

Green beams flattened the bush into powder behind them.

A moment of dislocation.

Nothing.

Bernice, Wolsey and Stokes appeared before the, now empty, rows of chairs that Bernice recognized from the last time she'd been amongst the audience.

'What the hell,' she asked Stokes, 'are you doing here? Apart from saving our lives, for which many thanks.'

The artist swiftly filled them in on his experiences. 'And after I was zapped, I just wandered around in the never never for ages. I visited a sort of purple void which I think was where toads go after they die, because there were just hundreds of them, and there was spawn everywhere. You should have heard the croaking. And I wandered around the edge of a singularity for a while, and saw all the people and things that were trapped there, their dreams flashing round and round like tracks on an ancient record. I talked to several of my ancestors, and spent an enjoyable few hours in a punt on the Serpentine in the early nineteen seventies. I have come such a long way to be here, I have seen so much.' Stokes smiled a slow and astonished smile. 'And I can't wait to get home and paint it.'

'But how did you find us?' asked Bernice.

'I seemed to be called here, after a timeless time.' Stokes looked around the theatre, as if it was as surprising as everything else he'd seen. 'I think it was that control box you've got on your finger.'

'You mean this?' Bernice indicated the ring.

'Yes. Odd place to keep it.'

'I found it . . . In a vase that had always been beside my bed.'

'A vase I transported there. These alien chaps can

manipulate all time and space.'

'But the coincidences . . . the accidents involved to bring that vase to me, for me to walk back into my own past when I walked out of this program, for that single planted object to bring you here . . .' Bernice sat down, suddenly and heavily. 'Gods and goddesses. Blessed be.'

Stokes shrugged. There was something about his half-smile, Bernice realized, that could never be fundamentally changed by even the most cosmic of experiences. Menlove Stokes knew who he was, and was content, no matter what his bluster said, to be that. Unlike herself, who'd been dragged from emotional pillar to post by a panto. 'That's comedy for you,' he said. 'There are no accidents, there's just a series of jokes. And most of them, I think you'll find, are on us.'

'Menlove, remind me to get drunk with you when we get out of this . . .' Bernice began. But just then the comedy caught up with them with a vengeance. From the stage behind them came a great cry. 'Aha!'

The Greater One and his minions were standing there, having followed them. 'Give us back our genie!' called the alien leader. 'Or face evaporation!'

Wolsey and Stokes pulled Bernice to her feet, and the three of them threw themselves between the seats as green energy beams splintered and charred the velvet.

They ran along one of the rows, dodging and leaping as blasts flickered around them, but a new column of Perfectons ran off stage left and stage right, and encircled them. More and more of them were flooding into the theatre.

'Split up!' Bernice called, and they ran in different directions just as an energy bolt landed where they'd been. Bernice dodged the clutches of a Perfecton, leapt over another's sprawling tackle, and threw the lamp to Wolsey, right over the head of another alien grabbing for it. Wolsey caught it, spun, kicked an alien aside, and sprinted down the central aisle, heading for a higher exit door. A row of

Perfectons leapt up from behind the rear seats, and he tottered backwards, trying desperately to reverse his steps. It was only because he fell over that the volley of neon green light missed his head.

He rolled, hopped upright on to a seat back and shouted, 'Stokes! Catch!'

'Hold on . . .' the artist started to say, but it was too late. He intercepted the lamp in a long dive, and thudded into the carpet, flat on his face. He grinned to see the thing intact in his hands, but his face fell as he looked up and saw a ring of Perfectons surrounding him. 'Now, don't do anything you'll regret later,' he advised them. 'I am a member of several important arts funding councils, and if any of you are even thinking of pursuing a career in the visual media, I can tell you this isn't going to do your case any good.'

During that puzzled interlude, Bernice had hauled herself over a seatback, and ran at the aliens from behind.

She broke through, and, remembering some smidgen of sporting skill from her days on the bloodsoaked fields of the girls' games pitches at the Academy, thumped the lamp as hard as she could with her foot. It spiralled into the air.

Everybody looked up.

Bernice used her momentum to grab Stokes and break free from the circle.

Wolsey barged three Perfectons aside, trod on several heads, and made a running catch. Bernice and Stokes joined him a moment later, and continued to run with him, a column of shouting Perfectons right behind them, the Greater One at its head.

The pursuit led right round the theatre, the Perfectons on the other side too scared to fire at the fugitives for fear of hitting their comrades. Benny, Wolsey and Stokes kept throwing the lamp back and forth between them as they ran.

On the third lap, Bernice panted. 'This is all very well, but unless we get this sorted out, done and dusted, we, them, Us, everybody, will be killed in a very terrible and final way by an exploding sun. What are we going to do?'

'Remember . . .' panted Wolsey. 'The magic words! That would help!'

'Magic words?' panted Stokes, looking puzzled.

'To get us back to the castle,' Benny explained, nearly fumbling her catch through exhaustion. 'Typically, the lives of over three billion beings depend on me remembering a couple of words, and I've gone absolutely blank.'

'It's as simple as that?' Stokes puffed. 'Just "Open Sesame" and we get away?'

Bernice stopped suddenly and spun on her heel to face the panting mass of her oppressors, 'I'm so sorry to put you to all this trouble,' she told the bemused aliens. 'I'll forget my head one of these days.' She hooked her arms through those of the stunned Wolsey and Stokes. 'Open Sesame.'

A cloud of scarlet smoke enveloped them.

From the *Informative Record of Recent Grel History*:

The brave Grel Master had released his dangerous prisoners, certain that his experienced Servitors could easily deal with them should they offer resistance. He was watching one of them expertly working one of the alien control boxes, about which the Grel had learnt so much, so quickly. An unforeseeable error had occurred: the Producer of Waste had evaded the control of the Grel control box.

(Note: 'Producer of Waste' is a term used frequently in the Grel archives. There is much debate over whether it refers to artists in general, or purely to Menlove Stokes.)

'Observation: it is as if another control box is operating,' the Grel Master swiftly concluded. 'The subject has been lured off course. Use another.'

The Servitors went to take another human to be fired into the Green. But at that moment, calamity of calamities, disaster of disasters, one of those annoying coincidences, those natural happenings beyond control that unfairly beset the Grel whenever we seem to have a chance of winning, occurred. The huge chamber shook and shuddered.

This really is so [expletive] unfair!

(Note: This is the last entry recorded in this particular sequence. It seems the scribe gave up any attempt to create a heroic ending.)

Extract Ends

Warrinder had been bracing his thick paw pads against the floor for minutes now, waiting for the first shock to strike the planet. When it did, he was the only creature not to be thrown off his feet. There were, he decided, some advantages to precognition after all. With a bound, he launched himself at the staggering Grel Master, flexed his powerful hind limbs as he flew, and delivered a kick that sent the alien flying into the wall of the enclosure.

Singh immediately leapt on to the back of one of the Grel Servitors and started wrestling with him. Wagstaff lashed about him with his walking stick, from where he was lying on the floor, and Farouk tripped one of the Grel as it struggled to rise. Epstein dived for the gun and the control box, and kicked them away from a Grel as it lunged for them.

They landed at Thooo's feet. He picked them up, then looked up as a wave of thunder rolled across the chamber. 'My world is dying,' he whispered.

Professor Owl opened her mouth in horror. 'The outer layers of the sun are being sloughed off. The surface of the planet will be molten by now. We've got about half an hour before that star goes supernova, and takes this entire solar system with it.'

The Grel Master staggered to his feet and pointed at Thooo. Warrinder was pleased to find his words were actually a surprise. 'Query: can you help us? Do you know a way to survive?'

Thooo glared back at him.

And fired the gun. He swept around the room, fingers expertly playing with the sphere on the butt of the toy, faster than the human eye could follow, the green beam sucking up and searching out the Grel with extraordinary swiftness.

Until there were no Grel left at all.

'Way to go!' Janes clapped his hands. 'But won't that throw the Grel into the same boat as your people?'

'No.' Thooo gave a final twist on the sphere. 'I have contained them elsewhere.'

'And are you going to save us all?' asked Lucinda. 'I gather you do know of a method of escape.'

'Sorry.' Thooo looked resigned, and Warrinder felt a terrible lump in his lower food pouch. 'They seemed so bad I just didn't want their company.'

'So . . .' Epstein closed his eyes, grappling with the air in an effort to express the concept. 'We are all going to die?'

'Yes.' The alien nodded. 'But at least we can go to one of the observation domes and watch the sun explode. What do you think?'

The scientists and humanities professors looked at each other, with an unexpected unanimity.

Epstein spoke for all of them. 'I think that if I were to choose an ending to my own story, it would be something as spectacular – and, considering we came here for a barbecue, something as ridiculous – as that.'

The others all nodded.

'Then let us go,' said Thooo.

He nodded upwards.

The ground they were standing on separated itself from

the floor, took a quick spin over the walls of the enclosure, and then flew straight up to the ceiling.

The dwarves had taken guard on the battlements, and, under Moody and Gushy's leadership, had persuaded Prince Charming's rather scared forces to at least run about and make a show of defence. The greater blasts of the genie had ceased, but a steady bombardment from the smaller weapons of the vast army of the audience continued.

Candy had supervized the launching of a giant catapult. It was, unfortunately, filled with sweets, but she felt sure that it would at least give the army below pause for thought. She'd already used a vast pair of her bloomers to create a hastily stitched army of her own – mannequins to make the battlements appear more heavily defended.

Now she looked over the side of the castle and gasped. The audience had blown down a tree, taken it up between them, and were running at the gate. She wiped her brow, gathered the dwarves, and followed them at a run down into the palace. This was certainly the toughest audience she'd ever faced.

The dwarves and the dame burst in on King Rupert as he was solemnly taking the A-bonbon from its niche, the pantomime horse watching nervously. 'We draw the line here,' the King declared. 'And we shall hope that history will remember the name Balsam. I intend to face the enemy standing on my own bulwarks.'

'Good trick if you can do it,' noted Candy.

'It can't end this way!' cried Cute. 'Where's Bernice?'

From higher up in the castle, there came yet another, new sort of explosion.

It took Bernice a moment to realize where they'd appeared, the smoke of their materialization was so thick. Princess Aurora and her sister Marian were staggering and coughing near a window. They held bows in their hands. Through the door of what was, apparently, the master bedroom, came rushing the dwarves, horse, King, Prince and dame. They were closely followed by the Vizier, who grinned as widely as he could possibly grin when he saw that they held the lamp. 'Oh, hello. You got it then?' Then his face fell. ' 'Ere, why'd you bring that lot with you?'

'That lot?'

'Behind you!' the assembled characters cried.

Bernice turned round.

Behind her stood the Greater One and a number of his warriors. They'd obviously been caught by the spell. The alien leader was tapping his foot.

'Give me the lamp,' he ordered.

Bernice put the lamp between herself and the aliens. From downstairs there came a crash. Candy coughed in embarrassment. 'I knew there was something I had to mention,' she said. 'There go the gates.'

Bernice turned slowly back to the Greater One and regarded him coolly. 'I didn't have time to tell you our bad news earlier. Your sun's going to explode within the hour.'

The Greater One pursed his lips. 'If you surrender the lamp, we will use the genie to create control surfaces and pilot this place into hyperspace. We will place you all in the Green, and may take you out in the future to be our slaves. If you're lucky.'

'What about if we use our computer program to stow you lot in the Green?' Bernice glanced at the Vizier, who suddenly blanched.

The Greater One regarded the Vizier with distaste. 'That program has been rather messily inserted into this world. He is very limited in his function, and could not do what you describe.'

Bernice considered that for a moment. The Vizier obviously had something to do with the remaining mystery of this adventure, the matter of the anomalous caves and the convenient plot device of the lamp. But that wasn't important now.

'I could rub the lamp and summon the genie. Make it work for me.'

The Greater One remained confident. 'And I would immediately use the control code to make it obey us once more.'

The sound of running feet came from the corridor. Before anybody could do anything, a squad of Perfectons ran in and covered Bernice's group from every angle. The new arrivals looked to the Greater One for guidance. He waved for them to wait.

Bernice paused. She was aware of the alien weapons trained on them. Aware of time running out. And aware that she couldn't think of any options other than the most awful one. She looked at Wolsey out of the corner of her eye. He was looking at the plinth, sitting unnoticed beside the bed. Their eyes met for a moment, and his glance carried a silent plea not to do it. There was something about his expression that reminded her of those evenings after Jason had left. The onset of night had always been the worst time, and her cat had seemed to sense that, climbing up on to her lap and kneading her until she responded and went to get him some milk or something. She'd felt like she still had love left, because of Wolsey.

It had been a delight to know him as a friend, as a person. How could she condemn him to that mindless sort of love again? The love of something that knew nothing but love, that didn't understand how complicated it all was.

Surprisingly at the time, but, as Bernice was later to think, right on cue, a new voice spoke up.

Cute had stepped forward into the aim of the guns.

He looked quite scared. He looked at Bernice for a moment, his mouth open, as if he'd surprised himself. He cleared his throat. 'I can't help but love,' he said. 'That's my character. I'm the littlest dwarf. I love beauty and intelligence and reason and bravery and all the other best things about women. Because I love like that, nobody really takes me seriously. I'm the one who just goes "She's beautiful" all the time. I love Bernice here, for instance, because she's so big and at the same time so little. Because she finds the big in the little. Because she's so young.'

'Young?' Bernice had been blushing, wondering what this most embarrassing and blundering of dwarves was blundering into now. She looked around the assembled factions, aware that her high-pitched exclamation had attracted attention. 'Sorry. Go on.'

Cute continued. 'Bernice says that a lot of us here are characters. Quick sketches of real people. I'm sure I'm much more complicated really. I'm sure that if you look at any quickly sketched character closely you can see many more lines, enough for whatever person you might come looking for. But for now, while I'm this adorable character, you –' he nodded to the Greater One '– can be absolutely certain you can trust me. If you go back into the audience, and let us avoid whatever terrible thing we need to avoid, then I promise that we'll let you all out again when we've escaped. I give you my word. And you know that you can trust the word of the littlest dwarf.'

Bernice looked at the Greater One. For a moment, it seemed that he might actually accept that.

Then he started to laugh. 'Why, this is pure comedy! You expect the Greater One to obey the wishes of one as small as you?' He gestured to his men. 'On the count of five, kill them all. Try not to damage the lamp.'

Bernice looked again at Wolsey. In the corner of his eye there was the glint of a tear.

The aliens all around them started to aim to the Greater One's count.

In the distance of the dying land outside, a bell began to toll.

Everybody looked at Bernice to save them. Her fingers tightened on the lamp.

The count and the bell came to one.

Wolsey's eyes met hers again. 'Five o'clock,' he sighed. 'And still no sign of Dick.'

And then he roared.

Everything seemed to happen in slow motion.

Wolsey became a bristling ball of fur, fangs gleaming, flying in a great leap straight at the Greater One. His sword had swung free of its scabbard.

Menlove Stokes threw himself at Cute, waving his arms like a windmill target, trying to attract the lightning to himself rather than the dwarf.

Bernice leapt at the pillar.

She landed beside it, the first flickers of green neon impacting and bursting the wall just past her head.

She looked quickly over her shoulder.

And saw Wolsey's sword and arm incinerated in hundreds of skittering bursts of light.

She thought of love and of how vulnerable and precious and funny it was.

And then she reached up and slammed the lamp down on to the top of the pillar.

A knot of space-time stood in orbit above the world. It was an electromagnetic blank: light fell into its labyrinth, rushed around it and was filtered out the other side, unchanged, on its original course. Inside the knot were melded the *Winton*, the world and culture of the Perfectons, and the complex intellectual matrix of English pantomime. The knot was in turbulence, straining against itself. One moment it was whole, and then, like a small universe in creation, it was exploding.

Above the planet, the *Winton* folded itself back into existence.

* * *

A moment of dislocation.

Nothing.

Bernice was lying face down on the floor, she realized. A new floor. The floor of the flight deck of the *Winton*. The whole deck was suffused with red light that shone through the vision ports. She poked her nose up a fraction. She was spreadeagled across the doorway between the deck and the navigation bubble that led off from it. The missile had penetrated the wall here, as well as in the fantasy world – only here the effect wasn't nearly so dramatic. The nosecone of the missile protruded from the computer banks, and was covered with the airtight white ceramic gel of the anti-meteor sprays. Scattered around Bernice were the seven members of her tutorial group, the ship's captain and three of his officers, Professor Candy, Menlove Stokes and the two mysterious agents of the People.

'Wolsey,' said Bernice. 'Where's Wolsey?'

'He's here.' Professor Candy had clambered to his feet near the navigation computers.

Bernice scrabbled across the floor, grabbing a medical pack as she went, and landed beside the cat. He was lying in a foetal position, curled around the blackened stub of his right front leg. He was mewling high and hard.

Bernice sprayed the leg with antiseptic bandage foam, thumbing the anaesthetic button frantically until Wolsey slept. 'Don't die,' she whispered.

Aurum Silvestra had scrambled back to her navigation position. She had just finished tapping a complicated data sequence into her lectern. Now she let out a little shriek. 'The star!' she cried. 'It's going to blow. We've got less than ten minutes.'

Bernice, carrying Wolsey in her arms, stumbled to one of the vision ports. The whole of the sky was filled by a red mist, at the heart of which lay a nub of brilliance. That starlike point was flickering rapidly as material fell into it, growing visibly brighter by the moment.

Captain Balsam started to hit controls frantically. 'Ready the hyperdrive.'

Stokes looked back and forth at the chaos around him, uncomprehendingly. 'But my friends,' he shouted. 'The other academics! They're still on the planet.'

'If so,' the Lieutenant Formerly Known As Prince Charming muttered, 'then they're history.'

'But they weren't on the surface,' Stokes insisted. 'They could have –'

The woman that Bernice knew as Princess Marian called from her position. 'We're getting a distress call . . . from the planet's surface!'

Balsam swung to look at Bernice. 'We can't mount an evacuation,' he insisted. 'There just isn't time.'

Bernice bit her lip, and looked down at Wolsey, dreaming in her arms.

Thooo stood in the translucent green dome on the molten surface of his planet, and watched the surface slide by under the red sky. The alien academics stood with him. They gazed at the dying sun overhead, and they shivered, and cried, and still couldn't stop talking.

Professor Wagstaff turned to Professor Blandish. 'If, as seems likely, time is about to shut up the book of all our days . . .'

'A misquote,' noted Blandish.

'I wasn't aware that it was a quotation at all,' sighed Wagstaff.

'Raleigh, surely. Or is it Drake?'

'Drake? Why would I be quoting Drake? We're about to be reduced to atoms, not fight the dratted Ar . . . Ar . . .' For a moment, Thooo thought that the stress had been too much for the old man's frail body, that he was having some sort of seizure. Then he realized that he was sobbing.

Blandish awkwardly stepped forward and put his arms

around his colleague. 'You did not lose that book that you borrowed from my library. I found it again and didn't tell you.'

'You should have had my office,' cried Wagstaff.

'It's all right,' said Blandish. 'I preferred mine. In the end.'

Hettie and Lucinda turned away from the two sobbing History professors. 'I hope we shall have none of that,' said Hettie.

'Indeed,' said Lucinda. 'Suffice it to say that I have found our unusual situation –'

'And it is certainly unusual.'

'– to be not without interest.'

'As have I.'

The dear ladies nodded to each other, and then, as one, reached into their purses and each extracted from them a miniature of some liquor. They threw them back together. 'Cheers.'

Singh had put down the communication device that he'd been uselessly yelling into, and had started to pace in small circles around Warrinder. 'It's never been anything personal,' he assured the Pakhar. 'I hope you understand that.'

'Yes,' said Warrinder.

'It's just that I've always been uncomfortable with the nature of your academic, or quasi-academic, discipline.'

'Yes.'

'And, as a consequence –' Singh suddenly stopped, and looked at the curl of the Pakhar's nose. 'You know something, don't you? Something that's going to happen.'

'Yes.' The Pakhar nodded.

'It's starting,' whispered Professor Owl. She was looking up at a spot of brighter light that had formed on the edge of the stellar mass that was compacting above them. The spot grew and grew. 'That will be one of the initial flares,' Owl noted. 'It'll vaporize the planet.'

Thooo was astonished that, at that moment, the professor began to laugh. 'Why –?' he began.

'If I'd been asked to choose a way to go,' Owl chuckled. 'This would be it! It's all quite fascinating.'

Singh's mouth fell open. He took one slow step forward. 'My friend, I think you are going to be disappointed. That isn't a solar flare.'

Owl screwed up her eyes. 'Oh yes it is.'

Epstein clapped his hands together and leapt into the air. 'Oh no it isn't!'

The academics all started to cheer. Thooo changed the shape of his eyes to better see what they were seeing. And felt pain. Because suddenly he had hope.

For powering towards them through the red sky, trailing vapour from every surface, was the stubby shape of the *Winton*.

Singh's communicator crackled into life. 'Bingo wotsit or whatever you're supposed to say. Professor Summerfield to all other professors. I'm told that we're going to get one go at this, so listen carefully . . .'

Bernice was curled up in a corner under the communications desk, Wolsey in her lap. She held a microphone close to her lips to muffle the sound of the stresses that were tearing at the hull outside. 'Most of the planet's atmosphere has been boiled away, which is good news, because we don't have time to bother with the jolly boats. We're going to make a low pass over the surface and open the cargo-bay doors.' She glanced at Stokes. 'I'm told you've got all sorts of alien magic stuff going on down there. Can you fly?'

Thooo grabbed Singh's communicator. 'We're flying now.'

The academics looked down. They were.

The hemispherical green dome swept straight past the ruddy golden shape of the *Winton* as it tore through the thin and swirling vapour of the planet's upper atmosphere. It spun to a halt right behind the craft, then whizzed straight through the open doors of the cargo bay.

They closed behind it.

Bernice felt Wolsey's breathing against her chin. They were all going to make it. Every single one of them.

As she thought that, the shadows across the cabin instantly lengthened and everything was silhouetted. The colour of the sky outside changed from red to white.

Which meant that the star had exploded.

The expanding sphere of the supernova swept past the planet.

Then swept through it.

The body of the world that had cradled a civilization became a lengthening stream of plasma.

The little golden shape of the *Winton* sped out of the solar system with a wall of fire racing just behind it, planets being vaporized in its trail. The fire blossomed into great flares that reached out for the spaceship, fingers of fire that pursued the craft right up to the edge of near-lightspeed.

Inside the juddering craft, Bernice reached out her hand.

Her fingers closed by accident on those of Michael Doran.

But there are no accidents, she thought as she stared seriously at him and he stared seriously back. There's only narrative.

The flares swept around the *Winton*.

Just as it impossibly passed lightspeed and vanished from the universe.

And was free.

EPILOGUE

MOMENTS OF PLEASURE

Extract from the Diary of Bernice Summerfield:

The leaves still stuck for a moment on the window of my rooms in Garland College, and then they were pushed away. I was lying back in my long low chair by the secondary ice bucket, cradling Wolsey in my arms. I was thinking that he was probably delighted with the new arm that the vets grew for him. But then I thought that I would think that, wouldn't I? He forced my hand on the matter of whether or not I played snakes and ladders with the tree of evolution, but I still felt very guilty about it. I stroke him, and try, through warmth and contact and soft words, to communicate the love I feel for a cat. But he just gives his animal love back, and, although that has its usual depth and beauty, I can't help but think of him as he was with a long coat and opposable thumbs.

Thooo has been offered a teaching place at St Oscar's, of course, and is considering it, along with the matter of where and how to start resurrecting his people. The entirety of his culture is stored in a single data module, Professor Archduke's pantomime thesis. The module had been carefully extracted from the *Winton*'s central computer a day after we returned, and had been given to the

Dean for safekeeping. Perhaps when we start waking up selected Perfectons we'll be able to learn the truth about what made that missile hit the *Winton* in so perfect a way, and why the program that we found ourselves in contained an exit device that so neatly parcelled up all of Perfecton culture.

I suspect, myself, that the module containing the thesis must have been fitted with some sort of homing device to attract the missile. I also suspect that the combination of the lamp and the pedestal upon which it was to be placed could only have occurred through deliberate intervention, that our whole adventure was designed, by whoever introduced such anachronistic elements as the mine where the lamp was stored, to deliver up the Perfecton data to them on a plate. Archduke has already appeared before the senate and declared his complete surprise at the whole matter. In his defence, he's said that he's only too pleased for the authorities to keep the thesis module and examine it for a homing device. I'm not sure who to believe. This conspiracy seems too big for a simple academic to have planned it.

Stokes has already started to paint his experiences, and the publicly displayed results are the subject of protests by a number of campus-based organizations.

I had, initially, decided not to take up the offer of employment put to me by the two agents of God. Then I got home to find a pile of bills on the doormat and decided that, as extra-curricular activities went, their job description sounded quite exciting. They reappeared that same night, of course, and we shook hands on it. I await their first assignment with some trepidation.

I've also dangled a few book proposals in front of the university publishing arm. These include an account of our adventures in pantoland as either a hard-hitting action novel, a solid piece of factual reporting, or a collection of limericks. But my favourite idea was that I'd write a volume about relationships, and how distance can give you an odd perspective on them. I think *Men Are From Mars, Women Are From Mars Too, Unfortunately* has a ring to it.

My musings were interrupted by Joseph sweeping imperiously into the room. He gave a little electronic cough. 'The young gentleman is here to see you, Rector.'

I let Wolsey trot off to find his dish and started to adjust all the bits of me that lose their shape when at rest. Then I stopped. 'Let him in, Joseph.'

I found my glasses on the sideboard, and, in one of those little gestures that only people who think that they're mistresses of their own narrative make, snapped them clean in two and dropped them into a vase.

Doran looked worried. He was dressed in the most profoundly adult way, in a casual suit which looked so ridiculous on him that I couldn't help but smile. He carried my book. 'I finished it, Professor,' he said. 'And I found that it had many interesting things to say about –'

'I don't think you're Cute,' I said.

'Oh,' he said.

'Not the definitive article, anyway. Do you remember much of what happened to us in pantoland?' Most of us did, but as a dream, with strange conflicts and bits missed out.

'No.' He took a seat near me and looked at me with anxious eyes. 'Well, actually yes. I'm not like that, you know.'

I went and sat by his knees and looked up at him over my shoulder. He got the idea after a moment and sank down to sit beside me, looking more worried than ever. 'So I take it you don't make good speeches? That you don't express love in an extraordinarily pure and refreshing fashion? That you don't think I'm young?'

'I do think you're young,' he whispered, with a nervy depth to his voice that made me smile a softer smile. 'That's why I like you so much. I don't think you're ever going to get old.'

We watched the leaves for a while, and I idly found his hand with mine once more. We were, after all, fellow survivors in need of comfort. Aren't we all? 'Oh yes I am,' I told him.

'Oh no you're not,' he said.

That went on for quite a while. And at some point during that conversation I found that I'd started to believe my student's theory. I opened the book he'd given back to me, and pointed out a passage that I wanted to hear him read.

At some point in that long autumn afternoon I was sure that I would ask for 'Lullaby of Birdland'. And good brandy.

And love.

Extract Ends

Late that night, Professor F. Archduke's *English Pantomime: A Critical Study*, in data module form, sat on the side of the Dean's desk.

From which it suddenly overbalanced.

The room was empty, so there was nobody to comment on the sudden movement.

The module stopped a few inches above the floor, and swung to the left and right. On its side appeared a graphic window, and in that window appeared the image of the program that had suddenly come to life to activate these hidden gravitic motors and move the module.

The image wore a turban and an all-consuming grin. It pointed upwards.

The module rose to the level of the Dean's porterhatch. Then sped out through it.

The module flew through the night, along the walkways of St Oscar's University. It flew past several colleges, over several islands, and down several tunnels.

Until it came to the cloisters of Pierce College.

The little box hopped a hedge, sped at surface level over gravel, took a left at the fountain, and stopped before one particular door.

The door opened.

Professor Ferdinand Archduke, specialist in Obscure Theatrical Forms, stood framed in the light from his rooms behind him. He reached out for the module and missed it. It wavered in the air, the power in its batteries failing.

'Stop messing about,' he said.

The module settled into his grasp. The Professor slipped the module into one of his gown's deepest pockets, glanced ruefully at some distant, imagined audience of his own, and then closed the door behind him.

COMING SOON IN THE NEW ADVENTURES

DRAGONS' WRATH

by Justin Richards

0 426 20508 1
Publication date: 19 June 1997

The Knights of Jeneve, a legendary chivalric order famed for their jewel-encrusted dragon emblem, were destroyed at the battle of Bocaro. But when a gifted forger is murdered on his way to meet her old friend Irving Braxiatel, and she comes into possession of a rather ornate dragon statue, Benny can't help thinking they're involved. So, suddenly embroiled in art fraud, murder and derring-do, she must discover the secret behind the dragon, and thwart the machinations of those seeking to control the sector.

BEYOND THE SUN

by Matthew Jones

ISBN: 0 426 20511 1
Publication date: 17 July 1997

Benny has drawn the short straw – she's forced to take two overlooked freshers on their very first dig. Just when she thinks things can't get any worse, her no-good ex-husband Jason turns up and promptly gets himself kidnapped. As no one else is going to rescue him, Benny resigns herself to the task. But her only clue is a dusty artefact Jason implausibly claimed was part of an ancient and powerful weapon – a weapon rumoured to have powers beyond the sun.

SHIP OF FOOLS

by Dave Stone

ISBN: 0 426 20510 3
Publication date: 21 August 1997

No hard-up archaeologist could resist the perks of working for the fabulously wealthy Krytell. Benny is given an unlimited expense account, an entire new wardrobe and all the jewels and pearls she could ever need. Also, her job, unofficial and shady though it is, requires her presence on the famed space cruise-liner, the *Titanian Queen*. But, as usual, there is a catch: those on board are being systematically bumped off, and the great detective, Emil Dupont, hasn't got a clue what's going on.